EVERYTHING SOLID HAS A SHADOW

# *Everything Solid has a Shadow*

Michael Antman

First Edition ISBN 13: 978-1-937484-57-6

AMIKA PRESS 466 Central AVE #23 Northfield IL 60093 847 920 8084
info@amikapress.com Available for purchase on amikapress.com

Edited by John Manos. Cover art by Dan McCarthy. Author photography by Marina Carsello. Designed and typeset by Sarah Koz. Set in ITC Týfa, designed by Josef Týfa in 1959, digitized by František Štorm in 1996. Title set in Duke, designed by James T Edmondson in 2009.
Thanks to Nathan Matteson.

I would like to thank, for their suggestions and support, Michele Rubin, John Manos, Kelly Notaras, Hannah Antman, Irina Velitskaya, Christopher Guerin, Mark Guerin, Phil Lanier and Cheryl Phillips and, for their research assistance, Dr. William Bender and Megan McGrath.

ONE

# *The Inner Surface of the Eye*

## (Alisa)

# 1

My name is Carlos Xavier Alessandro, though everyone calls me Charlie. My parents, of Southern Italian extraction, were born in Argentina, but I was born here in the States. When I was eight years old, something happened to me, or, rather, happened to someone else *because* of me, that forced my parents to decamp in a panic with me to Buenos Aires for a few years, and led them, after I was an adult, to move back there permanently, where they have remained until this day, filled with wine and shame.

What happened was that my little friend from down the block, a very shy and pretty brown-haired girl named Wilhelmina (though I called her Willa) invited me over to her house to help her babysit her infant sister. Her mom was out running errands, and as I remember it, Willa and I were talking in the middle of the sunlit sidewalk—it was the height of summer in Chicago, and it was hot enough that the stripes of tar between the sidewalk cracks were rubbery to the touch, like Black Jack chewing gum, and the actual wads of gum on the sidewalk were even softer and stickier than that—and she said, "Charlie, do you wanna watch Elizabeth with me, she's really cute and she doesn't cry or throw up much," and I said sure, because even at that young age, I loved little babies, and of course I loved Willa too, but in a different way.

Elizabeth and Wilhelmina. Her parents, whom I doubt were of an ironic cast, must have hoped their little girls would become queenlike, or maybe they just liked those regal-sounding, four-syllable names. I don't know, and in any event I don't remember their father at all, although I remember their mother far more clearly than I would prefer.

What puzzled me years later, when I was a rational adult and back in Chicago, was why Willa was standing in the middle of the sidewalk under one of those big elm trees that partially shaded our eyes from the implacable sun (this was in the days before the elms all became infested with disease and were chainsawed and carted away) asking me that question when her three-and-a-half-month-old sister Elizabeth was back in the apartment in her slatted wooden crib, all alone.

The tree itself was remarkable: It had fantastically gnarled above-ground roots that looked like the knobby knees of a kneeling person seated atop another kneeling person and a crown of leaves as infinitely complex as another galaxy adjacent to our own. This I remember much more clearly than any fleeting follow-up discussion about her sister, and why she had been left alone, that Willa and I might have had under those still, summer leaves.

Be that as it may, we eventually made our way back to Willa's neat little apartment on the second floor of a perfectly rectangular, red-brick, three-floor co-op, and we checked on Elizabeth, who was sleeping peacefully in her crib in her thin, gray swaddling blanket. And then we spent a little time hanging around in Willa's tiny room at the back of the apartment, with its view of the backyard that held a single crooked ash tree with a frayed scarlet mitten still dangling in its branches from last winter and a rusted swing set screwed together out of thin metal pipes, no more and no less fragile than that rickety crib within. We probably talked instead of played, because Willa's toys and stuffed animals wouldn't have held much interest for an eight-year-old boy—especially since she didn't own, as I recall, anything nearly as magical as a certain dollhouse that floats in the air above the dormer room floor in the rental house where I live now. Two years before, when I was six, I had given her a small gumball-machine "engagement" ring with a big green plastic jewel the color of a lime Jujyfruit while we were standing on the very same sidewalk where she'd asked me to help her babysit, but if that ring was still somewhere in her room, I didn't see it then.

We must have gotten bored after a little while, so we wandered into the kitchen and got a couple of Fla-Vor-Ices from the freezer, the kind you squeeze from the bottom with your thumb and forefingers out of its flattish cellophane tube and suck down bite by icy bite until all that's left is a little bit of warm fruit-flavored water at the bottom that you tip toward your mouth and drink, and it pains me to remember quite distinctly that my ice stick was orange flavored, though I do not remember many rather more important details of that afternoon. We had found a rusty pair of scissors in a kitchen drawer, and I'd snipped the cellophane top of Willa's Fla-Vor-Ice first, like the little gentleman that I was, and then my own, and, still clutching our sticky cellophane treats, we wandered out of the house to go "butterfly hunting."

I am certain that we didn't catch any butterflies, and in fact this whole story distresses me for trivial reasons, because you hardly ever see any butterflies flittering around anymore, or that Black Jack gum that tasted tangentially of licorice, or elm trees, or ribbons of tar between the squares of city sidewalks. But I remember these forgotten things distinctly, and yet I do not remember anything at all about our little sojourn, and I certainly do not remember taking Elizabeth out of her crib and placing her on Willa's bed that she shared with her cats, Willy and Willard, and the usual assortment of stuffed animals. Nor do I remember seeing Elizabeth in her diaper but out of her swaddling blanket, lying on that bed, but in fact by the time we returned from our fruitless summer hunt, Elizabeth had somehow managed to roll into the crack between Willa's bed and the sea-green wall.

What is a three-and-a-half-month-old baby capable of seeing? I have often speculated about this, and, from time to time, I have closed my eyes and tried to imagine the world from Elizabeth's perspective, looking up at a tangle of sheets and, beyond the sheets, at the white ceiling, not knowing what a "sheet" or a "ceiling" was, nor why with every exhalation her slender ribcage constricted a bit more and she slipped infinitesimally further toward the unforgiving floor.

It took about two minutes after that for everyone's lives to come to an end.

# 2

She entered through the back door of the club, a door that seemed, in the distance, far too small to accommodate an adult human being. She walked through the crowded and crooked tables, twisting and turning here and there because the absurdly wide organza-and-tulle ball gown she was wearing barely afforded her passage between the oddly crooked wooden chairs. They were chairs that looked somehow arthritic and impoverished, like they were out of one of van Gogh's later paintings from Arles. As she walked, she grew alarmingly larger, until by the time she was standing next to me, she was the size of a normal adult person. The club's walls were canted at a precipitous angle, so that when we stood side by side, each of us had to tilt our heads awkwardly in the direction of our own shoulders to peer into each other's eyes. Though her gown billowed out from below her waist all the way down to her ankles, somehow the lower half of her body didn't seem to exist at all.

Her name was MariAngela, and she was, like me, a singer and guitarist. I did not think to ask why she needed to wear a lilac-colored, organza-and-tulle ball gown in a funky little neighborhood Italian restaurant and music club, nor why the color of the gown at one point changed to an intense orange like a polluted sunset. Her eyes held a bit of metallic orange in them too as she spoke to me, her face held uncomfortably close to mine, as if she were peering through my eyes instead of into them. Well, that wasn't quite right either. It was as if she had entered my head through the back door of my brain and walked toward the front where my shuttered eyes slept, and thus was looking at my eyes from the inside rather than from the outside.

All she said was, "There's something wrong with my brain."

Her lips did not move when she said these six words, and in the time it took for my blood to course just once from my heart through my veins and clamber its way back again, she was gone.

When I saw the real MariAngela at the real music club the following evening, I of course thought nothing of telling her this funny little dream. I saw no reason not to; we were friendly, and not at all rivals as musicians. In fact, she was a waitress at the club and not a musician at all, as she had been in my dream. The nightclub, which was also a pretty good Italian restaurant, was called Berto's, unlike the dream version, which had no name, and its walls were straight, not painfully tilted like the dream-restaurant, and MariAngela was wearing a light lavender-colored sweater—spring was settling into summer, but none of us quite trusted it yet—and a pair of black denims. Most important of all, the real-world MariAngela, a South Side Irish Catholic girl, was glowing with good health. She had just gotten back from a vacation in Australia, where she'd surfed, snorkeled on the Great Barrier Reef, and partied with a lot of good-looking beach-bum types, whose twangy, relaxed, long-voweled accents, she claimed, made her think of the color blue.

So when she walked up to me as I was sitting on a stool and tuning my old Cordoba guitar, it was merely a funny and casual conversation opener to say to her, "Hey, MariAngela, guess what? You were in my dream last night!"

MariAngela, five six-and-a-half and with a black, pixie haircut and strong eyebrows the color of espresso, skinny and slim-hipped with a girlish swayback that thrust out her flat little belly and made her look just a bit parenthetical, blew some air out of the corner of her mouth that troubled a feathery black bang for just an instant. She laughed lightly. "Yeah, I'll bet I was."

"Nah, nah, nah, it wasn't a sex dream. Not that I don't have those about you too."

Actually, I hadn't, at least that I could remember, but Mari-Angela and I were comfortable flirting with each other, maybe because she alternated between musician boyfriends who disappointed her and terribly serious young lesbians who bored her, and maybe because it was rumored that when she wasn't waitressing at Berto's she worked at a local sports bar where all the servers wore skimpy halters, and thus was used to gently parrying horny male come-ons. Anyway, she always laughed when I made some comment or another about how I was the one who could put her back in tune, or pluck her strings, or help her hit a high C, or some such.

But this time she shrugged and said, in an impatient-sounding voice that made it sound like I was one wrong word away from her ending the conversation abruptly, "Yeah, so what was it about?"

I laughed to lighten her up a bit; it didn't work. I suddenly felt nervous for some indefinable reason and hesitated before continuing. I put my Cordoba back in its case to cover my unease. "Well, so, anyway, in this dream we were in Berto's just like now, except it wasn't Berto's, and it didn't smell like red sauce and wine or look anything at all like this place. And you were dressed in this bizarre ball gown for some reason, and you came into the room from some tiny back door like you were entering my skull from the back and then you walked forward until you were looking me right in the eyes with these weird orange eyes you had."

"Lovely." She sounded bored, and a little contemptuous. Not like her at all.

"Hey, I can't be responsible for my dreams. It's not like I can, you know, go back and *edit* them like I'm an *auteur* or whatever." Why was she making me feel so defensive about a stupid little dream? "So, anyway, that was pretty much the whole thing, except at the end you looked into my eyes—and, I don't know, it was more like you were looking *through* my eyes or something, except through the back of my eyes through to the front, if you know what I mean—and you said, 'There's something wrong with my brain.'"

Pretty, parenthetical little MariAngela opened her mouth and made an odd grunting sound that I'd never heard from her or from anyone for that matter—it sounded like a baby seal being clubbed. She put the three middle fingers of her right hand on my right bicep, so that her arm crossed both my body and her own, and at first I thought it was a friendly gesture, but I slowly realized that she was doing so to steady herself. She had become terribly pale, like she was about to vomit Berto's garlicky, overly sweet red sauce all over Berto's black-and-white tile floors.

A second passed like this, as she stood in her usual swayback stance, but for once actually, almost imperceptibly, *swaying,* and then she said, "I was diagnosed yesterday afternoon with something called amyotrophic lateral sclerosis."

I didn't say anything for a moment. She withdrew her hand from its awkward position on my arm and crossed her hands in front of her like a deferential schoolgirl.

I said, "I've heard of it." I couldn't think of anything else to say, because, having heard of it, I had also heard that it was about the worst thing any human being could get.

After a moment, MariAngela said, "After my doctor's appointment, I went out with Dani"—her girlfriend of the moment—"and we talked about it and I cried and I said I couldn't decide if I should tell my parents or my brothers or sisters yet, and I really didn't want them to get all drippy about it, but then I was telling Dani, and *she* was getting pretty weepy herself, which I already like totally hated, and I realized that I had to tell somebody who was a nice guy and would be sympathetic and all that but wouldn't get all gooey on me. And for some reason you crossed my mind, Charlie. I was planning to tell you tonight before you had to step in and ruin it."

MariAngela had never been an especially close friend, but nonetheless I used to encounter "her" all the time. I say "her" because

I am actually referring to two other women I'd observed that sort of looked like MariAngela but also reminded me of her for other reasons I couldn't explain. Not too long ago, I was in a little resort town in Illinois called Galena, one of those places that seems to consist of nothing but tea shops and bakeries and gimmicky gift shops and rock shops and bookstores and candy stores, and I saw a young couple coming toward my girlfriend and me. They were arm in arm and looking very much in love. But his left leg was in a hip-high cast, and his head was heavily swaddled in bandages, and he was supporting himself with a three-pronged cane. His girlfriend, upon whom he was leaning, had an enormous club-like cast on her left foot, and her face was largely obscured by her own bandages. She also had splints on the fingers of the hand opposite the one that she had around the waist of her crippled boyfriend. My girlfriend Alisa and I looked at each other, taking care to avoid staring at this terribly damaged couple, and an indefinable understanding passed through us (we must have talked about it later as well) that this couple had been on a honeymoon trip when they'd had a terrible car accident.

How did we know this? We just knew.

That was the part that haunted me. But I also found it of note that, of the little of this young woman's face I could glimpse through her bandages, her resemblance to MariAngela was strong —so strong that a few days later at work I nearly, for just a passing second, asked MariAngela if it were her before realizing that she was entirely unhurt. It was the eyebrows, mostly, I guess— the injured woman on the street had strong, coffee-colored eyebrows still visible through the bandages and light-brown eyes like MariAngela's as well, and there was something of her parenthetical quality, a subtle curvature through the middle of her body, though that no doubt had been a temporary condition due to her terrible injuries.

And both before and after my encounter with this woman and her boyfriend (or husband), I used to see another woman on the El who would get on a stop or two after I did and, if the train was not too crowded, slowly remove the contents of a large, cheap-looking, pink-straw knitting bag, piece by piece, onto the seat next to her. If I had nothing better to do or was sick of looking at my phone, I'd watch her as she would take out, say, a ham and cheese baguette, still in its crinkly cellophane wrapper, and a couple of knitting needles, and some earbuds, and a phone recharger, and a paperback book, and a green apple, and a tube of lipstick, and a toy wind-up duck, and etcetera, etcetera, as the King of Siam used to say. The first couple of times she did this—with great care and deliberateness, I might add—I watched her with some interest, wondering how she was going to integrate all of these disparate items into some coherent activity, and how this action was going to be completed in the few minutes before she got to her stop. But in fact, the "activity," such as it was, consisted solely of removing these items one by one from her flimsy pink knitting bag, and then, in the very order in which they had been removed, carefully placing them back into the bag again, just before she arrived at her stop. The second or third time I watched her perform this careful ritual, I concluded that she might be mildly mentally ill, and I would have turned my attention elsewhere except that she, too, looked like MariAngela.

# 3

*Having* lived in Buenos Aires only from age eight to twelve, I'm about as Americanized and un-Argentine as anyone I know, so everyone except my parents calls me Charlie instead of Carlos. I'm a junior partner in a Chicago integrated marketing communications consulting agency, I speak hardly any Spanish at all these days, I love to travel, and of course I love music, though I've long since given up any hopes of being a professional musician beyond my weekly gigs at Berto's. I've got a mild case of irritable bowel syndrome, but on the other hand I've got great hair, which shouldn't be a big deal for a twenty-eight-year-old, but I have friends my age in the agency business and even more friends in the music business who are already losing theirs. (I associate hair loss with heavy marijuana use, for some reason, and I hardly ever touch the stuff myself.) My hair is very straight and floppy and so deep brown it's almost black, and occasionally when I'm playing guitar I'll wear a funky little headband to keep it out of my eyes. I've got very pale skin, like a lot of Chicagoans who hibernate all winter, and an unfortunate little chin that gives up the ghost just when it should be getting started, and a permanent shaving rash over my Adam's apple. I'm skinny edging toward scrawny, and my shoulders hunch, probably from all that bending over my guitar to pick out notes, and bending over my laptop to write marketing proposals, but I've been told that, even with the weak chin and hunched shoulders and all, I'm pretty good-looking. I can't really see it myself, but I have very dark brown eyes that, with my almost-black hair, make a nice contrast with my pale skin. I guess it makes me look "sensitive," which, for a singer/songwriter, is a good thing, though in the agency world it's not a good thing at all, and that kind of sums up my life dilemma, or at least one of them, right there.

And one other thing about the way I look: My wardrobe changes depending on my girlfriend at the time. They all seem to like to tell me how to dress—one favored the lumberjack look, so I invested in a lot of flannel shirts and corduroy pants and hiking boots, and right after that another girlfriend who detested grunge made me dump the whole closet full of flannel and buy an upsettingly expensive preppie wardrobe. My guy friends have told me I'm too suggestible and too easily swayed (they use more colorful terms than that), but I couldn't tell them—because I hardly understood it myself—that ever since I was eight years old, I have been terrified of a woman's disapproval.

My dad is a taxi driver, an inveterate gambler, and an amateur Henry Moore-style sculptor of no repute in Buenos Aires or anywhere else, and my mom mostly putters around. I fly down to that glittering city of immense boulevards and dangerous little dives whenever I can afford it, and I take my parents out for dinner along the Puerto Madera docklands, where they would otherwise never think to go on their own. "Oh, it's too expensive," "oh, it's too far away," that sort of thing, but after dinner every time, they seem really happy and pleased to have me as their generous and successful son. They're good people, but I know for a fact that my father keeps a bottle of red wine in the seat next to him when he's driving his taxi, like it's his favorite passenger, and takes swigs whenever he's just dropped off some tourist at the San Telmo market and is waiting for the next fare to come along. And then when the next fare *does* come along, my father drives with his left hand and now and again pets with his right the bottle's rounded shoulders, as if to assure himself that it isn't going anywhere.

And when he's in his workshop or at the kiln, it's the same story—he sculpts these faceless reclining figures with holes in their chests or bellies and no discernible gender, and it's like he has a hole of his own he's never going to fill. There's a great old Ray Bradbury story about a man who hears a continual mysterious "clink" coming from the darkened house next to his. All night long, in thirty-minute intervals, he'll hear *clink, clink, clink.* Nothing else, no TV, no talking, no arguing. So one day, he sneaks over to his neighbors' window and looks inside and sees this old husband and wife sitting side by side in kitchen chairs drinking cheap red wine, not saying a single word to one another, and every time they polish off a bottle they just drop it to the tile floor with a clink and open another.

That's my parents: *clink, clink, clink.*

And it's all my fault.

I made them into alcoholics because of what I did when I was eight years old.

Because I allowed, albeit not directly or deliberately so, a little girl in my care to fall between the bed and sea-green wall and die of suffocation.

So now there's something else about me you need to know, beside the fact that I have floppy hair and play the guitar. I love children but cannot have any. Not because I ever got into any legal trouble as a result of Elizabeth's death—I was eight years old, for God's sake!— but because I am afraid to. I am afraid that if my girlfriend or a future wife gets pregnant and bears a child, I will unthinkingly commit some act of omission that causes our child to die. And that, I cannot bear.

This is of course not something that occurred to me when I was eight, but it did when I was eighteen, when I started having sex with my first girlfriend. In one sense, it wasn't any big deal. I was the opposite of many young men you hear about who spread their seed indiscriminately; by contrast, I was excessively choosy about my girlfriends and fanatically careful about birth control. But even so, the prospect of pregnancy, and my fear of being unable to take care of the child that would result, has cast a shadow over my life ever since.

Just to be clear, MariAngela was not my girlfriend. I never told her that my parents were alcoholics, and I never told her what had happened to me and Willa when we were eight years old. And why would I? MariAngela and I were only casual friends, and I would see her only at work, not counting the times I was reminded of her by that woman on the train and that other woman hobbling along the pavement in Galena.

To be equally clear, I am not otherwise lacking in female companionship. A shadow is just a shadow, as I like to say. Having stayed behind in Chicago when my parents moved back to Buenos Aires for good, I managed to assemble a life that was every bit as good as any urban dweller of my acquaintance. I never developed an unnatural affection for alcohol, unlike my parents, or for gambling or for fruitless artistic pursuits, unless one counts the guitar. I had a great job in marketing, pretty and athletic girlfriends with legs built for chasing down backhands, a brand-new Lexus, and the joyless, steely sort of normalcy that is the hallmark of someone with a lot of guilt to repress and a lot of strength to repress it—though no strength whatsoever for either facing that guilt or attempting to peel back the infinite layers of equivocation and pluck out the heart of what actually had occurred.

MariAngela caught up with me later that evening and picked up our conversation right where we'd left off, but with a distinctly lighter tone. "So, anyway," she continued, "I forgot all about telling you, not that it matters anymore because of your weird dream, because I had other things on my mind, especially spending like a thousand hours on the Internet and eating a pint of coffee ice cream researching the horrible ways in which I'm going to die, and so naturally I couldn't get to sleep between staring at a screen all evening and worrying about dying, and, you know, the actual fucking disease *itself* which has been making me really kind of shaky and fatigued—which is why I went to the doctor in the first place. So anyway I'm lying there at 3:00 in the fucking morning staring at the ceiling, and I'm thinking, *Wasn't there something important I was supposed to do today?* And it wasn't until that moment that I remembered that I was planning to tell you about my, you know, *disease.*" She enunciated this last word with a meticulous distaste in her tone, as if holding up for inspection between a blood-stained thumb and forefinger a nasty little orange-eyed insect she had just pinched.

"So this was at about 3:00 A.M. when you were thinking of telling me?"

"Yeah."

I took a moment before responding.

"Well, first of all, before I get to the rest of it, I'm so, so sorry to hear of your illness. I feel like I haven't really had a chance to say that to you yet, so anyway...anyway, I'm sorry and I know you'll beat it because you drink wheatgrass and vodka cocktails" —she really did; she couldn't decide if she was an organic locavore health type or just a party-girl, part-time cocktail waitress type, so she mixed up both at once in the form of sugary cocktails with ginger, echinacea, Red Bull, and various forms of booze. "But anyway, I'm glad you decided to tell me and you know I'll always be your friend and help you through this, and, you know..."

"I know." She smiled for the first time. "You don't have to say it. But let's get something straight right from the gecko, Charlie...."

"Yeah?"

"There *is* no prognosis. You know? My neurologist says they've recently tracked down what causes ALS, but it's one of those diseases that is"—and here she lowered her voice to sound comically portentous, like she was narrating a documentary about her own life—"intractable, untreatable, and incurable." She shrugged. "No one ever recovers from ALS. It's a rollercoaster ride, but with only the part that shoots straight down, and it's real fast, and you're out of control and can't even steer, and then you just choke to death on your spit and you're dead."

"They're sure? I mean, that what you have is ALS and not something else like MS or something?"

"Totally sure. My calves kept on quivering when I was bringing plates of lasagna to people. Then it was my thumb so I was having trouble gripping the plates and was slopping primavera all over my wrists. And I was really fatigued, you know, the kind of tired where your bones feel almost hollow. I figured it was stress or something, but I went to this neurologist and after he ran some tests he said, 'You know, people come to me with severe headaches and they're always sure it's a brain tumor, but 90 percent of the time it's just migraines or something benign like that. But a young person comes to me with sudden unexplained weakness in the muscles, and they always assume the opposite, I mean that it's just stress or too much caffeine or something, but I get a sinking feeling 'cause I know what these cases look like, and then after I run the tests it's really hard to deliver the news because it's far, far worse than anything they could have imagined.' "

"I know you probably don't want to talk about this, but what exactly happens? I mean, when you get really sick?"

"You know, trapped in your fucking fucked-up body. The mind works just fine all the way until the end, but you get weaker and more paralyzed until you start shitting yourself and can't talk anymore, and then you're in a high-tech wheelchair, and then you choke on your spit like I said or choke on your food, or suffocate, or some combination of all three. So you can watch it all happening to yourself and you don't even have the...the...you know, *luxury,* of being fucking *unconscious* or *demented* or shit. You know, it's like, whatever." She had tears in her eyes.

"I'm really sorry." I kept on thinking about how MariAngela had just said "right from the gecko" instead of "right from the get-go," and it was so cute and so typical of her that I couldn't get my mind around what she was saying.

She broke the silence. "Listen, Charlie, I know this is already pretty weird, but what time did you have your dream about me?"

"You mean could it have been 3:00 A.M.?"

"Yeah, I mean, of *course* that's what I mean."

I thought about it for a moment. "I don't know. It's not like in bad TV where you have a nightmare and you sit bolt upright in bed and then you look at your phone or clock or whatever so the audience can see what time it is. It was one of, you know, a dozen dreams I probably had last night. I happened to remember it because it was strange and because it was about you. There's no way I could tell you if I had it the same time you were thinking about telling me."

But she knew, and I knew, that it didn't matter. That night, she had been inside my skull, speaking to me.

# 4

So now you know about the two big things that slammed into my otherwise unremarkable existence like a rotted tree crashing into the roof of a house followed, years later, by another tree smashing through the rafters again—one when I was eight years old, and one just now. First was the "incident," as my mother called it, with little Elizabeth that caused me to be afraid to have children of my own, and, second, the inexplicable nighttime visitation of MariAngela.

There's one other item of note before I can get on with the story of what happened to Willa and my parents and me after Elizabeth's death; the other story, equally consequential, of why MariAngela came to me in a dream and told me she was going to die soon; and the utterly unexpected way in which these two life events turned out to be connected.

The other item is a very strange sight (I can't call it either an image or an object, as it isn't exactly either one of those) that I encountered in the house that I'm renting.

The thing is, not long after I moved in, I discovered a shadow that'd been left by what once had been a child's dollhouse against the wall of a small dormer room located at the very back of the top floor of my rental house. It isn't actually a shadow, of course, but rather the outline, in dusty and faded buttercream-yellow paint, of what the dollhouse in vertical cross-section had once looked like. It was a classic dollhouse shape, with a big, more-or-less-square, undifferentiated room on the left, a simplified chimney shape on top, and two smaller rooms, one on top of the other, on the right. It looked nothing at all like the real house in which it could be found.

Apparently (because I never actually saw the dollhouse itself) the open back of the dollhouse had been attached by five screws through minuscule projecting flanges to the drywall in the dormer wall, which then must have doubled as the dollhouse's own "back wall." I know this because, to this day, the sharp buttercream-colored edges of the shadow are "pinned" to the dormer wall by screw holes, each of which is still filled with the intimate, soft white dust that had been left when the screws had been unscrewed from the little flanges and the dollhouse thus removed. There was one screw hole at the top of the "chimney"; two at the left edge of the house, where the downstairs living room and master bedroom must have been (assuming the children in charge had possessed a classic sense of design); and two more at the much-smaller right side of the house where, I imagined, the top floor had served as the children's bedroom and the bottom floor as the kitchen.

Or maybe the top floor on the right-hand side had been a lunar observatory and the bottom floor an ice cream parlor, and perhaps the left-hand side had been filled with a tangle of plastic farm animals, hooves to heads to hindquarters, or out-of-scale tables and chairs. It was a dollhouse, after all, and the children could put whatever they wanted in it, wherever they wanted to.

As I said, the dollhouse itself was gone, and so were the ill-matched accoutrements that had undoubtedly jumbled up its rooms, and so were the children who played with it. All that was left was the shape that had been created accidentally when someone painted around it with a coat of fresh sea-green paint—and yes, that, quite coincidentally, was the same color as the walls in Willa's house that I remember all too well. The owners of my rental house probably insisted on unscrewing the dollhouse to complete the paint job, and the children must have insisted on keeping it in place, and the children must have won, and so the dollhouse had stayed in place until the family had moved—so only the buttercream-colored shadow of the dollhouse remained.

Only the shadow and, more or less in the middle of the "big" room that constituted the left-hand portion of the shadow, an actual pair of miniature wooden shutters.

These were approximating real French window shutters that opened inward, but of course they were Lilliputian in size and made from a fragile wood that probably was balsa, though with a single, slender brushstroke of light varnish to stiffen them a bit, and there they were, whole and complete in the middle of the buttercream-yellow shadow in the middle of the blank sea-green wall. The shutters were no bigger from top to bottom than a quarter, and each one no wider than a child's thumb, and they were attached on either side to the miniature "window" in the wall by a delicate hinge assembled with a Swiss watchmaker's skill.

The flat wall of the dormer room faced the street, and the clever adult who'd built the dollhouse and affixed it to the wall had also had the wonderful notion to cut through the drywall and brick and create a window that his children could open or close at will. For the marvelous thing was, when you slipped your fingernail under one of the shutters and then pried them both open with your fingertips, a diffuse beam of actual peachy sunlight appeared in the gloomy dormer room. The opposing wall of the dormer sloped, and the sea-green paint was covered with old crayon scribbles involving abstract loops and awkward stick figures. When the shutters were opened, the peach-colored light illuminated a sloping section of very old yellow crayon marks, and the buttercream yellow of the dollhouse shadow and the yellow of the crayon seemed to be winking at each other, as if they shared a kinship in what was otherwise a sea of green.

At night, the glow from the streetlights was bleary and weak, but it still illuminated, ever so slightly, the yellow crayon marks on the opposite wall. The sunlight and streetlight wouldn't have illuminated anything except the opposite wall's baseboard molding, in fact, if the dollhouse had been attached to the wall in a natural way, which is to say at a right angle to the floor, creating a kind of linoleum "sidewalk" leading to the house. But instead, the dollhouse had been affixed a foot or so above the floor, so that it appeared to float on the wall. I could almost see the children kneeling on their haunches on the worn, buckled white linoleum, delightedly opening and closing those clever little shutters at a level that would have been about even with their eyes. I could see, almost, the formless patch of sunlight that must have played on their innocent eyelids and unformed cheekbones and fine messy hair, and I could feel, as they must have felt, the infinitesimal piercing draft of cold when the weather turned. What a wonderful adult to have created such a thing, when the dormer room was so small (it was clearly intended only for storage) that anyone larger than a toddler would have had to kneel in order to install that dollhouse with its shutters, or to view it as I did now.

Kneel, or lie uncomfortably on one side, with one's legs extending into the bedroom that the dormer room adjoined. But lying on one side would have left only one arm free to cut that tiny rectangle through the wall of the house and install those precise hinges and featherlight shutters, so kneeling had been, I assumed, the way it had been done.

I would find out later that I was wrong.

Regardless of method, the shutters existed, and they opened and closed. And thus it was here, in this actual house, in this dormer room at the top of this actual house, in this shadow of a dollhouse that floated above the linoleum floor of the dormer room, and in the shuttered "window" that opened up a tiny sliver of the slanted and cramped little room to the actual sunlight outside, that I discovered why MariAngela had come to me in my dream, and what had actually happened to Willa and me when we were eight years old and to little Elizabeth when she was an infant. That's the story I want to tell—how I solved those two mysteries and, having solved them, where I went from there.

# 5

As far as the house itself is concerned, I'm just renting it for a couple of years from a family who moved to the Philippines to do some kind of Christian missionary work. There's something pretty weird about the family, but this is not a ghost story, at least not exactly, so don't get the idea that my house is haunted or anything along those lines. It's a rambling old house—once upon a time, the rental agent told me, a farmhouse—with a lot of little cupboards and cubbyholes and crawl spaces, many of which I have yet to explore, and many of which are still crammed with junk from the missionary family, or from their predecessors, or, who knows, from the farmers who originally built the place. For example, I'm not exactly sure what a "harrow" is, but I think I saw the spiky points of one, along with some ancient cardboard boxes of ant killer and some soiled spades, in one of the crawl spaces in the basement, but the space was crawling with earthworms, so I never investigated further.

I'm not home a lot, because I travel quite a bit to meet with clients and do marketing audits, and of course I fly down to Buenos Aires when I can to visit my parents. And, as I've noted, when I'm not working I like to play guitar and perform my music—a sort of alt-country, folk-soul hybrid leaning more to the folk side, with Michael Stipe phrasing because my lyrics are oblique and I like it that way. I perform mostly at Berto's on their "acoustic nights" and once in a blue moon (or as MariAngela calls it, a "blue mood") at a few other small clubs around town. I'm a pretty damn good songwriter, I think, though apparently not too many other people think so, based on my lack of success so far. Look me up in the Apple Store or Spotify, or just Google my name or something, and you'll see what I mean: You'll find me pretty much nowhere.

The point I want to make is that I'm a "sensitive songwriter" and all that, but in general, I'm no more or less sensitive than any other guy. I have an incredibly pretty girlfriend in Alisa, and I treat her a little more apathetically than I should from time to time—other than, of course, being extremely careful not to get her pregnant. And I'm not touchy-feely or new-agey, and I have no particular interest in my Argentine or Italian "heritage," since I was actually born here, and my parents didn't return there for good until I was in college, and most important of all, I have no psychic abilities whatsoever.

Whatever happened to me, and to MariAngela, and to my girlfriend Alisa, and to everyone else, was kind of thrust on me. Like electromagnetic waves in the atmosphere, or the ions that arrive every instant from the farthest reaches of the universe, it all just sort of floated in through an open window.

A couple of nights after my odd encounter with MariAngela, Alisa and I went out with Alisa's coworker at her PR agency, Frank, and his wife Diane. Alisa is twenty-nine and I'm twenty-eight, but this couple is about ten years older than us, and I think Alisa was drawn to them because she was holding them out to me as an example of what a successful marriage could look like ten years down the road. That was fine with me—I'm not one of those types of men who makes sparks on the sidewalk with his heels while his girlfriend drags him to the altar. I really *want* to get married and to feel as if a woman trusts me enough to spend her life with me, though with one understanding between the two of us that should be clear enough by now.

Frank was a little bit of the professorial type, but not in a superpompous way, and Diane, who's a labor-law attorney, was incredibly lively. She had those midlife braces on her teeth you see on some women that make them seem touchingly hopeful about the future, and she laughed constantly, though not at all in an annoying way, as if she were proud of the braces and wanted to show them off. The braces seemed like they were in a race against time with her laugh lines, but she didn't seem to care, and everything she said, just about, was full of happiness and good cheer, and she had a little chestnut-brown pixie cut that swished back and forth as she turned from face to face at the table, making sure that everyone was having a good time like she was. After one of our dinners, Alisa had said, "I just don't think she's vivacious enough," and we laughed for a good long time about that.

Alisa herself was a lot quieter and had some levels that weren't open to the public, if you know what I mean. She had amazing green eyes and light blondish-brown hair that made a straight line across the middle of her forehead, and she was very tall—my height, five foot eleven. She was very, very pretty, as I mentioned, with luminous pale skin, though her jaw seemed a bit too large for her face, and that alone kept her from being genuinely beautiful. When she was upset, which was often enough, she'd jut it out and lock it into position like a lantern fish, and at those times, she became ugly and fearsome to me, and I had trouble even looking at her.

There was something about all of these factors—her height, her temper, the fact that she was a year older than me, and the fact that she had an enigmatic quality where, even after nearly three years of dating, I wasn't sure I entirely knew her—that made me a little afraid of her, if I can be honest. She'd even played volleyball in college for a couple of years, at Coronado State in San Diego, and was a better athlete than me, and probably almost as strong as I was, which isn't a big deal, I guess, except my Latin heritage made it one. On top of everything else, it seemed very important to her to be smarter than me, and part of that meant rolling her eyes, a little bit, at some of the songs I wrote. She well understood the words "jejune" and "sophomoric" and "callow," and she wasn't hesitant to use them. I was afraid, at those times, to remind her that I was the one who'd taught her what those words meant to begin with.

But none of this really strikes at the heart of it. Even if Alisa had been perfect in every way, I still believe I would have felt unhappy all of the time, as I did with all of my girlfriends and my dwindling band of other acquaintances. There was a continual lump in my chest and stomach that corresponded with the holes in the chests and stomachs of my father's epicene odalisques. I didn't know what this lump was for the longest time, or how it related to the mystery of Elizabeth—because I didn't understand for the longest time that there *was* a mystery. So I just sort of navigated through my days with Alisa, attentive only to her insults and insensible to all of the rest of her.

Did she know about what had happened with Elizabeth? Sure. Did she hold it against me? Not at all. If anything, she was very careful to reassure me that it was the sort of careless thing that any little boy could have done, but there was always the implication, somehow, that the careless little boy in question was, in its present-day incarnation, me.

But I was always more relaxed with her when we went out with Frank and Diane because both of us respected them, and Alisa seemed to be impressed that Frank, in particular, was impressed by me. So I generally looked forward to our double dates. Maybe that meant there was something wrong in our relationship that I needed a buffer like Frank and Diane, but obviously so did Alisa, so there you go.

This night, we went to see a movie that was squirming and jumping all over with glittery CGI effects like a dead dog with maggots and fleas, and we were all pretty disgusted by how bad it was, but then we went to a steak house and had a few drinks, and I decided to tell them all the story about my prophetic dream. I figured it'd be at least a little more interesting to talk about than the movie.

Frank corrected me right away. "It wasn't prophetic. You told me she was already diagnosed when you had the dream. I think it was more of a 'clairvoyant' dream."

I said, "Claire who?" Alisa looked at me and snorted. She didn't especially like it when I played the fool, and that, in turn, made me feel foolish. The whole point of deliberately playing the fool was the humor that was inherent in the ironic contrast with one's actual intelligence, but it sometimes seemed as if Alisa missed the "intelligence" aspect of it entirely, and focused only on the "fool" part. And yet if I had indicated to Frank that I knew precisely what "clairvoyant" meant—and of course I did—that would have irritated Alisa even more.

"Clairvoyant," Frank said. "She was somehow communicating with you telepathically. I think we all have those skills but they're vestigial"—Alisa shot me a look in case I was planning to pretend I didn't know what that word meant either—"and it's only in times of high and low emotion that the connection gets made."

Alisa said, as if she were prompting the explanation along for my benefit rather than really needing to know, "What do you mean by high and low emotion?"

"Well, I'm just a PR guy, but I just think that when some insensitive, blockhead ass like your boyfriend"—I smiled at this; I'd heard worse, and I knew that Frank's comment was more of a statement of disapproval about Alisa's implied judgment of me than it was actually *about* me—"is sleeping, it's about the only time our defenses are completely down and relaxed, and we return to this animal state where our vestigial senses are awake. No bills, no work, no crappy movies, no relationship issues to get in the way and block the transmissions.

"But at the same time, your friend MaryAnn or whatever you said her name was, she's in a state of extremely *high* emotion because she's just been diagnosed with a deadly disease, so it's like water being poured from a full vessel into an empty one, if you will. You know, 'seeking its own level.' That's how she delivered her message to you, even though she wasn't aware that she was doing it."

I thought to myself, *If you will.* That was exactly the kind of thing Frank would say, because it was the kind of thing that professors would say. He was a big, rangy guy with a high forehead, muscular biceps and forearms, and a kind of soft, distant, "wise" look in his eyes that made him look like an especially vigorous emissary from the future. But I liked him; he respected me.

"And it doesn't only happen when you're dreaming. Let me give you an example. This was years ago; I'm coming down the down escalator at Midway from some flight to who-knows-where, and there's this flight attendant going up the up escalator, and just at the moment she passes me, in other words rises above me, she happens to turn around and glance down at me, and I saw this look on her face." He paused and closed his eyes for a moment. "She was young and slender and a lot better looking than most flight attendants these days, but I noticed that she had kind of a stiff, old-fashioned hairstyle and also a stiff posture, and her face, oh, man, that face, it was haughty, and imperious, and disappointed, and pretentious, and there were practically tears in her eyes. And it was like she was instantaneously communicating to me that she found men insufferable and her family uncultured and her fellow stewardesses stupid and cowlike and that I was someone, or maybe I was the *only* one, who could understand her and make her happy."

Diane snorted. "You knew all this from one glance she gave you?"

"Yeah, and more. It was because she was really upset about something at that very moment, probably a man who'd yet again let her down, and I was just diddling around on the escalator waiting to get down to baggage claim and pick up my bags and not thinking about anything in particular. So when it hit me, it hit me like an electric shock, and it wasn't only the things I told you either, it was like I instantaneously knew how she felt when she was having sex, and how she hated her mother, and how she couldn't find anyone to talk with about good books, and everything, and then by the time I looked up again, she'd hit the top of the escalator and was gone."

"Poor Frankie! The love of your life!" The way Diane said this, it was a little hard to interpret. She wasn't sarcastic or dismissive or angry, and indeed her tone was rather light, but there was a strained quality to it, too, which Alisa and I acknowledged to each other with a quick glance.

In any event, Alisa jumped in before Frank could answer. "Okay, I know what you're saying about high emotion and low emotion. It reminds me of this thing we learned in college English about 'negative capability,' where if you're a true poet, you can sort of let your mind go slack and become open to things you otherwise wouldn't have ever noticed. But I don't know what you mean about this 'vestigial senses' business. Just, like, ESP?"

"Not necessarily. I mean, I don't even believe in ESP, and I know Charlie doesn't either. It's all a load of bullshit and wishful thinking. But there's something else." He picked up his steak knife and said, "Okay, Alisa, since you were foolish enough to ask, I'm going to play a little game with you. Lean forward."

Obediently, without even asking why, Alisa did as she was told. I felt a pang about this, because if I picked up a knife in front of Alisa and tried to play whatever game it was Frank was about to play, she would have given me hell and implied I wanted to kill her or something.

Frank also leaned forward and brought the tip of the steak knife close to Alisa's eyes. Diane said "Whoa," and grabbed at Frank's wrist, but he just pushed her away with his other hand.

"Don't worry, there's relatively little eye gouging involved in this experiment." Then, in a softer voice that wasn't directed to anyone else at the table, he said, "Trust me, Alisa, I haven't stabbed anyone in a long time."

He took a deep breath and brought the knife back in front of Alisa's eyes. "Now close your eyes," he said. Again, although this time with a nervous laugh, Alisa did as she was told.

"Now, Diane and Charlie, watch carefully, but don't say anything." Now he very slowly brought the tip of the knife down to the bridge of Alisa's nose and held it there, less than a millimeter away from her skin. "Alisa? Okay. Keep your eyes closed and concentrate. Tell me what you're feeling right now."

Alisa thought for a moment and said, "Nothing." Then she said, "Oh, my God," and opened her eyes very suddenly. "It was bristling! It was like you were holding a magnet to my face and all the tiny hairs on my face were made out of iron filings or something and they were all moving! God, it felt creepy. Don't ever do that again!" And she mock-threatened Frank with a fork in her right hand, but with her left hand she had picked up her own steak knife and waved it in my direction.

It was my turn. I closed my eyes and Alisa carefully brought the knife to the bridge of my nose, and for a long time I felt nothing, and I forgot about my clairvoyant dream and reminded myself that I was an insensitive blockhead after all, but then I felt it—an infinitesimal cringing sensation on the skin between my eyes, a faint tingling at the bridge of my nose and, most of all, a sense that the tiny hairs on my face were erect, alert, and bristling. I thought of wolves and coyotes and badgers, and of a terrified opossum I'd once encountered standing stock-still behind my house at midnight, and of housecats puffed up in fear.

"So," Frank said, as Alisa put down her knife—though not without first mock stabbing me just for the hell of it—"that's a vestigial sense. Not a big deal. We all have 'em; we just almost never use 'em. Another one is when you stand at the edge of a cliff and peer over and you get a tingling or aching sensation in your groin. Some people claim they don't know what I'm talking about, but that's because they're not paying attention to themselves."

By this time, our food had arrived—veal Oscar for me, a steak salad for Diane, cliff-like slabs of pork chops for Frank, and a delicate little rack of lamb for Alisa that I couldn't bear to look at—and suddenly Diane spoke up for what seemed to be the first time in hours, even though we hadn't been at the restaurant for more than forty minutes in all. She was murmuring in a low voice, and it sounded so unlike her usual lively self that we all sort of sat up and paid attention.

"Did you ever notice the one thing all dreams have in common? In every dream I ever have, and maybe everyone's dreams?"

We all looked at each other.

I said, "They're boring if they're someone else's?"

Frank opened his mouth to say something more intelligent, but closed it again, stumped. Alisa said, "They're irrational?" But recognizing the inadequacy of her response, she just shrugged when no one said anything in response.

"So here it is. A lot of dreams are about sex, right? And a lot of dreams are about traveling. And a lot of dreams are about being unprepared for tests and being lost in strange cities and stuff like that. And yeah, Alisa, they're all irrational and strange, I mean, that goes without saying that we usually don't have dreams that make sense. And I would also say that most dreams are about feeling confused and at a loss in some way. But I'm talking about something else. I'm talking about, if you're dreaming that you're in your home, even if you've been living in your actual home for the past thirty years and know it inside out and backward, the dream home is going to look completely different. Why? I mean, why should this be the case, when even your unconscious mind knows perfectly well what your own house looks like?"

Everyone else was eating by now, but Diane just kept on going. I thought of the slanting wall in my house's dormer room, and of the slanting walls in the version of Berto's I had dreamed.

"And at some point during the dream, your home is going to turn into an airport or a Chinese restaurant or something. And if you're talking to your father in your dream, first of all he's not really going to look like your father, and maybe he'll have 'breasts' that you think are a little weird for some reason you can't quite put your finger on, and second of all, at some point he's suddenly going to turn into your college boyfriend or whatever, and *he's* not going to look like himself either, and then all of a sudden you're on a tour boat on the River Volga fishing for sturgeon with slices of pork."

We could tell she'd thought of that example because Frank had ordered the pork chops. He said, "Okay, let's grant what you're saying is true. In dreams, everything changes."

Diane said, "No, in dreams everything constantly *shifts*. That's a little bit different. Everything is constantly unstable, like it's all melting like a big bowl of sherbet and the colors are swirling together. And here's what I'm getting at."

Frank said, in his mock-professorial voice, "Yeah, Diane, why don't you tell us what you're getting at?" Big laughter all around the table. She waited for it to stop.

"Well, what is the one thing all of us have in common in our real, waking lives? No matter how important or unimportant or young or old we are, we are all getting older at exactly the same rate, one minute at a time, with every breath we take, no exceptions, no exemptions. If you're a kid, you're growing, and if you're an old fart, you're dying, but either way, every day you're one step closer to death. You...cannot...hold onto...anything. Ever."

Frank said, "Well, this isn't something any of us don't already know."

She looked at Frank directly now. "But our knowledge of this fact was inborn, or I should say *created* in us the moment we were ripped from that incredibly comfortable and safe and warm womb, so that we instantly knew in our bones that nothing was ever going to be safe and comfortable and predictable ever again, that we were going to change and grow old and then die, and sometimes at a young age from a horrible stupid disease like ALS, and this inherent knowledge, this *vestigial* knowledge that's as much of a reflex as the hairs bristling on our face, *that* is the thing that causes us to dream in a way in which everything is unstable and shifting and ripped away from us at any given moment. At the end of the day—"

"The end of the night," I interrupted.

"Yeah, at the end of the night. Okay. At the end of the night, all of our dreams are rehearsing and remembering and trying to work out this terrible knowledge that everything slips away, and that's why in our dreams we feel confused and lost and everything *does* slip away. What is underlying all of it, every time we 'lose' our home or our parents in a dream and they disappear and we forget about them and suddenly find ourselves fishing with pork on the Volga is the absolute shock and outrage we once felt about being born, because at that moment we also experience the shock and outrage we will feel when we realize we are going to die. And we never forget this, and it haunts us every time we close our eyes."

For the entire duration of Diane's speculations, I had been fighting an urge to flee to the bathroom or leave the restaurant entirely, stranding Alisa with her friends. I couldn't take it when Diane talked about feeling our deaths in our bones, and I especially couldn't take it when she talked about how our dreams shifted and transmuted, because it made me think not at all of MariAngela but rather of a long, white box of roses that, when opened, revealed instead of roses a tiny human skeleton.

But being the good and responsible person that I was, I shoved away this image (which was something real and certainly not a dream) and attended, if not so much to Diane's words, at the very least to the meaning behind the words. And so to avoid giving anyone at the table the impression that anything was disturbing me, I forced myself to ask a reasonable and perfectly apropos question.

"So you're saying that MariAngela's shock and outrage about dying from a neurological illness somehow communicated itself to me before I even knew she was sick?"

"No, not exactly. Or maybe that's part of it, too. But what I'm really saying is that your *own* shock and outrage about your *own* doomed existence is what made you pick up on her communication. You heard her with the little hairs on your face, or the little hairs inside of your ears, or whatever."

I took a long time to answer, and when I did, my voice sounded high and light, like someone else's. "I sort of understand, but why did it just happen for the first time that night? I've had other friends who were distraught or died." I started to say more, but

I was too close to the edge and too focused on Elizabeth's death to think about MariAngela's life, so I just sort of stared at the food on my plate for a moment.

"First of all, Charlie, I don't believe it's never happened to you before. I think if you searched your memory you'd see that it's happened many times before. But let's assume that it's happened rarely. Why, this one night, did you pick up on this one woman's transmission that wasn't even directed at you?"

"Because he's got a thing for her, that's why," Alisa said, and the three of them laughed.

"Well, maybe," Diane said, "and maybe she likes him, too." She said this as if it were a matter of the slightest consequence, and my opinion—and for that matter, Alisa's—didn't matter at all. "My point isn't about why he had this particular dream this particular night. For whatever reason, he was 'open' that night, like how every once in a while your neighbor's Wi-Fi music files used to pop up on your computer. But the point is that we're all dreaming the same thing every time we dream, no matter how stupid or random the surface subject matter might be: We're remembering what it was like to be born, when everything was shapeless and incomprehensible, and we're dealing with how we morph into something different every single moment of our lives, and we're dreading what it'll be like when we finally morph into something horrible and gruesome to look at and then we die."

I know that I haven't presented a very good portrait of Diane. I'd never even heard her refer to death before, and she really is incredibly vivacious most of the time.

But after that, it took us a few seconds—it felt like minutes—to pick up our forks and start eating again.

# 6

***That*** night, because we'd both had too much to drink, and perhaps because we were both a bit unsettled by what Frank and Diane had had to say, Alisa spent the night at my house. Normally, we spent the nights together only on the weekends. No big reason, and I really probably did want to marry her, but she's a morning person and I'm a night person, and we both travel a lot, so it's just easier to keep separate places. I'm not thrilled about her sterile condo, and she's equally unenthused about my creaky old house with the weird dormer room and the Christian missionary furniture, but that night, she was happy to be in bed with me.

The sex thing didn't seem to be happening that night, because she said she'd eaten too much and her tummy was a little sensitive, so I rubbed her stomach for her, being the good guy I am, and then I kneaded the little hollow area under her ribs, and then I slid slowly over the ribs and massaged her breasts for a while and nibbled the side of her neck, and then she must have felt better because she started to lift her hips up and down slowly at first and then really fast, and I got my underwear off in a big hurry before she'd changed her mind. She seemed more turned on than usual and grunted even louder than normal, and that turned *me* on even more, even though it sounded a little bit like the baby-seal noise that MariAngela had made.

Or maybe *because* it sounded like the noise that MariAngela had made.

She came so hard that her eyes actually rolled backward into her head for a second. Afterward, neither of us could get to sleep, and then Alisa said, lightly, "You know what would be cool? How about if I try to communicate my dream to you tonight? Like, I'll dream about something specific, you know, a rake or a shovel or something, and then in the morning you tell me the objects you had in your dream, and maybe one of them will be a rake or a shovel."

I laughed. "But how are you going to control what you dream about? Maybe while you're falling asleep, you'll plan on dreaming about a rake, but it'll end up that you're dreaming about an igloo instead, and then you'll forget what you dreamed about anyway, and then I'll wake up and it turns out that I dreamed about storing slices of American cheese under my armpits and then where'll we be?"

At this, Alisa laughed too. We dropped the subject and went to sleep.

Except we didn't really drop it at all. I had to go to New York for a couple of days to interview some job candidates for a creative director position, but when I got back, Alisa was all excited. I'd wanted to tell her about my walk along the High Line, and the Chelsea Market, and the Picasso show I'd seen at the Gagosian (speaking of suprarational transmutations!), but she had her own agenda.

"Okay, so I've been doing some research. Duke University used to do a bunch of investigations into psychic phenomena, and the results were pretty inconclusive, but I read about this one really simple experiment that I think we could do with your dreams."

We were sitting in Alisa's condo. I had come straight from the airport, and I was pretty fatigued, so I just flipped my palm up to indicate my apathy.

"C'mon, Charles. You can zone out later, but this is important. I won't even try to describe the Duke experiments themselves, and frankly I thought a lot of them were pretty pointless, but I've adapted one of them for us. It's basically about just sending the simplest possible message to you, without any emotional content at all, just a binary code like a computer."

"Meaning?"

"Just a yes or a no."

"But what about what Frank was saying at dinner about high emotion and low emotion?"

"That's all well and good, but it was a total fluke. He said so, even Diane said so. She had this big theory about why we dream the way we do, but even she was totally lame when it came to explaining why MariAngela came to you in your dream that particular night. If it was just a matter of high emotion and low emotion, we'd be having dreams with our distraught friends in them all the time."

"So if we can't explain why this happened to me this one time, how are we going to replicate it artificially? I mean, you can't will that kind of thing unless you're a professional psychic, which I'm not sure even exists."

"I'm not either, and I don't think the Duke experiments proved anything one way or another. But this is such a simple thing, either 'yes' or 'no,' that, I don't know, it's just a little blip that can leak through your defenses. Basically, what I'm going to do is just go down to the basement. You know that light switch just above the laundry table across from the washing machines?"

"You mean here, in your condo? Not really. No."

"No, I guess you wouldn't. That would mean you'd done my laundry for me at some point in our relationship."

"What are you talking about? When you had the flu? And that other time, after your 'margarita mistake?' " I didn't have to explain what I meant by that; both times, I had washed her clothes in her condo's laundry room, but I sure hadn't been paying attention to any light switch. I'd also been down there once or twice to search for an opening where chipmunks had been sneaking in; they'd scamper up a chink in the foundation walls and through a heating vent in the floor of Alisa's living room, where they'd proceed to pillage whatever oatmeal cookies and granola bars, or crumbs thereof, she'd left lying around in the kitchen.

She said, "Okay, so you've done my laundry a couple times. I stand corrected. But let's not get off track."

"You were the one who got off track with the laundry crack."

"Just listen. So what I'm going to do is go down to the basement tonight before I go to bed. Are you sleeping here tonight?" I shook my head. "Well, doesn't matter one way or another, I don't think. I mean, MariAngela wasn't in bed with you when you had the dream about her, was she? Ha ha. So anyway, I go down to the basement and flip the light switch either up or down. That's all I do. And when you're drifting off to sleep, you know, just at that point where you start to realize that you're falling asleep, I want you to concentrate on the image of me flipping the light switch. I'm going to do that every single night from now on."

"And then what?"

"And then nothing. I do this every single night before I go to bed, and eventually, one of these nights, I think you're going to have a dream about it. I mean, that's what I'm hoping, and that's what this research was talking about. You'll have a dream where you're seeing me flip the light switch, and you'll either see me flip it up or down, and then you'll remember it the next day and tell me."

I was quite unimpressed. "And then what?"

"And then we'll go to the basement together and see if the light switch is in the position you saw it in, in your dream."

"Yeah? So?"

"So then, I don't know if you've heard of this thing called lucid dreaming, but the idea is that if you really concentrate on your dreams before you go to sleep, then while you're sleeping, you can start to control the action of your dreams a little bit. You know how Diane was talking at dinner about how everything shifts in your dreams and nothing is stable? Well, if you're a lucid dreamer, you can start controlling the shifting and making things happen the way you want them to, just because you're aware in your dream that you're dreaming, so you can do anything you want to do. I mean, sometimes I'm dreaming that I'm walking in the middle of the air, and then suddenly I kind of will myself to wake up because I know it's just a dream, and then I wake up and get out of bed, but I'm *still* walking in the air, but it feels incredible because it's real."

"You mean, you've dreamt that you've woken up, but you're actually still sleeping."

"Exactly. But it just *feels* more real is what I'm saying. So in your case, if you really focus on the light switch and making it real, you can control that, too, and pretty soon every night if we're lucky you'll be dreaming about the light switch."

"Still not quite making the connection."

"If you dream every night about the light switch, and you're right about its position more or less just half of the time, then there is no connection. But if every time you have the dream, the light switch is in the position I left it in, then you're psychic. There's no other explanation. I mean, either you've picked up what I did with the light switch..."

"Or...?"

"Or, this just occurred to me, maybe the causality works in the other direction, and you somehow influence me, here in the waking world, to flip the switch one way or the other, and your dream just confirms what you already know. Either way, it's cool, and it works."

"Yeah, so what if I happen to guess right one night? I tell you the next morning that it's 'up' and you say, 'Wow, you're psychic!' Then the next night, since I know it's up to begin with, the only way you can flip it is down—wash, rinse, repeat, I'll be right every time."

"Nice try. But I can toggle the switch up and down as many times as I want, purely at random—I mean, unless you really are somehow influencing my supposedly random acts, though the more I think about it the less likely I think that is. No, it's all about me and how I communicate to you in your dreams the position I leave the switch in. I could leave it in the up position five nights in a row if I wanted. And there's no way you'd know the pattern, unless it came to you in your dreams."

I thought about this for a moment. "But why can't I just do the same thing you're talking about while I'm awake? I can just stare off into space and guess, or visualize, or whatever, the position of the light switch. And then I'll tell you what position it's in."

She took her forefinger and pointed it directly to the bridge of my nose. I swear at that moment, even though it wasn't a knife, the hairs bristled again. "That's why," she said. "Because it's something that's out of your conscious control. It can only happen when you dream."

A moment before, Alisa had said, "I stand corrected" in that supercilious way she had, as if she hadn't actually been wrong at all. But I suddenly thought of something so obvious and stupid about her plan that she would have to admit she was wrong no matter what.

"So what's to prevent your neighbors from flipping the switch themselves? Especially if the light is burning in the middle of the day or the middle of the night when it doesn't have to be, or it *isn't* on in the evening when it *should* be? You live in a four-flat. That's three other sets of neighbors who can flip the switch any time they come down to do the laundry."

"Ah, Charlie, Charlie, Charlie. You don't even know the light switch I'm talking about. The one right above that long folding table for the laundry? No one ever touches it because it's not connected to anything."

She was right again. Suddenly, I had an image of the little Gilbert science kit I'd received for my seventh or eighth birthday, not long before we'd been forced to move back to Buenos Aires for a few years. It had a miniature light bulb you screwed into a circuit board and a bunch of switches you had to flip in just the right order to complete the electrical series and make the connection work properly. I couldn't figure it out for a long while, and the bulb remained stubbornly un-illuminated, and I felt really disappointed and incompetent. But finally I'd gotten the switches in the right order and the miniature bulb suddenly *glowed*. It was incredibly beautiful, that minuscule glow. It had made me feel so happy and triumphant, even though I turned on and off lights all over the house all of the time, and those bulbs glowed in pretty much the same way. Maybe it was because I'd done it myself. My feelings now were a little more complicated, but inside of my head, right at about the spot where MariAngela had appeared, a little spot was glowing.

# 7

If anything, I felt even more excited than I had as an eight-year-old, so we tried the experiment for several nights running, but this time around, neither one of us could flip the switches in a way that worked. I couldn't remember my dreams for the most part, and when I did, they had nothing to do with the light switch in the basement of Alisa's condo, much less what position it was in. Most of them were my usual confused dreams about traveling and getting lost on trains and subways, and Diane would probably say that this was really all about my memories of passing through the birth canal or my fears of passing through that other tunnel into the bright white light at the moment of my death, or something. In any event, as Diane also said, my dreams were about being helpless and lost, and that helplessness extended itself to being utterly unable to "see" what Alisa was doing with the light switch.

Alisa and I went down to her basement once or twice, but to what end, I cannot say. We'd just stand there looking at the switch and at the laundry table, and Alisa would sigh, a bit wistfully, as if she'd been expecting more from me. As long as we were down there, I'd check the chipmunk trap that I'd periodically bait with a dab of chunky peanut butter. It was a cage the size of a toaster oven, placed in the corner behind the washing machines, and it was always empty. But the previous summer, the small cage had captured six or seven of the little guys, and so had a second trap

I'd set in Alisa's condo, right near the heating grate in the living room. One time I'd placed a granola bar, still in its silvery wrapper, about a foot away from the trap in the living room so I could catch one of them in the act. That same day, while Alisa and I were in the kitchen making sandwiches, we heard an unmistakable rustling, wrinkling sound and tiptoed back into the living room to see a chipmunk struggling to open the bar; he looked like a lumberjack trying to balance a log on his shoulders. After a while, the chipmunk gave up trying to tear through the wrapper (he didn't understand that there was a little notch in the wrapper, nor did he have the opposable thumbs to exploit it), so Alisa and I watched, fascinated, as he sniffed his way toward the peanut butter at the back of the trap, and then, when he triggered the mechanism and the barred gate slammed shut behind him, he twirled around and flung himself against the gate in a scrambling panic. I took the trap out to a nearby park and let the little guy go, and for all I know the basement and living-room traps were populated, all that summer, by the same two chipmunks making the same journey—over and over, from the park where I'd left them, across the busy street, and back into Alisa's condo.

Maybe the low emotion that Diane had referred to was out of the question, because I was in my own sort of caged, scrambling panic. I could barely sleep at all. Mostly it was because of my job. A lot of companies were pulling in their horns as far as traditional marketing programs were concerned, spending less on PR and advertising and building cross-platform social media programs—or taking all the work in-house. I wasn't exactly on the bubble, but I could sort of sense in my normal, non-psychic way that my boss was humming thoughtfully every time he passed my desk and I wasn't working on anything. It made me feel like even more of a failure than I already thought I was, and that made it very hard to get back to work. So during the day I was staring at the office walls a lot, and at night I was staring at the ceiling a lot.

In fact, I was examining the off-white wall in my office at the very moment when my father, for the first time in several months, called me on my cell.

He said, in his still-serviceable English, "Hello, Carlos. I've shattered my kneecap."

His tone was a little muzzy though; his voice seemed hollow and very weak, like the outline of an elaborate drawing that hadn't been shaded in.

"Your what? Your *kneecap?* Shit, Dad. How?"

"What does it matter how? I need you down here. I'm in agony."

"I know, I know. Let me—I have to see what I can do."

"Why?"

"I mean about when I can get down there."

"I know. Why?"

"Why? Because I have a job, and because what if this is another one of your false alarms?"

"What do you mean, fucking false alarm? I lost a lot of blood. The pain from the kneecap—it's beyond description. Thank God I lost consciousness. It was like the worst electric shock you could imagine. For the first few minutes, I prayed I would die. And then I prayed...and then the ambulance came."

"Shit, I'm so sorry. How did this happen?"

"Just come down here, and I'll explain the whole story."

"Dad, I have responsibilities. I can't just come down there. Especially when you're not being honest with me."

"You don't believe I've shattered my kneecap? I'll text you the picture. It'll make you puke your guts out."

"That's not what I mean by not being honest."

"What do you mean?"

"You know what I mean. You started to say 'and then I prayed....' What could you possibly pray for after you prayed to die?"

"Well, that I'd live, of course. That the ambulance would come. I changed my mind, okay?"

"Dad, that's not what I heard. What I heard was you starting to say 'and then I prayed *he'd* die.' "

"Who is he?"

"That's what I'm asking you, Dad. Who did this to you? If you'd just shattered your kneecap, you would've told me how it happened by now—you slipped on a step, another taxi hit you, some story with alcohol slopping around in it for sure. But you haven't told me how, so I have to think it's something bad, and that would mean that someone did this to you because of something you did."

"My God. My God. You should have been a detective."

"So someone did?"

"Shot me. Yes."

"Because of Trilenium?" That was the casino he frequented; I'd had a vague idea that he'd been losing a lot of money there, just as, when I was a child, I'd remembered my mother fighting with him about his visits to Chicago-area racetracks like Maywood and Arlington Park.

"It doesn't matter why."

"So, because of Trilenium. I figured."

"All I want is for you to come down here and take care of me."

"Father, you know I can't do that. Not now. Isn't Mother taking care of you?"

"I'm on so many painkillers right now I couldn't tell you who's doing what. I just can't go through that again."

"Wait. Go through what again?"

"Shithead, being shot again."

"Again, why again?"

"Because the first two kneecaps were just to get me to pay attention."

"Wait a minute. First *two?* You said 'kneecap' before. Now it's *both?* And just how many kneecaps do you have?"

"You know what I mean, idiot. Your mother has two of her own, plus they said they'd shoot me in the head next. God, I can't tell you. The first one was such a shock and such agony, but the second one was far worse. Far worse. Because by then I *knew* how painful it was, and when I saw this gigantic shithead in a shiny blue-green suit aiming for the other one, the, I don't know how to call, the dread, and the outrage, and the unfairness of it, my God, it was overwhelming. And that guy, the guy who shot me, I mean, he was so *wide*, it was like a block long of nothing but shiny blue-green fabric so that even if that first shot hadn't blown apart my kneecap, I think it would've taken me a week to run around him, it just left me feeling so hopeless and, I don't know, shit."

"And how are you still alive after all of this ostensible trauma?"

"I don't know the meaning of this 'ostensible.' Like I said, it was a warning. He made a point of showing me it was a .22. He said, I mean before the first knee, 'We don't want to kill you. But it's still gonna hurt.' "

"And you want me to come down there to protect you? Me? I don't know anything about the Argentine Mafia or whatever it is. They'd just laugh at me. And a .22 can still kill you if it's aimed at your head, you know."

"No, not protect me exactly."

"So what, exactly? If the first two kneecaps were just to get you to pay attention, then I wonder pay attention to what? Do you mean pay attention or just pay?"

There was a long pause.

Then he said, "Just pay."

"So you really just need my money, right? So you can pay these guys your gambling debts before they shoot you in the head? Is that it? Why don't I just wire the money to you?"

"Because you're going to need to come down here to negotiate for me."

"And why is that?"

"Because, in U.S. dollars, I owe over sixty thousand."

I paused for a long moment and looked up at the ceiling as a respite from the identically colored wall.

"So you need me to give you sixty thousand bucks, is that about the size of it?"

"The size, the amount, however you want to say it, yes."

"And not visit?"

"No, not unless you would like to, of course. Your mother and I are always delighted to see you."

"Delighted to *see* me? Are you serious, Father? I thought you wanted me down there to take care of you! What about your two shattered kneecaps, then?"

"Yes! This is exactly what I said! They threatened to shoot them off without the money!"

"Father, your English sometimes goes in and out with the tides. Do you know exactly what the word 'threatened' means?"

"Yes, Carlos, you idiot. I know better English than you do."

"So, father, if I have this clear, your kneecaps are still intact."

"In what? Yes, they are still not shot, but they will be soon. That's what I've been trying to say from the beginning of this conversation, idiot."

This was not the first conversation along these lines that I'd had with my father when he was drunk. On the previous occasions, when the putative injury was a broken leg, I'd given him the money he'd asked for out of weariness and sheer admiration for his brazen prevarication, but he'd never asked for $60,000 before. I couldn't afford it; I couldn't afford anything, really, and yet I had no doubt that someone was threatening him and my mother over his gambling debts, and I feared for him. But the fear was tempered by past and present disgust.

I did have one disturbing dream during this period, but it wasn't about my father or the Argentine Mafia, or about light switches and dark tunnels, and it wasn't even psychic. In the dream, I was in a grammar school classroom filled with a bunch of twelve-year-old kids running around and whooping it up, I guess because the teacher wasn't there for some reason. I'm not even sure I was in the dream myself, or whether I was just an observer. But one of the little girls was seated very calmly at the desk instead of running around like the others, and the weird thing was that she was transparent. It was like she was made of clear, uncolored gelatin or something, so you could see her bones beneath the clear jelly.

And you couldn't just see them, you could hear them, bumping softly against each other, the sound muffled—and therefore, oddly, magnified—by the jellied flesh that covered them.

I knew exactly who that girl was. It was little Elizabeth, of course, and although I'd been responsible for her death at the age of three-and-a-half months, I was somehow imagining her as a twelve-year-old, a clanking skeleton, and thus just as dead as she actually was anyway. But why twelve? My guess was that it took me until I was twelve to understand the significance and the horror of her death, so I saw her death in my dream as taking place at the same time that death became real for me.

It also could have something to do with the fact that when I returned from Buenos Aires to Chicago, I was about twelve, and, back on familiar ground, I might have begun thinking about her again, even though when I was twelve she would have been four, had she survived the slow process of being suffocated in a tangle of blankets and sheets between her sister's bed and the wall. Or it could have been that when I returned to Chicago, Willa herself, who really *would* have been twelve at the time, like me, was nowhere to be found, in my school or in my neighborhood, and so I was thinking subconsciously about how she wasn't there, and somehow she'd become dead too, in my mind. Either way, it seemed plausible that the first iteration of this dream had happened when I myself was twelve, though this was, of course, impossible to determine.

Maybe the transparent girl in the dream was some sort of amalgam between Willa and Elizabeth or, as Diane would put it, was unstably "shifting" between those two souls. Maybe part of that little girl was actually me, too, though I doubt it. All I know is that I couldn't stop thinking of her, and the faintly clattering bones that I could hear through the transparent, jellylike flesh.

# 8

*Every* day, I got a little bit more worried about my job situation, but as summer began to take hold of the city, I got a call that would lead me to everything I would come to discover about me and Alisa and Willa and MariAngela.

The call came from my friend and coworker Mon Bowen, who also was, in a manner of speaking, my "agent." My musical career was so moribund, and so below the radar, that I didn't have an actual agent, but Bowen, who was a moderately successful soundtrack composer for documentaries and basic cable television programs in his off-hours from the agency, would sometimes keep his eye open for paying gigs other than Berto's. He'd also post an occasional performance of mine on YouTube, and once I actually got a favorable comment from someone I didn't know, and I was so excited I couldn't sleep, so that gives you an idea of the level of my fame. Anyway, when he connected me with a weekend gig at some other club in the area besides Berto's, I'd pay him by buying him dinner, the value of which approximately equaled the amount I'd get paid for the gig, and a couple of beers, which put me in the red. We were both fine with this arrangement, though Alisa thought the whole thing was a childish waste of time.

But this was something unexpected. He and his girlfriend had been in Hawaii on vacation, and they had befriended the manager of the lounge in their hotel in Honolulu. Bowen had bragged on me, as he was wont to do, and had somehow managed to convince the manager to book me for a full week of shows. It wouldn't even pay the cost of my airfare, much less Alisa's, but I'd never been to Hawaii, and I had some vacation time built up. Maybe if I wasn't around to be fired, they wouldn't fire me. Stupid, I know, but that's the way I liked to think.

Bowen was pretty excited himself. The "Mon" part was just a joke; his first name was Malcolm, but he was the product of a union between an Irish father and a Jamaican mother and had grown up in Jamaica. He had a high-pitched voice and a lilting speaking pattern that accentuated the near-indistinguishability, under the right conditions, of Jamaican and Irish accents, those right conditions being, respectively, ganja or Guinness. He tried to get me to partake of both, but other than the occasional pint of stout, I wasn't all that interested. In fact, his curly hair was receding and his eyes always were a little or a lot red, and it made me think that with every spliff he smoked, he, rather than the spliff, was inexorably burning away. Still, he was a genial guy and a good friend, and he kept me from getting too broody in my music.

I yanked out my cell and called Alisa.

"Guess where we're going?"

She sounded distracted. "I don't know. I'm not psychic."

"Hey, did you hear about the guy with the psychic girlfriend? She broke up with him before they met."

"Ha, ha. So where're we going?"

"Okay, get this. Hawaii. The week of June 22nd."

"Really? Why?

"Why? *Why?* Because why the hell not? Because Bowen got me a gig there, can you believe it?"

"Bowen? Your so-called agent? How much ravioli does he get?"

"Ha. Actually, I mean, you're right. It's going to pay only about fifteen hundred for the week, so the most he'll get is his usual meal. But I've told you before he's fine with that!"

"Uh huh."

"Plus I'll have to pay our airfare, but our room will be free, and so will any meals we eat at the hotel, so all we need is a rental car and snorkeling equipment and stuff like that, and if we want to eat somewhere else, we can probably get a Groupon or something..."

My voice trailed off. Alisa wasn't saying anything.

"What's the matter? We both need a vacation. I've never been to Hawaii. Have you?"

She said, firmly, "No."

"So what's the holdup? Don't you *want* to go to Hawaii?"

"I guess. Yeah." A pause. "Not really, no."

"Hmm. Now, this is interesting. I mean, who doesn't want to go to Hawaii?"

"Me. Your *girlfriend.*" She said it almost bitterly. I could see her jaw beginning to jut. I was glad I wasn't in the same room with her.

"So I'm not paying attention to your needs, is that it? Should I call Bowen back and tell him to find me a gig in Venice, Italy, instead? Would that suit your needs better?"

"I don't care. I don't care about your 'gigs.' "

"Oh, so is this about my music, then? Goddamn it, Alisa, you claimed that's what made you like me in the first place, but every chance I get to do something with it, you're not there for me."

"*Do* something with it? Are you kidding me? How is working as a marketing communications consultant 'doing something for it?' You don't do anything as far as I can tell, except tune your guitar and write a few songs..."

"You left out 'shitty.' Don't you mean, a few shitty songs?"

"Don't you fucking put words in my mouth. I think your music is beautiful. But this whole business of your music 'career' is just so fucking half-assed. You have this comfortable little thing where you go to the club and flirt with MariAngela..."

"Oh, so is that what this is about? A woman who's dying of a terrible disease? And you're using her to get at me by claiming I flirt with her? Real nice."

"Oh, don't give me that. First of all, she has a neurological disorder; she isn't dying. And how do you think she'd feel to hear you say she is just to score a point in an argument with me? Huh?"

I felt ashamed, and couldn't respond.

And yet it was indisputably the case that MariAngela was dying.

"Anyway," Alisa said, "I've seen you flirt with her a thousand times. And then you have a *dream* about her."

"Yeah, a dream that she's *sick*. Do you think it was somehow, in some twisted and demented way in your brain, somehow sexual?"

"No, I'm sure you keep *those* dreams to yourself."

"Oh, fuck you."

"Yeah, Charlie, fuck me. You want to go to Hawaii for a gig at a little hotel *cocktail* lounge where they probably have a two-for-one mai tai special on the weekends and little pineapple spears in the drinks, and it'll cost more for the drinks than you'll earn from the gig."

"The drinks are free!" I shouted this into my cell phone, and of course it goes without saying that the agency's owner, whose name was Gilbert Bick, was walking by right at that moment. He gave me a sharp look, and when it came to sharp looks, he was a master. Gilbert was a stocky and ponderous fellow who was mostly bald and had skin on his forehead that was so tight and shiny that you could practically see a diminished version of yourself in it when he was lecturing you about something or other. Gilbert and his death's head had lectured himself right out of two beautiful wives and his three daughters, all of whom hated his guts, along with many clients, and several business partners. So I braced myself for one of my encounters with him, but he kept on walking and then I braced myself a second time for whatever Alisa had to say next, but when I brought my cell back to my ear, she was laughing.

"Free drinks! Woo hoo! We get free drinks!" The amazing thing was, she wasn't being mocking about this. I think the absurdity of my claiming that this was somehow an adequate form of compensation for having to pay for the airfare out of my own pocket somehow struck her as childishly funny.

"Okay, Alisa. I get it. Never mind. It's the idea that I'm trying to *justify* this trip as some kind of business trip that's getting to you, isn't it?"

"What do you mean?"

"I mean, if I had just said, 'Drop everything, we're going to Hawaii on vacation because we fucking *deserve* a vacation,' you'd be packing even while we speak."

There was a long silence at her end.

"Wait a minute. No? *No?* That wasn't it either? You mean to say that you don't want to go to Hawaii, period? Is it about my father? I can't help him any more from Chicago than I can from Hawaii, even if I wanted to."

"It's not about your father. I just don't want to go."

"Well, why on earth not? Who doesn't want to go to Hawaii?"

"Charlie, everybody's different. I mean, couldn't we just go somewhere else like Lake Tahoe or something?"

"Sure, instead of going someplace really hot where everybody drinks frou frou drinks, we could just go someplace really hot where everybody drinks frou frou drinks. I get it."

"I'm really sorry, Charles, but you *don't* get it."

"You're right, I don't. I'll swing by later, and maybe you can try again to explain whatever the hell you mean." But I said this softly, because I knew that whatever she *did* mean, it wasn't just some sort of whim.

I didn't figure it out until the next morning. More accurately, I didn't figure it out at all; she just told me. We'd had a pretty good night together at her condo, no light-switch guessing or anything, and the next morning, she was using her fingertip to play with the condensation on the outside of her orange juice glass when she suddenly said, just like that, "I'm afraid of the water."

"What water? What are you talking about?"

"I don't know how to swim. I never learned."

I was so relieved that that was all it was that I laughed. We'd been dating for two years, and only now, for the first time, did it occur to me that we'd never gone on an island vacation or gone to a swimming pool or the beach. It was hardly the kind of thing I would have noticed—we'd taken vacations to New York, to Maine in the autumn, to Sedona Red Rocks, and to Santa Fe and Taos, and when we weren't on vacation, we were too busy going to concerts and plays and movies and jogging and working out and having sex and going to our jobs. "So that's it? That's the big explanation of why you don't want to go to Hawaii? Because you won't be able to go *snorkeling?*"

She didn't say anything for a moment.

Then something occurred to me. "What the hell, if you hate the water, why would you've suggested Lake Tahoe? Isn't Lake Tahoe on a, you know, a lake?

"Yeah, but we could drive there, or, I mean, just take a taxi from the Lake Tahoe airport or something."

"Huh? Meaning what?"

"Meaning I'm *really* afraid of the water."

"Meaning what, again?"

"That I can't be in an airplane that's flying over water. I mean, it's bad enough flying from the mainland to Hawaii. But then you have to take those little planes from island to island, right? Cause there's no other way to get around, is there? You'd literally have to kill me first before I'd do that. Next year, one of my clients has a big show in London and I'm *terrified* they're gonna want me to staff it. I mean it, Charlie. *Kill* me."

I took a deep breath. "Okay, let's take this one step at a time. Why are you afraid of water?"

She shook her head. "Forget it. You can psychoanalyze me all you want, but you're still not going to get me to go. I think it's because when I was in the first grade, a friend pushed me in the deep end and I was flailing and the bubbles and everything, and the sound of the water roaring in my ears, and I couldn't grab onto *anything.* It was the most terrifying moment of my life. So okay, I got permanently warped, alright? And then when I became this big volleyball 'star,' everybody just assumed an athlete is an athlete, and then if they found out I couldn't swim, they'd make a big deal out of it like I was somehow weird, which I guess I am.

So I just stopped talking about it after a while. And obviously I don't have any problem with flying per se, just flying over water, and all of our matches were in our conference, so that wasn't ever an issue. But talking about it or not talking about it, or figuring out my motivations or whatever just isn't going to change anything. I'm just not gonna go."

"Look, if it makes you feel any better, I have an irrational fear, too."

"Success?"

Why did she always have to ruin things by saying shit like that? "No, not success. I was gonna tell you, but never mind." The more I thought about it, the more upset I was starting to get, so I said, "Just forget about it, okay? Don't worry about Hawaii. I'll go there by myself, do the gig, come home, and maybe we can take a vacation together in the fall. I mean, who wants to go to Hawaii in the summer anyway?"

So that should've been that, but after work, I kept on brooding about the conversation—the "success" crack, the fact that she was right about my lack of accomplishment, my shaky job situation and shitty music career, her fear of water and how it was that after two years of dating I hadn't even discovered this, the pointlessness of the gig in Hawaii, everything. So almost without wanting to, I ended up driving over to her condo. I apologized first, but at least she apologized too, and we ordered in Thai. She had green curry with shrimp, and I had some Thai version of sweet and sour with little wedges of pineapple that made me think of Hawaii, so I smiled, and then I remembered our argument, so then I lost my smile.

I was a mess.

That night, I dreamed for the first time of the light switch. I couldn't tell when I recalled my dream the next morning if it was the same as the real one, but the laundry room itself looked different, just as Diane would have said. It was narrower and much darker, and there seemed to be a skylight that was letting in a soft, diffuse light from somewhere up above, and despite this light there seemed to be a violent, roiling thunderstorm high in the sky. In my memory of the dream, all I saw at first was the light switch above the long, aluminum laundry table, in the up position. After a second, I saw Alisa's bikinied white butt hovering over the table, like she was lying on her back but supporting herself on her elbows, but I couldn't see her face. It was like a video that was the wrong aspect ratio, and the sides of the scene were cut off. Then I saw the torso of a man, and the torso was pressing down on Alisa's belly like he was trying to enter her even though she still had the bikini bottom on and he had swimming trunks on, and when he pressed against her, her butt inadvertently flipped the switch to the down position.

The dream came back to me a few minutes after I woke up, while I was standing in Alisa's bathroom, peeing. She was still asleep. The more I thought about the dream, the more excited I got. She hadn't told me last night whether or not she was still doing our little experiment, but regardless, if I went down to the condo basement and the switch was in the down position, that might really mean something. So I threw on some pants, raced down the two flights of stairs to the basement, and located the switch, just above the long, aluminum laundry-folding table.

It was in the up position.

Laughing at my credulousness—I mean, even if the switch had been down, what exactly would it have proven?—I came back upstairs. Alisa was still asleep. I pulled the light sheet off of her and admired, as I did whenever I had the chance, her long, sleek torso. Two years of dating, and I still hadn't tired of seeing her body in the morning. She was on her side, wearing only her panties, which allowed me to admire her flat belly and pink-nippled breasts and incredibly long and strong legs all at the same time. My cock was throbbing, so I pulled off my pants and started rubbing it against her panties to wake her up so we could have sex, and then I realized that the butt I'd seen in the dream was exactly the same as Alisa's. And why shouldn't it have been? After all, it was Alisa I was dreaming about. But according to Diane, and according to my own experience as well, it should have looked, somehow, different. Again, I had no idea what this was supposed to mean, if anything, but I stopped poking at Alisa like a fifteen-year-old, and I closed my eyes for a second to see if I could remember if the male torso had been mine.

# 9

I *stopped* by Berto's after work the next day because it was a night that MariAngela usually worked, and I wanted to see how she was doing. I guess I also wanted to brag a little bit about my gig in Hawaii, but only because I knew that, even in the wake of her devastating diagnosis, she'd be happy for me.

She and I ended up ordering a plate of gnocchi with bacon and an endive, blue cheese, and walnut salad to share, but MariAngela hadn't eaten anything all day, so I just sat there and sipped my vodka gimlet and watched her vacuum up everything and wash it down with a glass of apple-beet juice with a splash of vodka. It made me feel good to see her eat so heartily; it made me think that maybe she wasn't really that sick.

She wasn't too bad at all, in fact. "It's kind of an illusion," she said, waving her fork around like a magic wand. "The early stages are just like this muscle weakness here and there, like I told you about in my calves and my hands. But you start to get used to it after a while, and it really isn't that hard. It's like that feeling when you're carrying some really heavy grocery bags and then you put them down on the table and your forearm is trembling and it's kind of scary, but you're not really scared because you know the trembling will go away in a couple of minutes? It's exactly like that."

"Except that in your case, eventually the trembling won't go away in a couple of minutes."

"Except that in my case, eventually the trembling won't go away in a couple of minutes. You nailed it. But I'm still at the stage where it's easy for me to pretend that it will. So I go to Berto's or wherever, I forget about it, I hardly notice it, but it's like I'm lying on my back at the bottom of a kayak that's floating down a beautiful lazy river, except that it's only a half mile from a waterfall. And I ain't got no paddles, baby."

"MariAngela, I mean, I don't know how to ask this, but what are you going to do when you can't work?"

"Ha! That's the kind of question you ask someone who's got cancer. She's got chemo coming up, she can't go to work during the chemo, but she needs a job waiting for her for when she recovers, which these days thank God she probably will. But in my case, when I can't work anymore, I can't do *anything* anymore, and then I just, you know, die. Okay? So. Hawaii. Why don't you tell me about that instead?"

"You sure?"

"I'm sure."

"Well, it's the most I've ever been paid for a gig, and also at the same time it's the most money I'll ever *lose* from a gig, when you factor in the airfare and everything. I mean, you pretty much just factor in a new Speedo, and I'm screwed. And Alisa doesn't even want to go."

"Doesn't surprise me."

"Why do you say that?"

"Well, her being scared of the water and all."

"Wait, what?" This one really caught me unawares. Alisa had met MariAngela on a half-dozen occasions, mostly when Alisa had come to the club to see me play and MariAngela had served her dinner, and maybe we'd had drinks once or twice afterward. But that was the extent of their direct connection. "How did you know that Alisa was afraid of the water?"

MariAngela shrugged. "I don't know. You must've told me."

"Uh-uh. I just found out myself, when she finally admitted why she didn't want to go."

"Then I don't know, I guess it was just sort of in the air, like comet knowledge."

"Common knowledge."

She laughed. "What'd I just say?"

"Comet knowledge."

"Ha! They say one of the first symptoms is slurred speech, but I thought I pronounced that very well, didn't I?"

"Well, but wrong."

We both laughed at that and clinked glasses. "Or wrong but well, maybe. Let's hope it stays that way for a long, long time."

After our dessert came, I rather hesitantly advanced the topic of my dream experiments with Alisa. I was a bit torn. On the one hand, the experiments were absurd on the face of them and hadn't worked at all so far. Plus, I didn't really want to remind MariAngela of my dream about her. I couldn't articulate why, exactly, but somehow it seemed to me that she must have felt somehow violated by me, however inadvertently. Even though she had been the one inside *my* head, and not the other way around, the fact remained that I had somehow become privy to thoughts she believed to be private.

On the other hand, MariAngela was my friend, and I wanted to use the pretext of the dream experiments to slide into a discussion about Alisa, and whether or not I was right to feel let down by her on the whole Hawaii thing, and how it was that her own boyfriend wouldn't have known a secret about her that seemed to be "comet" knowledge otherwise.

And I suppose I also wanted her to know that I actually had seen the light switch last night; even though it'd been in the wrong position, I was still a little excited by the dream and wanted to share it with someone.

But when I told MariAngela the whole story, she smiled indulgently and said, "I don't know that you and Alisa really needed to go to all that trouble of doing experiments. I've been thinking about your dream too, and, really, the simple explanation is that there was nothing psychic about it at all. Why did I go to my doctor to begin with? Because I was just feeling so fatigued and weird lately and feeling weak and shaky in my hands and calves. So how implausible is it that the last few times we were talking at the club, you subconsciously picked something up? I mean, I don't remember complaining to you that I was tired or anything, but maybe you picked up my body language, slumped shoulders, maybe my eyes looked a little dull, maybe you saw my hands trembling, who knows? That's really all there is to it, I think."

She signaled for the check, even though, having eaten only a bit of our dinner, I'd been contemplating a cup of coffee and maybe a biscotti. While we waited for the check to arrive, she smiled distantly but didn't say much more to me. There was definitely something wrong. Maybe she really had felt violated by my dream, or merely, for lack of a better term, freaked out. Maybe she didn't want me around to remind her and just didn't want to talk about it at all. Her explanation for my dream sounded more like a rationalization. After all, when she had spoken to me in my dream, she hadn't merely said she was sick or fatigued or shaky, she had said there was something wrong with her brain.

And there was.

So I let it go until after I'd paid the check, and I waited until we walked back out onto the sidewalk. It was a glorious summer evening, and the sun, though low in the sky, was still bright and hot. Suddenly, on impulse, I said, "Hey, you're still feeling really pretty good, right? And I'm not trying to minimize the seriousness of what you're facing, but hopefully you *will* be for a long, long time. And I know you like snorkeling and surfing and everything. Anyway, so if Alisa's not going to be able to go with me to Hawaii, how about you join me instead? See something beautiful instead of the inside of a club or a doctor's office, have a little fun, take your mind off of being sick."

MariAngela looked at me, a little startled, and the lowering sun made her eyes look almost like they'd appeared in the dream—

unnaturally bright, and with a tinge of orange in them. Then she said "no" so definitively and so abruptly that I knew that things with us would never be the same.

"No" was the only thing she said.

And then she walked away.

# 10

It was another bad evening. I went back to my house, and instead of calling Alisa as I'd said I would, I sat cross-legged on my bed, working on the chord changes for a new song. It was a tricky one, and just at the moment I was concentrating hardest on it, a sudden image flashed into my mind: It was Alisa's bottom half, stretched out over the laundry table in her condo basement, being pressed slowly down again by a male torso so that her bare butt—no bikini bottom this time—was pressing against the light switch and flipping it to the off position.

Except this time, I could see who the man was. It wasn't me, and it wasn't some shape-shifting, generic dream character. It was Frank.

I laid my guitar on the foot of my bed and went into the kitchen to make a late dinner. But I stood there at the open refrigerator, and I felt more frozen than anything in the freezer compartment. I was having trouble sorting out what was bothering me, because there was just so much. There was the argument with Alisa, and her comment about my "fear of success." That was one thing. But MariAngela's reaction to my Hawaii invitation was another. Her simple no kept on echoing in my head, and it wasn't just a rejection, it was a rebuke. It seemed to be implying that I was a bad person for even asking, but why? Because I already had a girlfriend? But Alisa had said no, and I was starting to wonder how much longer our relationship was going to last. Or was it because MariAngela thought it was unfeeling to ask her so soon after her diagnosis? Maybe, but wouldn't a good friend invite a good friend to a beautiful and peaceful place to get her mind off of that diagnosis?

Or maybe it was because MariAngela thought that I was asking her *despite* her diagnosis, in order to have sex with her. But that didn't make sense—if I'd never hit on her before, why would I do so now, when she was sick? Anyway, whatever MariAngela might be thinking, I knew my own mind and knew that I certainly didn't have any notion whatsoever of having sex with her in Hawaii. And yet if that were the case, wouldn't I have had to get her her own room? And how could I afford that if I couldn't even afford a new Speedo?

And wasn't it true that, sick or not, I had been attracted to MariAngela for a long time?

Or was MariAngela's rejection based on quite the opposite—on her knowledge that, as her illness progressed, she might never have sex again? Had she been insulted not by some imagined supposition on my part that we would share a room and have sex, but rather by some imagined supposition on my part that sex was completely out of the question?

Had she imagined, in short, that I had invited her out of a completely asexual sort of pity? And could it possibly be the case?

And then there was the image of Alisa having sex with Frank. I found it very hard to get it out of my head, even though it, too, like whatever the hell it was that MariAngela was imagining, existed purely in the realm of supposition. Alisa having sex with Frank and me *not* having sex with MariAngela were somehow all tangled together in a way that made me very, very unhappy indeed.

I went on like this for a while, feeling miserable, although I suppose that standing there with the refrigerator and freezer doors open wasn't so bad, because it was a hot evening, and my old house didn't have any air conditioning. But after a while, I started sweating and feeling weak in my legs, and that made me think of what it must be like to have ALS, so I shut the refrigerator, grabbed a dusty granola bar from the cabinet, and went to the couch to lie down.

It only got worse. I was developing a headache from the lack of food, and I wondered why I hadn't told MariAngela that I wanted some of that gnocchi too, or why I hadn't just ordered my own dish or even flagged the waiter down for some coffee and biscotti before the check came. Was it because I wanted MariAngela to get all the nutrition she needed? Or was it because I was afraid to interrupt her as she told me of her illness? Did I think she would accuse me of being unsympathetic for eating while she talked about her incurable disease? That was ridiculous, of course, but then that raised the larger question of why I was so afraid of women and of what they thought of me. And then that got me off onto a tangent that was too dark for me to handle, because of what had happened when I was a child and Elizabeth died and her mother said I was responsible, and maybe I was in a way, because why else would my family have moved back to Buenos Aires so quickly and then stayed there for three years?

I couldn't dwell on this for long, so I started worrying about my job situation, which, as scary as it was, was a big comfort compared to thinking about that little girl's horrible death. By the time I fell asleep on my couch, though, the one terrible thing that seemed to resound in my head worse than all the other terrible things was the sound of MariAngela saying no to me in such a definitive and preemptory manner.

I was a very bad person, and MariAngela, who was sweeter and less judgmental than anyone I knew, had me pegged.

# 11

*The* next morning, I felt a little better, and before work I went to the pancake place down the street from my house for a big breakfast of three poached eggs, turkey bacon, coffee, orange juice, and a pecan roll, and by the time I strolled into the office, I was doing pretty well.

Gilbert was in his "wise man" mode that day. His self-definition required him to imagine that others found him to be intimidating, controlling, and a memorable "character," though his inclination to be seen in this manner was so transparent that it made his tendency to dominate seem ugly and insincere, because it was in service to his self-image and not to the work we performed on behalf of our clients. Understanding this at some level, he would sometimes take a softer tack, where he spoke loftily of meanings and intimations, though, without his being fully aware of it, this was doubly insincere, as its purpose was to obscure, or artificially ennoble, his naked need to intimidate.

But there was a peaceful, if inadvertently comic, element to this softer mode of his. He pulled a chair up next to mine and started massaging my shoulder as if I were his prize horse.

"This business of ours."

"Yes," I said. "What about it?"

"You happy?"

"Sure, I guess." I shrugged a little bit to get his hand off of my shoulder. I felt relieved, because when he'd said "this business of ours" I thought he was talking about the marketing business in general, and that was usually the prologue for him to say something along the lines of, "It's a funny business, don't you think? I mean, at the end of the day…." And then he'd be off to the races.

But he was talking about our agency, specifically, so that was a bit better.

"I know we've had some tough times here lately, Charlie boy. And I think I know why."

"Why?"

"I think we're looking at this business backward. We've got a stable of clients that we serve 24/7, and we put everything we have into meeting their needs."

"So you're saying we should put our own needs first?" The irony, of course, was that this was exactly what Gilbert did every day—put our own needs first. That was what kept us, I believed, in the third tier of companies in our industry, though I wasn't about to point this out to Gilbert. It was easy for me to be contemptuous of him and his self-serving ways, but starting my own agency, and doing a better job of it, was well beyond my capabilities.

"No, I just mean that our clients really don't know what they need. Oh, they *think* they do, they think they do. 'Get me a social media presence.' 'Get me a content-marketing capability.' But do we ever stop and ask ourselves, or ask *them,* if what they say they need really serves a purpose?"

"Well, to some extent, we do."

"Like when, Charlie? Like when?"

"Well, like when I switched Gennaro to a Google AdWords campaign instead of the regular banner ads because I didn't see us getting much traction from them."

"Wait a minute, what? You did what?"

"I, uh, you know, I just felt because they depended so much on search results and it's a lot cheaper, and…"

"Just fuckin' with you, Charlie. Just fuckin' with you. Keep up the good work. Enjoy the islands, and we'll talk about Gennaro when you get back."

With that, he gave my shoulder another unnecessary squeeze and walked away.

So my job was off my fretting agenda for a while. I had a lot of other things on my mind, but no one to talk to about them. Obviously after her rejection and all that had come before, there was no way I could call MariAngela. Bowen was more of a buddy than a friend I could confide in. I thought fleetingly about calling either Frank or Diane, but I rarely saw or talked to either one except when Alisa was around, and besides, I suddenly remembered the image I'd had of Frank having sex with Alisa, which I'd almost forgotten about in the rush of other dark images last night. I really didn't have any other friends to speak of, but then it occurred to me that Alisa was still my girlfriend, at least for now, and I could at least give her a call on FaceTime.

I'd planned to keep it all kind of light at first, but instead what I said was, "Man, I had a terrible night last night."

A bit to my surprise, she said, "I'm sorry, sweetie. I hope you're feeling better today."

But instead of following her lead and asking her how she felt and, in general, making up with her, I said, "One of the reasons I had a terrible night was that I had this weird image of you having sex with Frank on the laundry table in your condo. I know it was just part of this whole light-switch thing, because that was part of the image, too, but I gotta admit, it bothered me a little."

Alisa surprised me again. "I'm beginning to think you really are psychic, Charlie. First of all, you actually dreamed about the light switch for a second time!"

"I didn't dream it. It was just this image that popped into my head while I was awake."

She shrugged, as if this were of the most supreme unimportance. "And second of all, I get where you're coming from with the whole Frank thing."

"What are you saying?"

"I'm saying that I haven't really been mentioning it lately, but pretty much every night, especially when you're not sleeping over, I'll run down to the basement and flip the switch because I'm hoping it'll make you have another dream."

"Like I said, it wasn't a dream. It was just an image that flashed into my head while I was awake."

"Same difference."

"Well, maybe, but in any event, that wasn't what I was asking. I was asking what you meant when you said you saw where I was coming from about the whole Frank thing."

"What I'm saying is that Frank's been coming on to me big time at work. He and Diane aren't getting along at all, and I'm guessing that's why she was so dark at dinner the other night, all that death talk and rumination about how everything changes and stuff. Frank said they haven't had sex in six months."

"So he's after you now?"

"You must've picked up subconsciously on some signals he was sending at dinner. Or maybe it really was one of those vestigial communications, but the fact is, Frank keeps on coming over to my desk and talking about all the things he'd like to do to me. Not super-direct or anything, but hinting, which is somehow worse."

"So you're saying he's sexually harassing you."

"I guess you could call it that. He's very proud of his huge dick and he keeps on telling me how he's going to use it on me."

"What huge dick? He has a huge dick? And how do you know this?"

"I don't, Charles. He's just bragging. He's trying to get me turned on. He doesn't understand women at all, if he thinks that'll do it. I'm thinking of going to HR and complaining."

"I'm still not clear on all of this." I often wasn't clear on things when I was talking to Alisa. "You just said he was more like hinting, but then you tell me he's talking about his huge penis. That hardly sounds like hinting to me."

"You'd have to be a woman to understand. He's hinting in a really obvious way, so that he knows I get the message that he thinks I want to hear, but without saying it directly so he doesn't get into trouble if I report him to HR."

"You don't report to him, do you?"

"No, he's in a different account group. Technically, we're almost at the same level. I suppose I could just tell him to shut the fuck up. But I'm a little afraid that if I do that, or if I go to HR for that matter, that he'll make more trouble for me."

"So you're not turned on by him at all?"

"Are you kidding? Absolutely not."

"And you haven't had sex with him at all? On the laundry table in your condo, or anywhere else?"

"C'mon, Charles, you're being ridiculous. The laundry table? It would collapse under the weight."

"Of his huge dick."

"Ha ha. No. I have not had sex with him on the laundry table or anywhere else. I just want to get away from him."

"So then how about you change your mind and come to Hawaii with me?"

"Okay."

"What? Okay? I mean, you'll really go?"

"Sure."

"What about your fear of flying over water and everything?"

"I've been thinking about that. That's why God invented Xanax. I figure one Xanax when we take off, one when we're over the water, and I'll fill in the gaps with vodka."

"Now you're talking!" I couldn't have felt more buoyant than I did at that moment. It was as if everything from the past few weeks—MariAngela's illness, her rejection, Frank and his putative big penis, my job situation, my father's $60,000 gambling debt if in fact it existed, even that horrible CGI movie we'd seen with Frank and Diane—all of it had been wiped away by a brilliant blue wave.

"So will you even try to go snorkeling with me?"

"I'll come to the beach with you. I promise. This is Honolulu where the club is, right?"

"Right."

"Oh, so wait a minute, we might not even have to fly to the other islands at all, right?"

"Well, I kind of wanted to see the rest of Hawaii, but we'll play that one by ear."

"Good. So anyway, sure, I'll go to Diamond Head beach, or whatever it's called, and I'll bring that white bikini, and maybe we'll find some beach volleyball players and I'll kick their asses so you can feel proud of me."

"I'm proud of you already, just for going."

"And if there's a topless beach, you can really show me off."

"Cool. And snorkeling?"

"I promise I'll think about it. Maybe. Yes. Not off of a boat in the middle of the ocean, but maybe some place where we can wade in from the beach or something. Get a couple of drinks in me and hold me around the waist, and maybe I'll give it a shot."

It was weird how nice she was being. But I didn't question it. All I could think of was me teaching *her* something for once, because, skinny and hunched shoulders and all, I was nonetheless a strong swimmer. And watching all the guys on the beach admiring her in her white bikini, or in just the bottom half of her white bikini. Seeing other guys admiring her body and her breasts would be a big turn-on for me, I had to admit. And so was watching her in the audience, smiling proudly as I performed—though I had trouble picturing this last one, and suddenly I was nervous all over again that no one would show up to my shows, or that I'd perform poorly, or something. I didn't have stage fright, per se, but I did have Alisa-fright, and I didn't want her to lose respect for me if she didn't care for my performance.

Because, I thought again, it was *really* weird how nice she was being.

# 12

*That* night, MariAngela came into my brain for a second time. Just as she had the first time, she arrived from the back of my head, where everything was very black, and walked slowly forward. This time around, I wasn't "anywhere." In other words, everything in my dream, not just the back of my head, was completely black, and all I could see was MariAngela, getting larger and larger as she approached the back side of my eyes. This time, she leaned all the way over, with her hands on her knees as if the space in my skull were as cramped as the little dormer room, and said, "Hey, Charlie, are you sleeping?"

"Yes," I said in my dream.

"And is Alisa sleeping next to you?"

"Yeah, she is."

"Well, could you roll over and wake her up? I need to talk to her about something."

This was all that I remembered of my dream. I probably did not wake up, even for a moment, and am fairly certain that I did not do as MariAngela "instructed" and wake up Alisa, because I asked Alisa about it the next morning, and she had no memory of my disturbing her sleep, and certainly no memory of MariAngela coming to her in her own dreams—not that I would have expected her to. What could MariAngela possibly have to say to Alisa, anyway? But then, if she had nothing to say to her, why did she come to me in my own dream and ask me to awaken her? That was a question that no one, including (or perhaps especially) MariAngela could possibly answer. It was even more puzzling than the first dream, because this time around, MariAngela had not delivered any information about her life as she had the first time.

And it was doubly puzzling because—as it suddenly occurred to me—in both of the "walk-in" dreams, MariAngela looked the same as she did in her waking existence. In the first dream, she had been wearing a ball gown for some reason, and in this one, I couldn't even remember what she wore. But despite everything that Diane had said at dinner about the fluid, ever-shifting nature of our dreams, in both of the walk-ins, MariAngela had *remained* MariAngela, not shifted her shape or become another person, not even that woman in Galena or the other woman on the El, or become an ambiguous being who could have been any of a number of people I knew or had never met. It wasn't my dream version of MariAngela, in other words, or my interpretation of her filtered through my fears or transformed into something or someone else. It was her, the actual MariAngela, and once again, while I was completely vulnerable and unaware, and for reasons neither one of us could understand, she had entered into my head.

The next morning, I called MariAngela and happened to catch her while she was out doing something with her girlfriend. She sounded annoyed and a little bit distracted, and this time around, she was even more dismissive of my dream than she'd been that night at Berto's.

"Why on earth would I want to talk to Alisa?"

"Exactly! That's what I was thinking!"

"So if we're both agreed that it doesn't make any sense, can't we both agree that it, you know, doesn't make any *sense?*"

"You mean that the dream has no significance?"

"Exactly."

"But I don't know, it isn't like any other dream I've ever had, or ever heard of anyone else having. 'You' looked exactly like you, and you spoke to me, directly, and looked into my eyes from the other side. You must have been trying to tell me something."

"Well, if I can think of what it was, I'll call you, okay? And if I can't think of what it was, but you have another dream where I tell you, how about you call *me* and let *me* know so that we're both on the same page, okay?"

"Sorry to have bothered you. You seem pretty upset."

"No problem, Charlie. Listen, I'll tell you the truth. I did want to talk to Alisa about something last night, believe it or not, so I guess your dream was kinda true, but it was about something really trivial, okay? I don't even remember what it was, and now I've got call waiting, so I'll try to get back to you before the next acoustic night at Berto's or maybe I'll see you there, and we can sort it all out, okay? I gotta run."

And that was not only that, it also was the last time I talked to MariAngela for a long, long time. In retrospect, I wished that I asked her how she was doing, or wished her luck on the difficult journey she was embarking upon all alone, but I did neither of those things, and I guess you can't change what's happened, so there you go. But at least I know now that we weren't finished, not by a long shot, and that's something, at least.

The main thing I took away from that hurried conversation with MariAngela was not her irritation about me and my dreams, though I confess to not understanding what that was all about, but rather her hurried and belated admission that she had indeed wanted to ask Alisa something. That something might have been "trivial," but the sudden knowledge that I was indeed a little bit psychic was not.

Work was a bit busier than it had been lately, and I got distracted by some client problems, and by the end of the day I had more or less forgotten about everything that had happened. But after work, as I walked into the parking lot, the sun was shining at just the right angle, and the red brake lights on all of the cars were lit by the sun, and I fell into a kind of state where everything not only seemed more beautiful than usual but more beautiful for *me,* I imagined, than it must be for anyone else alive. Who, after all, really notices the taillights on cars, of all things, and yet the intricate assemblages on display, the endless variety of squarish and rhomboid and ovoid shapes, the way they molded themselves so elegantly into the backs of the cars, the little red and white galaxies of glass and bulbs and colored partitions within, the subtle shades of pomegranate and cherry and strawberry and bright arterial blood, all of this was a revelation. I was high on myself and my superior perceptual capabilities, especially because I didn't believe in psychic phenomena to begin with. Nobody, I was sure, could see the world the way I did.

I suppose you could say that I'd become a little puffed up. Somehow this created in me a hunger to see and feel even more, so instead of going home, or going over to Alisa's condo, I decided to visit the sports bar where MariAngela was reputed to work.

It was at least twelve miles away via highway and a long, industrial road near the airport, and by the time I passed the first tollbooth—it was now dark and the taillights of the cars in front of me were now nothing more than indistinguishable red streaks, all those sublime and beautiful designs blurred together and erased —I had started to wonder why I was going.

Of course, the odds that she would still be working there were pretty small. I remembered what she had had to say about her post-diagnosis working existence, and the possibility of her serving Stoli, gin and tonics, and Jägermeister to lonely men and sports fans at this point in her life seemed close to grotesque. No, I really didn't want to see her in a sports club or a music club, nor even, apparently, in my dreams.

The whole thing had me flummoxed, and a few miles away from the club, I pulled my Lexus into the parking lot of a Burger King, turned the car around, and, a bit more deflated than I'd been that morning, headed home, becoming just another one of the indistinguishable taillights.

After I got off the highway, I called Alisa's cell, but she didn't pick up. Then, when I got home, I sent her a text and a Facebook private message that both read, "it's up" as a little ambiguous joke, but, unusually for her, she didn't answer and was nowhere to be found. I tried Frank, whom I rarely called on my own, but he didn't pick up, either. Something about their unreachability frustrated and depressed me, and I couldn't put my finger on it, though I suppose at some subconscious level the idea that I was psychic but had hardly any friends and couldn't communicate with the ones I *did* have, tasted like rust. So, too, did the not implausible thought that both of them were unreachable because they were together.

Next, I turned on the downstairs TV, found nothing there, spent a little time on my own Facebook page, and then, frustrated, went upstairs to look at my shelf of old DVDs. I watched most movies on Netflix or Amazon Prime, but I had a backlog of DVDs I'd never seen and decided that, since I had no friends anyway, I might as well devote my time to catching up. I picked out *Once Upon a Time in the West,* which I hadn't seen in ages, went downstairs, stuck it in the DVD player, grabbed the remote, and settled back.

But I'd either picked up the wrong remote or hit the wrong button, because there was a complicated and anachronistically mechanical-sounding whirring noise, and, instead of the menu screen for *Once Upon a Time in the West,* I was greeted by an old black and white Felix the Cat cartoon. I had somehow managed to activate the missionaries' ancient videocassette player, which I hadn't even noticed was still there, on a lower shelf of the TV stand, and the long-forgotten tape it still contained. I hadn't watched a video on cassette for more than a decade and certainly hadn't seen a Felix the Cat cartoon since I was a child, but I was too lazy to hit "eject" or figure out how to switch to the DVD player, so I settled back to watch.

In the cartoon, Felix discovered a loose thread in his sweater, so of course he pulled it, which caused the sweater to completely unravel. The thread seemed to be connected to everything else in the room, because as Felix kept on pulling, it unraveled a coat tree and all the coats and hats hanging from it, and then in turn the ceiling and floor, and then the whole room, and then the planet Earth, and then our galaxy and the entire universe, leaving only Felix himself, floating around in a cold and lonely primeval void.

"Your fault," I thought, "you could have stopped pulling that thread at any point."

Before I found out what happened to Felix, however, there was a burst of static, and I suddenly saw, there on the screen, the upstairs room of my own house, the one with the dormer room attached. It startled me so badly that I actually ran upstairs (though I couldn't explain exactly why I did this), and there was the actual dormer room, more or less exactly the way I had just seen it on the screen. But by the time I got back downstairs, I saw that this was nothing more than a homemade video that had been recorded over the cassette, as people used to do years ago.

Sitting on the couch—the actual couch I sometimes sat in myself, against the life-size window looking out onto the street and adjacent to the dormer room with its own miniature window—was a very skinny, one-armed man wearing a dirty, sleeveless T-shirt and holding a little boy, about six, in his lap. The man had floppy black hair and a recessive chin and very large brown eyes that—perhaps because they were obscured from time to time by the longish hair—made him look furtive and weak. His right arm had been amputated below the elbow, and he had a metal hook for a right hand. This was clearly something I did not want to see. But these were (or so I surmised) the very people, the Christian missionaries, from whom I'd rented the house, and I felt duty bound, at least for as long as I could bear to watch it, to see what this man would do to this little boy.

The sound quality was very poor, as it usually was in home-recorded videocassettes, and the picture quality was not much better. The boy said something unintelligible to the man, and the man said something that sounded like, "after dinner." And then the boy, who was about six, said, "Okay, but I got another move I'm gonna try."

The man laughed and said, "Okay, but does it involve my having to stare out the window while you move my pieces around?" This part was clearly audible for whatever reason, and the way he said it was so full of rich amusement and warmth that I immediately let go of whatever ugly thoughts had been forming in my mind and actually began to enjoy this accidental eavesdropping on a father and his son.

They talked a bit more about this long-ago game (chess? Monopoly? Stratego?), and then a rather plump, youngish woman walked in, followed by a girl about the same age as her brother—fraternal twins, perhaps, or "Irish twins." Each was holding a Fiesta plate of something that looked, as best as I could determine from the poor-quality video, to be egg rolls. The woman—the wife—said, "Here's a little sampler." And then the man said, "Okay, we'll be right down. We're just discussing 'stragety.' " And the boy said, "Dad, I think it's 'strategy,' " and then the little girl took a bite of her egg roll and got upset about something or other (it appeared that she didn't like the way it tasted, or thought it had too many vegetables in it) and threw it at her father. It bounced off his cheek, and he growled a little at her and picked it up off the couch and took a big bite out of it, and then everyone headed downstairs for their Chinese dinner. There was a blip in the video, and then I saw the one-armed man and his daughter, and she walked into the dormer room (she had to duck her head a bit, even at her age) and then the father got down on his side and slid in after her, the lower portion of his legs sticking out into the room.

The video camera was somewhere on the opposite wall, near where I'd stored my DVDs, so I couldn't see what was happening in the dormer room, but I really didn't have to. The little girl came out a couple of times and "stomped" on her father's legs, and I could hear both of them laughing, and that was all I really needed to see and hear. This was a normal family, and perhaps better than normal, because the father had clearly been the one who had built the floating dollhouse.

I wished I could see the dollhouse, but the camera was on a tripod or resting on a table facing the couch, and though I fast-forwarded through the rest of the cassette, it never moved from its location. Still, I had seen a lot. I had seen the couple from whom I had rented the house, and their two children who had played with the dollhouse, and had met the man who had built it not by kneeling painfully inside the tiny dormer room, as I had once surmised, but by lying on one side, the side with only a hook for an arm, and using his good arm and hand to cut the tiny hole in the wall with a DeWalt drill and a jigsaw and create the intricate assemblage of the shutters.

I'm embarrassed to admit that, that very same weekend, I wasted several hours looking through a utility closet in the second bedroom (the room that adjoined the family room next to the dormer) for other home-recorded videocassettes. I even found one. This one had been recorded on a new videocassette, rather than by taping over an old cartoon, and most of it consisted of the same four family members playing with a beach ball in the backyard.

At one point, they took a break and were eating tangerines and slices of watermelon, and the way the one-armed man would hold each slice of tangerine up to the sun to check whether or not there were any seeds inside before handing it to his daughter (evidently a very fussy eater) only solidified my view of this person. True, every time he swatted at the beach ball with his hook, I must admit to cringing a bit, but it never burst, and I never saw anything else of any particular interest.

The rest of the videocassettes were the normal sort of Disney and Pixar products you'd expect to see from a family with children, though there were no new movies after about 2006 or so, at which time they must have switched over to DVD, and then, presumably, Netflix or Hulu. A couple years after that, they had left for the Philippines, and I had moved in.

But none of this is really important. All that mattered was that seeing the way the one-armed man had carved out a little window in the wall for his children gave me an idea that transmogrified—as in a face glimpsed in a dream that would not stay itself but shifted from moment to moment to others unknown—everything I thought I knew up until then.

# 13

**Diane,** who's very big on internal exploration—"spelunking" she calls it, referring both to Western psychiatry and Eastern mystical arts like meditation and weeks-long yoga retreats—had evidently been thinking about our conversation at dinner, because she called me and recommended that I see a psychiatrist that she was impressed with. I didn't tell her about the second dream, not wanting to make it sound like I needed a psychiatrist as much as, in fact, I did. But I was willing and curious. In any event, though I wouldn't have dreamed of telling her this, I had been thinking about seeing someone for a long time, long before the dreams had begun, just because of the residual guilt about Elizabeth and how it made me afraid of a lot of things that I shouldn't have been afraid of.

Alisa had water; I had women. So be it. At least I was doing something about it.

His name was Donte Nemerov. Dr. Nemerov's office was in his apartment on a small side street near University Place on the South Side of Chicago. It'd taken me forever to find a place to park, and I was running late, so I dashed into the front door of his apartment building, gasping a bit for air.

But that first lungful of air inside his humid vestibule would have been my last, if I had had a choice. The vestibule reeked, and it got worse as I walked up the stairs—a mix of kitty litter heavily soaked in cat urine, cat turds, and cigar smoke. When Dr. Nemerov opened the door, though, I almost forgot the smell, because he was such an odd-looking example of a human being—six foot four or so, with a lumpy bald head, coarse and potato-like features, and a very dark complexion but only from the neck up, as if he'd been basking, lizard-like, under a sunlamp. He had a pair of eyeglasses with bright red frames dangling from a gold chain around his neck. He was wearing denim overalls over a light gray T-shirt and a pair of redundant leather suspenders under the overalls that must have been attached to a second, tighter pair of pants, undoubtedly leather, under the denim. In the pockets of the overalls, he had a number of very shiny or burled old-fashioned cartridge pens—some gold, some silver, some with a wood or kilt pattern. He clutched in his mouth the stub of a very wet and slimy but unlit cigar. He looked like a slovenly, gay intellectual Freudian motorcycle-club member—quite possibly the only member of that particular species on the planet.

We sat down in his living room, which was crowded with hundreds of books. Though I looked at the spines in vain for names like Adler, Jung, or Freud, most were volumes of European history or fiction. There were dozens of framed woodcuts, every one of them, without exception, hanging askew. And yet not a single one of them was hanging at the same angle, so I surmised that it couldn't have been the fault of a tremor or a passing moving van.

"So," Dr. Nemerov said. "My first name is Donte. Please call me that. Not Dante with an 'a,' Donte with an 'o.' And you're Carlos, or Charlie?"

"Correct."

"I hope you don't mind if I finish this cigar," he said with a clear lack of expectation that I would object. His voice was measured and calm, and, if I had closed my eyes and pinched my nostrils, I would have guessed that it issued from someone with regular features wearing a pair of well-pressed slacks and a crisp dress shirt.

"I don't mind," I said, though I did, a bit; I guess my thinking was something along the lines of "in for a dime, in for a dollar," and I supposed, as well, that the cigar smell would keep the cat stench at bay.

"So I read the form you filled out. We're not going to start at the very beginning, although that's where everyone's troubles come from without exception. The beginning, that is, infancy and the few years that follow, the years where all the damage is done.

"But just for today, let's start from today. Now. This moment. Tell me what's troubling you and what led you to make an appointment with me, and we'll work our way backward and see if we can help you feel better and be more effective. Because that's the goal, isn't it? If you can walk out of here and be more effective in your daily life, then I've done my job. But I want you to bear something in mind. If you are a murderer, for example, and my treatment makes you feel better about murdering people and more effective at this task, then I will have done my job but I will have failed at the same time. I'm telling you this because there's a common misperception that a psychiatric patient can say anything he wants to say in the course of treatment, and the therapist is there merely to listen rather than to judge. But I am a moral and ethical human being, and I do, in fact, judge, and in the process I try to help guide people toward what I would call right and just behavior. This is my responsibility as a therapist and as a human being. I have never walked away from a patient, but under certain extreme circumstances, I would do so. Just so you understand the ground rules."

"Is there a particular reason you're warning me about this?" I thought for a moment of Elizabeth.

"Don't take it personally, Carlos. I'm only telling you the rules. Rules are incredibly important, don't you think? Without rules, we have no civilization. But once you know the boundaries of any given situation, you can act with complete freedom within those boundaries with no self-censoring or timidity. And you should know that I detest timidity. So tell me what's troubling you."

"Well, I hardly know where to begin, because it's too strange, I guess."

"I have seen and heard a lot of strangeness in my career."

*Yeah, just looking in the mirror,* I thought to myself, and a little semi-laugh inadvertently escaped my lips. And to my delight, Dr. Nemerov laughed too, and spread his arms wide to indicate his surroundings, and then pointed both hands at himself. He'd understood my silent joke and, incredibly, appreciated it.

Right there, he had me.

"Well," I continued, "on a practical level, all of a sudden I'm having some very disturbing dreams."

Dr. Nemerov stubbed out the last little bit of the cigar he'd been smoking, fished in one of the myriad deep pockets of his overalls for another one, and lit it with a gold lighter he extracted from still another pocket. "So what is the nature of these dreams? Are they nightmares?"

"No, I don't really have nightmares per se. Nightmares I can handle. It's just that this woman, this casual friend, is dying of ALS, and she keeps coming into my brain. I mean it's not like a normal dream, it's like she walks right into my head while I'm sleeping and says things that I shouldn't be able to know."

"Such as?"

"Well, the first time, she told me in my dream that there was something wrong with her brain. And this was before I knew she'd been diagnosed with ALS. When I told her about the dream the next day, she was shocked, I mean she almost fainted, because no one knew except her girlfriend. And we were never even that close. She's just a waitress at a club where I play music sometimes. I'm afraid of losing my job and my father has huge gambling debts, but I don't dream about those things, just this waitress."

"So you're fearful of several different things, I would imagine. The first is that she, this 'waitress' as you call her, really is communicating with you in a telepathic way, which would mean that not only can you read her mind, but she's inside your brain so perhaps she can read yours."

"Which she denies. She says she has no idea why I'm having these dreams."

"So the second thing you might be fearful of is that by seeing things that you believe people shouldn't be able to see, like the thoughts of others, you are doing something that is somehow forbidden, and worse, you are doing so without any conscious control. I will tell you that from the moment we are first placed on the potty to learn how to shit, most of our energies are devoted to maintaining control over our bodies, our minds, and our social connections. This is where civilization comes from, controlling where and when we shit, so to speak. You think this civilization is corrupt? Try living in a place where people shit in the streets and tell me what you think then. So suddenly, when you are asleep, you have lost this control over your thoughts, over all the shitty stuff you like to keep inside, and suddenly things enter your skull without your permission. Is this a possibility? Yes? And are you torn between wanting this all to just go away and wanting to experience it even more often, except at your own volition instead of as a sort of frightening random occurrence?"

"I would say that both are possible. Maybe both at the same time, kind of swirled together. Like I'm proud of this gift I've been given, but terrified of it, and embarrassed when I can't just pluck it out of my, you know..."

"Quiver. Like an arrow you can aim. So tell me about the other dream."

"Well, I had this other dream where she told me to wake up my girlfriend Alisa and tell her something, but I don't know what it was because the dream just ended."

"You've described this young woman as only a colleague and a casual acquaintance. Does she know your girlfriend?"

"No, I mean only casually, not really."

"So what could this young woman possibly have to say of any importance to your girlfriend, other than that she loves you? Or that you love her? Is there anything else? 'What are you wearing to the prince's royal ball?' I don't think so. This is a dream about love."

I sat there, stunned. "But it's only a dream!"

"Ah, *now* it's only a dream. But it wasn't only a dream when you called me and made an appointment, and it wasn't only a dream a few seconds ago. The moment I point out consequences to you, you retreat behind this 'only a dream' business."

"But I don't understand, exactly. What consequences are you referring to?"

"Well, there are a couple. One is that you do indeed love her, but you've been suppressing this for some reason. All this business about this so-called 'waitress,' and 'she's just an acquaintance' and 'I really don't know her that well,' and referring to her as 'her' instead of by a name."

"MariAngela," I said.

"Okay, MariAngela. That's a pretty name. Who is she?"

"South Side Irish girl. Very nice."

"So: the suppression I'm referring to. We don't know what the reason for this is yet, and we don't even know if it's the case. You mentioned her girlfriend; is she gay? Partially, at least?" I nodded. "Well, maybe that 'partially' is part of the problem. It isn't easy to deal with ambiguity, though as I'm sure you're aware, women's sexuality is far more fluid than ours or certainly mine. On the other hand, it may be that this is utterly irrelevant to your situation. And the second is that *she* is the one who loves you and, equally, has been suppressing this fact for some reason. Except now we know the reason for both of your suppressions, don't we?"

"We do?"

"Understand that dreams are funny things. There are a lot of dream theories out there, but very few of them acknowledge that there are many different categories of dreams, some that might mean a great deal to the dreamer, and some that are merely ways of passing the time while the body repairs itself during sleep. Yours, I think, mean a great deal."

"Yeah, but..."

He held up his slimy cigar. It looked like the fetus of an alligator, fished from an algae-covered lagoon. "Let me finish. Most of the dreams that mean a great deal reveal those meanings only with a tremendous amount of effort on behalf of the dreamer, sometimes with the help of a therapist like me. But yours? Yours are right on the surface, it would seem to me, and the only difficulty here is in your facing the terror you feel at acknowledging the obvious."

"What obvious? That I love her and she loves me? Again, we don't really know—"

"No, you have mentioned your girlfriend, and we'll delve deeper on that score, but I don't get an initial sense that you're the type who's afraid of being in a relationship or afraid of sex."

"I'm not. Getting a girl pregnant, that's another matter."

He laughed, not fully understanding my meaning. "Nor on the other hand that you are prone to playing around with multiple women at once. So if we accept that for the time being, then we have to draw the conclusion that what is terrorizing you is the thought of loving someone who is about to die. Either because you will lose her, which of course is painful enough even if I believed that business about 'acquaintance,' or because she, by dying, will lose *you,* or because somehow, I don't know how, you will feel as if you will have been responsible for her death." He paused. "Or, to put it more accurately, that after her death, you will contrive to feel a certain guilt about her death that will stay with you long after she is gone."

He waited a moment. "These are all just initial speculations. I need to know you much, much better. And like I said, we'll need to start at the very beginning, with your parents and your upbringing, because invariably, that is where these false perceptions or inefficient ways of dealing with reality invariably begin."

It was my turn to laugh. "I don't think you'll have to dig too deeply in my case."

He said, "We'll see. People don't want to acknowledge the reality that their personalities and their characters are formed either in vitro or while they are still too young and helpless to have any influence over the process. That's why they don't want to talk about their parents. They say, let's talk about the here and now.

Let's talk about the 'practical level,' as your very first words to me said. Well, fine, we can do that at our first session, but what got you to the kind of 'here and now' that's so 'practical' that it's making you see a psychiatrist is inevitably something your parents or others quite close to you did to you, whether they intended to or not, when you were young. Does that mean it's hopeless? No, but it means we have to acknowledge the damage before addressing it."

He took a deep drag of his cigar and went on. "And let's bear in mind, as we explore who you are in the here and now, the very particular nature of your dreams. They came on suddenly as I understand you to say, correct?"

"Correct."

"And they are not symbolic, as we've discussed, but rather very direct, as if she's walked right into your brain. Correct?"

"Yes."

"This would suggest a certain desperation on your part to break through your very thick defenses after many years of allowing those defenses, these euphemisms you use, this 'acquaintance' stuff, to control your life. Please pardon the expression, Mr. Alessandro, but as skinny as you are, you strike me as a pipe backed up with so much sewage that it's about to explode."

Again, I thought to myself, *Yeah, you'd know about sewage, in this stink hole of an apartment,* and I laughed again, and again he caught on, but this time he raised a minatory eyebrow at me. "You are a very blocked-up person, because the kind of people who have dreams literally knocking on the inside of their skulls are either very open to these sorts of phenomena, or very closed, and you are certainly not the type that strikes me as the least bit open."

"No."

"And I have yet to hear you object to my somewhat insulting description of you as a blocked-up sewer pipe filled with shit."

"Maybe I am."

"You agree with me a lot. You seem to be very respectful of authority. Would you say this is the case?"

"Yes."

"In my case, that's a wise course." He laughed and then thought for a moment. "You are respectful, above all else, I think, to your own authority, which is to say your conscious mind. But as I hope you understand by now, we can do things deliberately without doing them consciously. Do you understand what I mean?"

"I think so, yes."

"I also don't want to entirely discount the possibility that this young woman really *is* walking into your brain at night, which is to say that her consciousness is somehow becoming implicated in yours. I have read quite a bit in the literature and am more or less of an agnostic tending toward outright skeptic on the question of psychic phenomena, although I think some of us may have weak vestigial powers and a very tiny minority may have something more than that."

There was that word again, I thought. *Vestigial!*

"So let us assume that there is a psychic element at play here, and either you are somehow capturing her thoughts at night without her knowledge, or she is sending her thoughts your way, either with volition or without. With any of these possibilities, but especially with the latter two, there is another thing that I think you are, in a very deeply buried way, terrified about."

My lips were so dry in that overheated, malodorous room that I had to actually wiggle my jaw a bit to peel them apart and speak. I said, slowly, "What is that?"

"Well, you said she had ALS, correct? I think you may well be terrified that she will continue to communicate with you after she has died."

There was a long and odiferous silence. I didn't especially like where this conversation had gone and how quickly it had gotten there. I suddenly couldn't wait to get on the plane for Hawaii and drink mai tais. "Dr. Nemerov, all of what you say is very interesting and insightful, but dreams strike me as being mostly pretty random, and maybe I just randomly happened to have a couple of dreams that in my waking hours strike me as more meaningful than most. And maybe, coincidentally, one of them happened to coincide with something real."

"Yes, Charlie, dreams are so random that you coincidentally drove all the way down to Hyde Park to see me. Let me ask you a question, okay? Where do you think dreams come from?"

"Well, I know you said there are a lot of theories and—"

"They come from *you.* You yourself *create* your dreams. I said a moment ago that I don't entirely discount the possibility that she is either inadvertently or with volition sending her thoughts your way. But I think that is very, very unlikely—at the outer edges of human possibility. No, when you are asleep, you are partially unconscious and for all intents and purposes you might as well be in a darkened cellar somewhere, with no sound and no light and no way for any external stimuli to reach you. But note that I say partially unconscious. You have just enough consciousness to feel bored and thus to create stories to alleviate that boredom. But you cannot see and you cannot hear, and more importantly you cannot remember where you are and how you got there, so the stories you tell yourself have only the slightest relationship to your waking reality. They're nonsense. You've forgotten, even despite a lifetime of knowing, what you look like and what other people look like, and if you could dream yourself looking at a mirror, you wouldn't recognize your face if you remembered it upon waking. Are you with me so far? Good. So every dream you dream is like a sock puppet acting out a primitive story, except that you are controlling the sock puppet yourself, and your eyes are closed so you cannot even see what you, yourself, are making the puppet do. The dreams are *yours,* Charlie, not that woman's, not your girlfriend's, no one else's, and as fragmentary and puzzling as they may be, they are *you* trying in a very awkward but real way to tell yourself something, and I think by now you must know what that something is."

# 14

The day before my Hawaii trip, Bowen popped into my office looking excited, so I naturally assumed that he'd managed to negotiate a higher cut of the gate, or an extra day's stay at the hotel, or something of that sort. But I was way off.

After I opened up the office door, he sort of waddled forward to force me to walk backward into my office. Then he shut the door very slowly, so that the click echoed in the silence. He ran his fingers—seven out of ten of which contained rings of various sorts—through his thinning, curly hair.

"So, Charlie, my man? Pumped about Hawaii? Alisa? She okay with it?" I'd told him earlier that day about our argument, but before I could explain, Bowen rushed ahead. I noticed the Jamaican/Irish accent he deployed in order to impress clients and women was practically gone; that would mean this was a serious matter. "Listen, I don't have much time, we can talk about the gig later, but I've got some bombshell news. Gilbert is selling out to a bigger agency in New York called Glennis Communications, or Glennis Partners, something like that. And wait, that's not even half of it. Gilbert's already planning his retirement, but the whole sale is predicated on Glennis getting their hands on ClickEver. I mean, that's the only reason they'd want us, right?"

"So we're out of jobs, basically?"

"Not that simple, buddy. That's why Gilbert's been so anxious lately about our client base, because he needs to keep it together to make the sale worthwhile to Glennis. But Jason"—a go-getter colleague of ours—"well, Glennis loves him, he's been ClickEver's account guy forever, so they've been talking about getting around Jason's non-compete, but they don't realize that as soon as our contract with ClickEver is up in a couple months, Jason's going independent and taking ClickEver with him. And no offense, Charlie, but Jason is the only reason they've stuck with us."

"So what you're saying is Gilbert has nothing to sell once Glennis finds out they don't get ClickEver?"

"Bingo, baby. Which means we'll have no choice but to keep on limping along independently, which means that unless we lose another account, we keep our jobs, I guess, for a while longer."

And so I left for Hawaii with a clear conscience.

There must have been something real to Alisa's fears, because, in the security line at the airport, I went to hold her hand and found it was gripped tightly around a small plastic bottle of Xanax, and when I went to grab her other hand instead, I discovered that she was clutching, along with her boarding pass and driver's license, a single thin, salmon-colored, ovoid pill, also Xanax, that the heat of her skin had partially melted into a pinkish smear. No matter; she no doubt had plenty more where that one came from.

It all seemed a little childish to me, though I knew as well as anyone about childish fears, so I let it go. Once we got settled into our seats, she stuck her boarding pass in her purse because she liked to save souvenirs of her trips, and I couldn't help but notice that the salmon-colored stain had smeared the word "Honolulu," so that all that was left was "lulu." Pathetic, I thought. She popped her first pill and then, after we'd hit cruising altitude (I wasn't around in the '70s, but something about the phrase "cruising altitude" made me think of discos and cocaine), she ordered a child's-size bottle of vodka, and then another, and later on a bottle of Campari, the one with "Bitter" in florid golden script on the label, to help her level off.

And then she reached into her purse for wintergreen Altoids

and one more Xanax, and for a few suspenseful moments all of the chemicals made her affectionate, and we had a trembly wet kiss in the middle of a cloud, which was wonderful. But then we pierced through all that fluff and we were suddenly over the ocean, and that clearly wasn't going to work for her, so she slipped back into her alprazolam mist and, for the remainder of the flight, slept deeply.

Life is not for amateurs, as Alisa herself once instructed me in a different and, for her, less subordinate situation, so I understand that we all do whatever we can to cope with our various terrors. But after the airport, I dragged her in a semi-comatose state into a taxi, while steering our luggage at the same time, and then into the Eva Waikiki Hotel, where the club was, and then to our bedroom, and by the time I'd pulled off most of her clothes and gotten her straightened out into a position that roughly conformed to the shape of the bed, I wasn't quite so understanding any more. She woke up once to take a pee and laughed in a wheezing kind of way at how badly overdosed she was, and then she collapsed back into bed. After about an hour of listening to her rattling snores, I went downstairs to explore the club, which was called Palmyra and had a slightly incongruous oasis theme, but it was only 3:00 P.M. local time and the place wasn't open yet; the one wall I could see had a dramatic, diorama-like camel caravan fashioned out of what looked like hammered copper and a bright but bleak orange light behind it to simulate the setting desert sun. It was spooky-looking in the otherwise blackened room, and a bit lonely.

So I walked down Kuhio Avenue by myself for a simple poke dinner and a beer and then came back to Palmyra at 6:30, as Bowen had arranged, to meet the house band and run through my set list for the next night's first performance. The room was much more inviting with the house lights up; I didn't understand how an oasis theme fit in with a lush tropical island like Oahu, but it looked contemporary, like the owners had thrown a few bucks at the project.

I always played solo at Berto's and had rarely worked with a backing band, so I was eager to do a bit of rehearsal, but that wasn't in the cards. One of the two side guys, a burly, middle-aged bass player wearing a sweatshirt with ragged sleeves to show off his biceps and a brown leather cap with a little button on top that looked like a miniature hassock, said, "We do this all the time, Mr. Allesandro."

"Charles. Charlie."

"Charles, Charlie. Gotcha. Okay if we stick with Charlie and keep things loose?"

"And I didn't catch your name?"

"Don. The drummer's eating dinner. He might stop by later. Old friend of mine, Zach. We've played it all, you name it. Toured with Leon, Gregg, Neil, all of the big guys."

"So when do we get started?"

"Tonight? We get started and finished at the same time. All's we do is fart around for a half hour, alright? We go through your set list, you give us the keys and the chords, bing, bam, we're outta here. Zach and me got another gig tonight. Tomorrow's when the rubber hits the road."

"I've got some originals."

"No problem. Originals, all's we do is follow you and make you look good. All's you need's a clean finish, and everything else is forgiven, am I right? Covers we got covered, lemme see the list."

I showed him my handwritten set list. "Okay, you got Garcia, that Garcia solo album is the bomb, nobody remembers that one; Richard Buckner, that's a good one; Willie Nelson, can't go wrong; Joseph Arthur; that one Jeb Loy Nichols, okay; plus some good old honky-tonk, we know alla these so no worries. Might have to brush up on the Buckner."

"When?"

"All in good time, my man. And then these originals, what kinda style would you say they are, like, druggy country, same as the covers?"

"Well, I don't know if 'druggy country' is right, but kinda country soul or folk soul, with a little psychedelic feel to them, mostly in my singing."

"'You Don't Know What Love Is.' Is that the standard? You say original here on your list."

"It's mine, just the same title, but a different song."

"The White Stripes got one too. But that song, the standard I mean, always left me hanging. It starts out, 'You don't know what love is, until...' You know, 'Until you know the meaning of the blues.' I fuckin' *hate* that 'until,' because up until that point, you think the guy's gonna really get it in the ball sack like he deserves —'you don't know what love is'...period, *dick.* Because you just... don't...get it. Am I right? I've known a lot of women, probably should a said something like that to me 'cause I deserved it. That was before I grew up and learned to act like a man." He took his hat off and scratched his scalp for a moment. "I hope your version's better."

"Well, I don't know about better, but it's definitely more along the lines like you said of just not knowing what love is, period."

"Okay, and 'It's Time to Not Try,' 'Everyone But Me,' 'In Tears Everywhere,' 'How Many Summers?,' 'Someone Just Like You,' minor key stuff, lonely feel, I get it, I hope you're happier in real life."

"Pretty much."

"You don't look happy. If I could observe. Right now."

"I'm just nervous. I usually play solo, and I've never played out of stage, I mean, out of state, or in front of an audience I haven't, you know, *recruited.*"

"Relax, my good man. Smoke something illegal. We've got all the chords, so let's just run through one so you can hear how fucking good we are." He peered into the darkness at the back of the club. "Chad, my man, you there? The drums await!"

"Chad? I thought you said your drummer was named, what's his name, now I forgot it, but I don't think it was Chad."

"Zach? You mean Zach?"

"Yeah, I guess so. Isn't that the name you told me? Zach?"

"Zach's not here tonight. I told you, I've got the gig with Zach.

So Chad'll help us out. Relax your mind, drummer's only got to get the time. And Zach's way smarter and more talented than Chad, right Chad?"

Chad, stepping up on to the stage, laughed and said, "Whatever you say, my man."

"So you'll kick ass tomorrow, Charlie. I guar-an-*tee* it. We'll run through a honky-tonk progression, then one of your minor-key masterpieces, I'm not being a smart-ass either, I think they're gonna be great, and we'll be good to go for tomorrow, okay?"

"I guess. I'll follow your lead."

"No, tomorrow night we follow *yours*, remember? Just go back to your room and save your creativity for your girlfriend. Alright, my man?"

I shrugged, not entirely convinced, but if these guys—Don and, apparently, Zach—were good enough for Leon Russell and Gregg Allman, they were good enough for me.

So I wandered out of there and explored Kuhio for a little longer, but suddenly I felt terribly fatigued, so I did a little loop on the sidewalk, went back up to our room, and discovered that Alisa was still sleeping. So I brushed my teeth and then slipped under the covers and joined her. It was only 8:00 P.M., but from the sound of it, she was down for the duration.

# 15

≈

The next morning, Alisa felt fine and refreshed, and she put on a brown and gold bikini (I know that combination sounds strange, but it looked spectacular on her, and it did a neat override on my fantasies about a white bikini bottom) and we walked down to the beach at about 11:00. My show wasn't until 8:30 that evening, so we had all day for her to lie around and get as brown and gold as her bikini, and for me to stay pale and worried about Don and Zach and Gilbert and everyone else.

We only lasted for about ninety minutes in the midday sun, as it turned out. We didn't talk much, and I spent a lot of time looking down the curve of the shore into the distance at Diamond Head, which was at the opposite end of the beach from the low-budget Eva Hotel, and sifting the sand through my fingers. It was really marvelous sand, consisting of very fine, evenly sized bits of poppy-seed black and dusty-rose colored sand mixed in with other grains that looked like very tiny sesame seeds and white bits of shell. I couldn't stop playing with it and stirring it around with my fingers and pouring it onto our thick turquoise L.L.Bean beach towel and onto Alisa's belly and silky brown bikini bottom with the raised gold striping. She was wearing a big, bulgy tigereye lune ring with tiny brown diamonds and yellow gold that she'd picked up for a song at a consignment shop, and she grumbled a bit when some of the sand got on the ring.

I was starting to be afraid that this would be our entire trip—

Alisa sleeping, me analyzing sand. And in fact, at just this moment, Alisa stirred and said, "Man, I guess I slept a lot yesterday."

"Yeah, you did. Basically from the plane ride all the way through to this morning."

"Listen, I know you don't want a complete drunken slut of a girlfriend after your parents and everything, but I want you to understand that all that pills and booze on the plane wasn't just about the water."

"Oh?" I said this rather neutrally and, I'll admit, a bit coolly. "So, then, what was it about?"

She picked at her brown tigereye ring for one moment with one pink fingernail, and I noticed that there was a single rosy grain of sand clinging pluckily to her nail; I was reluctant to look at her fully in the face. Then she said, "I think you know what it's about, Cha'. Frank. It's bad."

"I know. You told me."

"No, I really *didn't* tell you." She closed her eyes for a second, and then seemed to gather her resolve. I found it easier to look her in the face, now that I at least knew the subject matter. "He's got this thing where he lays out these, I don't know, scenarios. And they're all in the subjunctive tense, if you know what that means."

"Yes, sweetie, I know what that means."

"So, in other words, he'll whisper to me, 'If I were to meet you at the Candlewood Suites today after work, and I were to spend the entire time—I mean, the *entire* time—going down on you, I mean, how could you possibly object? I mean, I wouldn't ask anything of myself'—oh, he's so fucking self-sacrificing, that prick—'it would all be for you and only for you. So if I were to do something like that, I mean, could you possibly say no?' "

"So he was saying this in this sub rosa..."

"Subjunctive."

"Yeah, but I mean, I actually meant 'sub rosa,' or, I mean, I don't know, suggestive, but you know, in a sneaky way.'"

"Nice save, Charlie."

"No, really." It was frustrating to have a bigger vocabulary than someone while pretending in fact that it was smaller. "But, anyway, I mean, really sleazy, too. Because he thinks that somehow it's more enticing?"

"No, dumb shit, he's saying it that way because he thinks it somehow protects him from litigation if I were to ever sue his ass for sexual harassment. 'Hey, it was only a hypothetical situation, we were only speculating, it was only idle talk.' "

"Goddamn it, Alisa, don't you think you should have told me this was going on?"

"What do you think I'm doing now?" She said this so softly, so plaintively, that I felt myself melting a bit under the slowly setting sun.

"Is this just one example?"

"Oh, yeah, he'll come up behind me at work and be like, 'What would you do if I were to accidentally brush my hard dick against your ass like it was an accident?' Again, all hypothetical."

"And?"

"And what?"

"And so did he walk past your desk and brush his dick against you?"

For some strange reason, I expected Alisa to laugh at this question, but instead she said, "Yeah. He did. Once or twice."

"And how did you feel about this?"

"How did I feel about this? What are you, a fucking psychiatrist? I felt violated and humiliated is how I felt! He was acting like he could get away with anything, because everything he did came with plausible deniability. He even said that once! He said, 'I could fuck you for three hours straight, and you'd love every minute of it, but if you did some typical female thing later and changed your mind and complained to Diane or management or something, I have two different buddies—two—who would both claim I was with them the whole time, playing poker or reading Socrates or shit. That's plausible deniability, baby!' He actually said it that way, with the 'baby.' Disgusting. It made me feel totally powerless."

"You don't have to be powerless. You're telling me now. You could tell Diane and she'd probably believe you, because Frank has probably done this sort of thing before."

"Yeah, I guess. I'd hate to burst her bubble, though."

"You're an athlete, for God's sake. You're a winner. You don't have to take shit from some frustrated would-be college professor prick just because you don't want to hurt Diane. Do something!"

"I'm *planning* on doing something. When we get back from Hawaii and Frank gets back from Cleveland, I'm going to sit down with management and tell them everything."

"What's Frank doing in Cleveland?"

"I don't know. Business trip."

"Okay, whatever. The thing is, you're doing something, right?" Then I had a thought. "So do something now."

"What, call?"

"No, I mean, do something with me now. You're going to fight back, that's great. But *show* me you're strong. *Show* me you can overcome your fears. Get in the water."

"The water?"

"The water."

"What the hell does that have to do with anything?"

"It has to do with the fact that I've never seen you weak, and now you're being weak about two different things at once, so show me I'm wrong. Show me you can actually walk into the water. That's all I'm asking, walk into the water with me and show me you trust me." I opened my mouth to say something else, but stopped myself.

"You were going to say, 'Because I'm trusting you right now about Frank,' am I right? You were going to say that you trust me that I'm not going to let anything happen with Frank."

That was exactly what I was about to say. And I could tell she saw it in my face.

She sighed theatrically and started collecting her suntan lotion, sandals, snacks, and the other odds and ends we had collected after a day on the beach. Then she carefully wrapped them up in our towel. I really couldn't tell at first if she was planning to stalk off with this bundle, which reminded me of the kind that children prepare when they're planning to run away from home, and head back to the Eva Hotel, or whether she just wanted to keep our possessions in sight while she edged her way toward the ocean. It turned out to be the latter—she walked toward the water in a slow and sidewise fashion and left the bundle just outside the darker and smoother arc of sand that marked the farthest extent of the waves.

Then, taking my hand, she walked into the shallow water.

Her hand was dry and warm. It contained no hidden pills, and it did not tremble.

We waded in to the warm water up to our waists and stopped, me facing out toward the ocean and Alisa, of course, facing the shore and the long line of white hotels. I looked into her eyes, which were steady and calm. She said, softly, "Everything I just said was true. About Frank, I mean."

"Of course it was. I know that."

"I just wanted to tell you."

"You don't have to tell me. I know." And then we switched positions and I held her around her submerged hips, the warm water slopping around us and hitting me in my back with every wave, and with each little gentle slap, I thought that the way our bodies were positioned prevented her from feeling a corresponding slap on her belly and chest. I wanted her to know, in other words, that I, at least, knew what love was. I gave her a nice, long kiss, and then I dove into the waves.

I'm not sure what I was expecting, but when I emerged, there she was, twenty yards or so away from me, in exactly the same spot I had left her. I motioned for her to wade out a little farther to join me, but she shook her head curtly, and I couldn't help but notice that the waves were now hitting her directly in the belly and chest, and she winced with every little blow.

I swam back to her and, as if I had never left, put my arms on her submerged hips, and when I looked down through the water at my wavering hands and forearms, I felt subtly ashamed, as if it were my will that were wavering. But I wasn't about to give up.

"Look, I don't know why this is important to me, but I'm so proud of you for doing something about Frank, so I guess I just think this is your day to really break through all of the barriers. I mean, I'm breaking a barrier tonight and playing in front of a strange audience with a backing band, right? So head under the water, that's all. Do you think you could do that, put your head under the water?"

"I don't have a bathing cap."

That's when I knew I had her. If she wasn't panicking and flailing, and her primary concern was the lack of a bathing cap and what the saltwater might do to her hair, well, the hardest part was over.

"Okay, just stoop with me until the water reaches your chin." I held her more firmly around the waist and, without terribly much coaxing, got her to stoop along with me until the water reached her chin, but then a wave hit us and her face was splashed with water and she leaped upward and backward like a spooked Appaloosa.

I took a deep breath. "You have to expect the waves. They're regular, but I mean, sometimes one is bigger than the others."

"I know. I'm not a moron."

"Okay, just get used to their rhythm is what I mean. Take it slowly. Okay?"

"Okay."

"Alright, now dip down again with me, slowly, until your chin hits the water, and then when the next wave hits, think of it like this is no different from what it'll feel like when your head is actually *under* the water. You know, *wet.* You'll just feel wet is all."

Eventually, after several attempts, I got her to lower her head as far as the underside of her nostrils and then, though I should have known better, for I was the one reminding her of the irregularity of the waves, a bigger-than-usual wave hit and it completely drenched us. She flailed and lost her balance and fell all the way into the water, and before she could recover, another big wave came in, and I could see her clutching helplessly at the water with her mouth open, taking in big gulps of the sea.

We were still in waist-deep water, remember, so it was completely ridiculous; you would have to be a child to drown, I thought. But then as I thought that I felt an awful inner wave of shame and stupidity and reached down to scoop her up by her armpits, but as she came up, spluttering and spitting, she punched me, hard, in the left eye. It was an overhand right, and it came straight out of the sun without any warning at all, like the sun itself had plummeted out the sky and walloped me.

If you've ever been punched, really hard, in the inner part of the eye that's near the bridge of the nose, you know that tears instantaneously spring up in your eyes. It's some kind of automatic response—yes, vestigial, if you will—and if you're a man, you feel instantly humiliated because everyone thinks you're crying because of the pain, but it's just an autonomic response, and there's nothing you can do about it.

So I stood there with salty seawater and saltier tears stinging my eyes and feeling, now, a double sense of shame, and I started to yell against the noise of the beach and the waves, "What the fuck do you—" when Alisa grabbed the skin around my left eye and twisted it, hard, in the process digging the knuckle of her forefinger into the eye. I screamed like a woman and sank to my knees back into the water, and I dragged her down with me as if to punish her. I fell into the water with a great slapping sound, and Alisa fell on top of me, and as she fell, she scrambled with her hands and feet to avoid going back underwater once again. And then suddenly I was the one who was flailing with my mouth open, and the water was rushing in, and I thought Alisa was actually trying to drown me. But then she got back to her feet, and she stormed back to shore and grabbed our towel and was gone.

TWO

# *The Truth Rises Up from December*
## (Willa)

# 1

Alisa had taken everything with her, and all I had on was my wet trunks—not even a pair of sandals to walk through the hotel lobby, not even my room key. I couldn't bear to think about how, and why, my girlfriend had just punched me in the eye, so instead I obsessed about how my eye would look under the spotlights tonight, and where, with nothing in my hands and nothing on my body, I might wipe the tears and sand and suntan lotion off my face. I used the back of my hand and then I found a napkin dispenser in the Starbucks in the hotel lobby, but riding up in the elevator, somewhat drier but with my orbital bone and eye throbbing and bits of sand grinding between my molars, I started to become enraged.

The door, fortunately, was unlocked, propped open just a crack by one of Alisa's flip-flops. Alisa was lying, face down, still in her brown and gold bikini, and I was comforted, in some small way, by the fact that she had not yet changed, that she wasn't, at least, headed right now for the airport. And, too, that she was crying and not laughing; upset and not gloating; defeated and not triumphant. This made me feel, at some level, like we were in the same swamped boat.

I spoke first. "You alright?"

"I guess. It was kind of horrible, actually. It was the sound."

"What sound?"

"You know, of the water in your ears. The difference between the water up to your nostrils and over your nostrils is no big deal, I mean I can hold my breath, I'm not a child, but then when the wave hit me and I fell and the water was over my head, I heard this horrific rushing sound and then at the same time this immense muffled silence, and it felt like I'd been hit by a bomb and was dead all over again. It was awful."

"Dead all over again?"

"You know, like when it happened to me when I was a little girl. A friend pushed me in to the deep end. I thought I told you. It wasn't so much that I thought I was drowning, though I guess I thought that, too. It was more like it was what I thought it must be to be dead."

"I'm sorry. I mean, for taking you out into the water."

I saw her shoulders shrug from the back and that reminded me, in some small way, of how I had tried to shield her front from the waves, and I stood there, still dripping just a bit on the nice carpet, and expected her, somehow, to reciprocate. To apologize, not for the flailing, which was inadvertent, but for deliberately and with great force and skill punching me in the eye. The eye, and the orbital bone around it, was throbbing, and every throb arrived at about the same interval at which the waves had crashed against my back as I had stood there protecting her, and with every crash, the anger that had faded when I found the door open and Alisa lying helplessly on the bed began to return.

But five or so throbs into this mounting rage, she flipped around on the bed and looked up at me and smiled beautifully and said, "I'm really sorry I hit you."

"That's okay."

"It was instinct. But that's no excuse."

"It's okay."

"I was still in a panic mode, but it wasn't your fault the wave hit me. It was just that when it hit me, I hit back, but since you can't punch a wave, I guess I just punched you instead."

I had to laugh at that one—the image of "punching a wave"—but when I laughed my eye hurt more, and then Alisa started laughing too, and I jumped onto the bed with her even though that made my orbital bone hurt so badly I thought I was going to cry for real this time. She kissed me right on the spot where she'd twisted the skin and said, "Listen, first of all, I *promise,* so don't worry, okay? I absolutely *promise* I will go to tomorrow night's show, but please don't be mad at me, after what happened today at the beach, plus I'm still so dragged out from the jet lag and the vodka and everything, I just want to sleep in this bed until tomorrow morning. Okay? I mean, you promise?"

"I thought you were the one promising."

"I am, I mean, I promise I'll come to your show, I just want you to promise not to be mad that it won't be tonight's show, which you're really nervous about anyway, so you probably wouldn't even want me there."

"I'm not mad. I'm really not."

And I really wasn't. I put on my best jeans and a crisp blue shirt, picked up my Guild D-40 and my Martin DM, and headed downstairs to the club.

In the hour that it took me to do my sound check with Don and the real drummer, Zach, I started to feel a lot better. We ran through a couple of complete songs so that Zach could pick up the times, and before I even had a chance to think about it, it was nearly 7:00. No one, not even the voluble Don, had said anything about the deep black bruise that stood out so starkly against the white skin of the inner part of my left eye; maybe the low lighting and the orange glow from the camel caravan made it hard to see.

Bowen had known what he was doing, the whole losing-money aspect of it aside, and so had the club's manager, a cherubic half-Japanese, half-Dutch fellow named Reese "the Knack" Nakamura. What I called my "folk-soul meets Michael Stipe" style of music did all of the genres involved a bit of a disservice, but I had a kind of subdued affinity for murmured lyrics and lilting melodies that seemed to say "island," or, at least, some lonely islet. My minor-key tunes, the originals, seemed to go over with the crowd of about thirty-five or forty people better than the country and honky-tonk covers, and that was nice. Of course my back was to the drummer the whole time, but Don winked over at me once or twice as we settled into a groove, as if to say, "See, I know what the fuck I'm doing." Near the end of my set, he was smiling broadly, and I imagined that what he was saying now was, instead, something along the lines of "hey, you're no fucking Willie or Leon, but maybe you know what *you're* doing, too."

About halfway through "How Many Summers?" my third song in the set, I noticed a young woman seated stage left who looked different, in some way, from everyone else in the room. Since this was a hotel lounge in Honolulu, there were probably no more than a couple of locals in the audience, and everyone else seemed to be out-of-season, cheap package-deal tourists—mostly Asians with a few Germans and Americans.

This young woman, who appeared to be about my age, seemed more avid, for lack of a better term, than all of the other rum-sippers scattered around the stage. She was leaning forward, for one thing, while everyone else was leaning back, surreptitiously checking cell phones, relaxing, or quietly talking. She was petite, with a slightly broader-than-normal forehead, and a very erect posture—when she leaned forward, she did so only at the waist, and kept her shoulders square and her butt firmly in her seat.

She had very round and wide-spaced brown eyes and a rather small nose with an unusually flat bridge that accentuated the wide-eyed look and gave her the aspect, somehow, of an illustration from a fairy-tale book—a Little Red Riding Hood without the hood, perhaps, or a brunette Goldilocks. Her short brown hair was worn in a kind of asymmetrical flip that was cute enough but looked as if she had just come back from the stylist and was trying to make an impression on someone. She must have succeeded, because I forgot the lyrics to "How Many Summers" for a moment—something I never ordinarily do. I certainly didn't have any actual fans as such, but if I hadn't known better, I would have sworn that this woman had been following me on the last seven stops of my Asian tour—if, in fact, I had been on such a tour.

Of course, the next morning, I didn't mention the young woman to Alisa, who in any event was very focused on going shopping on Kalakaua Avenue; she'd had enough of the beach, and I'd had enough of her having enough of the beach. I, on the other hand, was just getting started.

I went to breakfast in a restaurant near the hotel, in a fine mood thanks to my performance, and then I wandered the streets for a while, feeling almost euphoric.

When I got back to the beach, I laid on the turquoise towel thinking about not much at all for the first time in a long time, drowsing, and listening to some Emmylou Harris on my earbuds. I awakened from my drowse every time I rolled onto my side so that the earbuds, and the tiny grains of sand they'd picked up over the course of the morning, pressed into my ear canal.

After the third or fourth awakening, the music was getting a bit too soporific for my taste, so I turned off my MP3 but remained prone on my towel and raised my head slightly to have a look around me.

Standing so close to me that she cast a shadow over me, and facing partially away from me, was the young woman from the nightclub, shaking some stray droplets from her too-new asymmetrical haircut. She was wearing the same pure white bikini I had "seen" in my dream and in my vision in Alisa's laundry room.

Then she turned her head slightly in my direction, and I realized that this young woman who had been listening so avidly to my music in the nightclub was Wilhelmina.

Willa.

I said the name to myself a couple of times, and suddenly remembered that, for a time, she had had the nickname Nilla, either because she liked to eat Nilla Wafers or because she was sweet and simple and bland, or maybe just because it rhymed.

Though she was standing so close to me she cast a shadow over my legs, she clearly thought I was still snoozing and was waiting patiently and politely for me to awaken. That gave me a chance to observe her, with my left hand in a downward-tilted salute above my left brow to keep the powerful sun out and, I suppose, to keep anyone from seeing my black eye. She had a compact but full-figured body; she couldn't have been any taller than about five foot four, but she had an unusually erect posture, very much as I'd remembered from childhood, with a slightly up-tilted chin and those big, resolute, unblinking eyes, as if she were bravely bracing for an impending impact. It accorded exactly with my earliest memory of her, when we were both four or so, and she had announced to me that she was mad at me about some nonsense or other, and, with a "humph," had stalked off with her arms crossed tightly and her head held comically high, whereupon she walked straight into an elm tree, bounced off of it, and fell backward onto her bum. I'd laughed, of course, but she'd picked herself up from the ground and, with the same up-tilted chin and erect posture, walked back to her home and her mommy.

She turned slightly further in my direction as if surreptitiously checking to see if I'd awakened, and I realized, though I had seen this as well in the club, that she was indeed a brunette now, though her hair had been much lighter—almost blonde—in her Nilla days. Her nails and toenails had a nice, light coral-colored polish, and I reminded myself that, while the eyes and the posture were unmistakably that of the little girl I'd once known, she was as much an adult now as I was.

I could see that she still wasn't quite sure if I was awake because I was still lying there, my eyes mostly closed against the sun, and I wondered if it was best if it stayed that way, because once she knew for certain I was awake, we would have to talk, and that conversation would inevitably turn to the very thing I didn't quite know how to talk about.

I couldn't talk about it because I didn't understand clearly then, and couldn't recall clearly now, why Willa's mother Isabelle—Mrs. Dunleavy, as I had known her—had blamed only me and not Willa, since both of us had been charged with watching Willa's baby sister. And I thought that this odd, though clearly not coincidental, meeting would be, as no doubt Willa intended it to be, a good chance to clear the air—not to blame Willa, nor even to ask her to share the blame with me, but merely to understand why it had not been shared to begin with.

Or perhaps it had. Perhaps Mrs. Dunleavy had spoken to Willa much as she had done to me, except that the mother had no intention of self-exiling her family to Buenos Aires or anywhere else. And maybe Willa was feeling much of the same guilt that I felt, and maybe I could help to relieve her of some of it. It was worth taking the chance of being the first to bring up this subject that she had traveled all the way to Hawaii to discuss in order to remind her that we had only been kids.

So I said, softly, but loud enough for her to hear, "Nilla," but Willa didn't turn around. I tried again more loudly, and still she did not acknowledge me, maybe because of the clamor of the waves and the other bathers, or maybe because she had seawater in her ears.

Or more likely because she had utterly forgotten that long-ago nickname.

So this time I said, loudly enough for anyone in her vicinity to hear, "Willa Dunleavy?" And she turned around and looked at me, still holding my down-tilted salute, and gave me a slow, shy smile that showed no teeth. She wore pale pink lip gloss on her thin and soft-looking lips.

Then she said, simply, "Hi."

"I recognized you right away."

"I did, too. I mean at the club last night."

"Well, I more recognized you here on the beach, I wasn't completely sure at the club, because it was so out of context for me. How are you, Willa, it's been quite a while!"

She gave me that slow smile again. It was one of those smiles that took a long time to gather itself and a long time to disappear. It was as if she had chosen to ration her expressions with care, or rather as if she valued each one individually, which wasn't precisely the same thing. And then she made a little murmuring motion with her lips without saying anything, and I instantly remembered that she would do this all the time when we were children, too—moving her lips infinitesimally for a moment before she spoke, as if she were rehearsing what she was about to say. It made her look a little like a bunny rabbit that twitches a bit about the mouth as it contemplates a tender dandelion.

"I'm doing good, Charlie. How are you?" Her voice, too, was not unfamiliar, though of course it was the voice of an adult woman. It sounded like soft, crumbled petals.

"I'm okay."

"Would you be better than okay if you didn't have that black eye?"

I laughed. "Yeah." I suddenly realized my hand hadn't really succeeded in covering my eye as I'd thought it would and, worse, that it was very evident to Willa that I was trying to hide it. I dropped my hand to my side, but the sun was so strong that I lost Willa in the glare and brought my hand up to my forehead again.

"Did your girlfriend sock you?"

"Were you on the beach yesterday?"

"Me? No. Why?"

"Because I was on the beach yesterday with my girlfriend, and she socked me."

She laughed. "Oh, she really literally did! I was just like trying to make a joke."

"Well, you nailed it. She socked me and we tried to drown each other."

"Wow, same old Charlie."

I suddenly felt a powerful wave of acid wash through my stomach. Somehow, in the course of this brief conversation in the blinding sun, I had almost forgotten how my connection with Willa had originally come about. I said, cautiously, "What do you mean?"

She laughed lightly. "You know, the fistfight with Winfred, that tall German kid with like the seven-foot wingspan. Among others. You always seemed to be in some kind of tussle."

I thought about this for a moment. "Winfred? I remember that fight, but I was in high school then. How do you know about it?"

"Know about it? I witnessed it, Charlie. I was proud of you Charlie, you beat him *down*." She laughed lightly.

"You witnessed it? But you moved away after, I mean somewhere during the time when I moved back to Argentina, because when I came back to Chicago I was only twelve and you were gone."

She laughed again. "Gone from your mind, apparently. I think that I just wasn't on your radar screen is all. Yeah, my family moved a few blocks away, but I graduated from grade school when you did, and I went to high school with you. I can't believe you don't remember that."

I was stunned. How could I not have noticed her back then?

And then I thought to myself, *Well, maybe I blocked her out because we shared something awful. Or because I was angry with her mother and, through her mother, with her. Maybe I just didn't want to be reminded by seeing her every day of what she and I had done, and what I'd been blamed for. Maybe I noticed her then, but I forgot it later.* But out loud, I just said, "Hey, it was a big school. What was it, 3,400 students or something? At least I recognized you now on the beach." I stood up from the towel then, so we could talk eye to eye, without me having to squint up at her, and her down at me.

She looked at me closely and smiled again.

"Funny I didn't notice your black eye at the club."

"A little dark, I guess." I paused, nervous and hopeful that she'd say something about my performance, and quite a bit more nervous that she'd get started on the real purpose of her visit, but she did neither.

"So you're here with your girlfriend?"

"Uh huh. It was just a fight. I mean, she's never hit me before and I've never hit her, but I guess it was just one of those things that happens. She's terrified of the water and she panicked. How about you?"

"How about me what?"

"Who you here with?"

She shook her head. "You know, you're lucky. My last three boyfriends broke up with me either by text message or e-mail. I guess e-mail's a little more formal and businesslike these days, so that makes it okay. Nobody does anything face-to-face anymore because they're all too cowards. I'd almost *rather* be socked in the eye, but I guess it's easier just to, you know, disappear."

I felt incredibly nervous at this moment, standing there squinting into the strong sun with my left hand shielding my eyes. My left arm was dripping with sweat, and most of it was running down my arm and off my elbow, but some of the sweat from my hand was running into my left eye and making it sting. I was trying to say something to her.

I was trying to say, "I'm not a coward, and I'm willing to talk face-to-face if you're also not a coward. I'm willing to discuss Elizabeth."

But I couldn't bring myself to say it. So I guess I was a coward after all.

But then, what did that make Willa?

As if to change the subject from what it was we weren't, in fact, actually discussing, Willa said, "So, I don't mean to probe, but did you and your girlfriend like break up or something?"

"No. I mean, not really. It's just really awkward because my show you saw last night was kind of amateur hour..."

"I thought it was good."

At last. It wasn't much, but it was something.

"No, I mean, thank you, that backing band was great, I just mean, it's earning me less than what it's costing for me and Alisa—that's her name—to stay here, plus I mentioned she's terrified of the water, and she doesn't even want to be here to begin with."

Willa suddenly put the three middle fingers of her right hand on my left forearm, and as she did, I suddenly had a terrible thought that I was forgetting something very important. She must have sensed my sudden stiffening or abstraction, because she said, a little defensively, "No, I was just gonna say, we're standing here in the hot sun, and I've got somewhere to be, but how about we meet at the beach, right at this spot, tomorrow at this time?"

"I'm good with that."

"Let me give you my cell in case something changes. What's yours?"

I told her my number and she called it. "There, now my number's on yours and yours is on mine. And wear some sunglasses tomorrow, okay?" She laughed, and I did too. Who comes to Hawaii without sunglasses? Only a morose, country-soul singer-songwriter from Chicago, I suppose.

And then she walked away, leaving behind, like a vapor trail, the words, "I think we both need to catch up."

Indeed we did.

# 2

*That* night, Alisa came downstairs to the club as promised. I was simultaneously relieved and disappointed to see that Willa was not there, though she hadn't said she would be.

Don was still on bass, but Chad was sitting in on drums instead of Zach, and maybe that threw me off a bit. Where the hell was Zach? Another gig, again? That pissed me off, though what could you expect from a house band? Plus, I'd decided at the last minute to switch to my Guild D-40 because I thought the sound would be a little mellower for my originals, which everyone last night had seemed to like. But I'd changed the strings just before leaving for Hawaii, so I kept on going flat at the beginning of songs; I couldn't even form a chord because the G and D were both off.

I was able to vamp a bit on the honky-tonk stuff, but when I started "You Don't Know What Love Is" in the wrong key, I had to start all over again, and Don shot me a look. Though I couldn't really see Alisa in the audience, I knew she was probably giving me a look, too. I only hoped that she wasn't actually holding her head in her hands, like she sometimes did when I performed.

I thought about switching back to my Martin DM, but I could picture myself glancing down at the tuner all night and seeing that damned red light every time I went flat and getting obsessed about it. I decided, instead, to tough it out with the D-40, and, with my back to Alisa and the rest of the audience, I took the three middle fingers of my right hand and pulled the strings really, really hard to get the slack out, which made me think of the way Alisa had taken her fingers and twisted the skin around my eye, just as hard.

But God and Don must have been smiling on me, not to mention Leon and Willie, because the stretching worked, and I played the rest of my set in tune. I felt soulful and relaxed and high, and my eye didn't hurt, and I kept on picturing Alisa in the audience, smiling, except in my mind the face kept on shifting from Alisa to Willa. After the set was over, she—Alisa, that is—said, "Great job, sweetie," and didn't even mention the early songs that I'd started out of tune. She and I and Don and Zach—who'd reappeared after the set was over, even as Chad had disappeared—hung around the club after the crowd cleared out and threw back a few tequila shots, and I'd made some reference to "fuckin' drummers," and Zach laughed heartily and it was all good.

The next day I went back to the same spot on the beach. I swear I was standing on the precise same patch of sand I'd lain on yesterday, because that was how much I didn't want to miss Willa. She showed up only a couple of minutes late, and I didn't want to start out of tune, so to speak, so I began our second adult conversation with something I'd rehearsed while waiting for her.

"Listen, I don't know if you remember this or not, but my family used to have one of those big, round aboveground pools that smelled of plastic and would take three hours to fill with a garden hose. And you came over a couple of times and we splashed around and played Marco Polo."

"What's Marco Polo?"

"You know, the kid's game."

"Yeah, I guess I remember." She laughed. "Well, not really. I loved your show, by the way. I didn't really tell you that when we talked yesterday, but I should've. Especially those slow, kind of lonely songs."

"What else do you remember? I mean, not about the show, I wanna talk about when we were kids." That didn't come out right at all. Just as I'd feared, my strings were loose and I was, once again, abrupt and off-key.

She looked at me a little wearily.

"Charlie, instead of talking about all of that right now, why don't we go for a swim?"

I smiled in relief. "Good idea."

We walked into the water together but apart—there was a good three or four feet between us all the way into the ocean. An observer on the shore would have assumed we didn't know each other at all, which I guess had been our point, intentional or otherwise.

But the moment we slipped into the water, it became difficult to determine where her body ended and mine began. I had never swum so beautifully before with another human being; I felt like we were a pair of sleek Monterey Bay otters, spinning around each other and through the vortices our spinning left behind and then back out again, as if we were untying a very complicated knot. We swam farther out than any of the other bathers, who in any event were mostly obese or timid tourist types, and we stayed in the water for a long time. Now and again, as we swam closer to shore, we stood facing each other just as I had with Alisa, but I of course felt no need to protect Willa from the waves, and yet I had this tender feeling about Willa, as if she were still the child I remembered. So I wanted to protect her in some deeper way I couldn't articulate, and when I held my hand up to my forehead to block out the sun, I felt for a moment like the one-armed man, inspecting the slice of tangerine against the sun lest his little daughter choke on a seed.

After we were finished with the water, we lay on my turquoise towel for a while, and then I said, "That was nice."

"Yeah, it really was."

"So Willa, what do you do for a living?"

"I'm a nurse in a long-term-care facility for the mentally and physically challenged in Seattle. Hawaii's not a huge trip for me like it is for someone like you from Chicago, so I come here once every couple of years."

"I hope you don't mind my saying so, but seems a little weird to see someone come to Hawaii by herself."

"It's the whole ex-boyfriend thing. I guess I got tired of the whole routine of breaking up and being broken up with. So the past two times, I've just come to Hawaii by myself. Off-season like this, it's super-cheap, I can just swim all day and club all night and not worry about running into someone I know on the beach wondering what I'm doing all by myself." She laughed. "Well, at least until you." Then she laughed again. "Not that I exactly 'ran into' you, though."

"Sorry. Didn't mean to make you self-conscious."

"You didn't, Charlie."

"So you wanna know what I do?"

"Sure. I mean, I guess I didn't ask because I know you're a musician."

This pleased me immensely. *Immensely.* "No, I just do that as a kind of hobby or whatever. I got this gig here just as a sort of accident. I have a day job in marketing."

She smiled her slow smile. "Do you enjoy it?"

"Eh, when I'm not on the verge of being fired, and when my boss isn't...listen, I hope you don't mind my being too direct, but are you ready to talk about what happened that day?" My heart was pounding and I felt sick to my stomach.

She did that little murmur-y thing again with her lips. "With my sister? I guess so, sure. I mean, that's what I came here for. I guess Hawaii's sort of neutral territory, right?"

"That's why you picked here?"

"Yeah, I guess. I Googled you once in a while for about a year after I finally decided we should talk, you know, trying to get my courage up, and when I saw you'd be here, I figured it'd be more relaxed or whatever."

"Look, I don't want to cover old ground or anything, but I want to tell you what I remember."

"Okay."

"We went 'butterfly hunting' is what we called it, right in the middle of the babysitting, but basically it involved just wandering around the empty lots in the neighborhood. We both had those Fla-Vor-Ice pops from your freezer because it was as hot then as it is today, and at some point, we ate them, and we must've thrown the plastic tubes in the garbage somewhere, because I don't remember having them when we came back to your house."

"You mean, came back and discovered that Elizabeth wasn't in her crib."

"Yeah. And I guess what I really don't remember at all was placing her on your bed, or even why we decided to *do* that. Or even finding her jammed up against the wall." I suddenly saw that Willa was quietly weeping. "I'm sorry, I didn't mean to upset you. You said you were willing to talk about it."

"And I am. I just can't help it. I don't cry that often, maybe once or twice a year when I remember, but then I remind myself that it was a long time ago. I just feel so fucking guilty, that's all."

"We were too young to be watching a baby. We have no reason to feel guilty."

"No, I know. It's not so much about me, because I know we were too young. I mean more like guilty about you, because I remember what happened with my mother."

What happened with her mother will never leave me, ever. The evening of the accident, after everyone had returned from the hospital, Mrs. Dunleavy—in front of Willa and in front of my own parents—had waved her forefinger in front of my face and said, "I never should have trusted you with a baby, *never.* There is something wrong with you! Wrong! You are not normal! You are a sick, sick child and you belong in a mental institution!" And who knows what she'd said directly to my parents—something as bad, probably, or perhaps far worse, because in their shame and cowardice they'd packed up shortly thereafter and fled to

Buenos Aires and into the waiting arms of their precious wine.

How could that leave anyone, ever, the words themselves, or the sudden flight that I couldn't comprehend at the time, and the sudden shamefaced goodbyes to all my school friends? It clearly had not left Willa because she looked at me and said, "I'm sorry. It must have been very difficult for you after that."

"It was, I guess. But more in later years." What I had no intention of telling Willa was that in my early twenties a UPS delivery person dropped off a long, white box, the kind that contains a dozen red roses. From time to time I'd sent roses to a few girls, but of course had never received any, but my girlfriend at the time was the playful type, so I'd assumed it was just a loving little joke, a turning of the tables. So I'd signed for the package, set it on the kitchen table of my old apartment, and snipped off the ribbon with a scissors. I was excited and flattered, to be honest. I pulled off the lid, and inside I saw the complete skeleton of an infant human being.

I screamed and fell backward from the table and knocked over a chair as I backed away from that cardboard coffin and the horror it contained. After about a half hour, I called the police, and they told me to bring the box of bones to the station, but not to touch the bones myself—as if I needed to be told that.

I told them all I could surmise was that the box, which of course bore no return address, had been sent by Mrs. Dunleavy to punish and terrify me, and of course I told them of the last address I knew of where she, her husband, and the girls had lived. After a few minutes of bemused examination, a couple of the policemen informed me that the skeleton, though seemingly real, was a high-quality replica that had been purchased at a medical-supply shop. They thought it was some kind of expensive prank. I buried the whole mess, bones and box and ribbon and all, in the backyard of my apartment, and when I was just finishing up with the spade and shovel, my landlord came by and asked me what I was doing, and I told him it was a deceased pet guinea pig.

But all I said to Willa was, "It kind of stuck with me, Elizabeth herself of course, what happened to her, but more this sense that your mother was right."

Now, this was a stupid thing to say, because her mother had behaved like a lunatic, but I couldn't quite tell Willa that. And it also was stupid because by saying Willa's mother was right, I was acknowledging that, as she had claimed, I was mentally ill. And I didn't want Willa to think that, not for even a second, so in my practiced way, I allowed the box to remain buried and I switched gears. "I mean, I've lived a very normal life, and I get up and go to work every day and in the evening I write my songs...."

"Your songs are beautiful. 'Heaven Right Here' was amazing."

"Thank you." I didn't have the heart to tell her that "Heaven Right Here" was a cover, but I was so pleased that she'd like one of the songs I'd sung that I lost my train of thought for a moment. "Anyway, what was I saying? Oh yeah, I live a pretty normal life, I'm nice to my girlfriend, well, at least most of the time..."

"Nicer to her than she is to you, sounds like."

"Yeah, I guess. Oh, you mean the eye. Yeah."

"That was pretty radical."

"I was forcing her to try to swim, even though I knew she was scared of it, and when I saw her flailing in the water with her mouth open, all those horrible feelings from what your mother said came rushing back."

"How deep was the water, again?"

"Waist, maybe chest."

She laughed. "She was in no danger of dying from anything other than severe over-dramatic-ness, if that's a word."

I laughed again. "If it isn't, it should be. Anyway, my point is that ever since then, I mean since your mother, I guess I've been a little, I don't know, I hate to kind of admit this, scared of women."

"Scared how?"

"Not sexually." I felt foolish about saying this so abruptly, as if Willa would think I wanted to reassure her on this score, and thus was attracted to her sexually, both of which were of course true. "And not in some anti-feminist, they need to stay in their place kind of way. More like just the opposite. I'm scared of their opinions, of what they think of me, of how they might judge me."

"Are you scared of me?"

I looked, closely, at Willa, and I realized that just as I had loved her back then on the sidewalk when we were both eight, and before that at six, when I'd given her that green ring in those days before Elizabeth had even been born, I loved her just as much now.

# 3

It took a moment after I realized that I loved her still—or, rather, again—before I could say or do anything. I just kept on looking at her, and while I was looking, I was wondering whatever happened to that toy ring, and whether Willa still owned it. But then, without thinking about what I was doing—I was barely aware I was even doing it—I scooted over on the turquoise towel just a bit and kissed her. I've kissed a few women in my time where they really didn't want to be kissed, or weren't expecting it, and I knew it instantaneously; it's a horrible feeling, those dry lips, and the cringing humiliation afterward. But this was the opposite: Her pink lips were warm and wet and soft, and she smelled faintly of the salt on our skins.

It was like we were swimming together again.

I pulled myself even closer to her and put my hand on the bare small of her back, which was hot to the touch, and we kissed some more. I looked into her soft brown eyes, which rarely blinked, but rather looked at me steadily and calmly and acceptingly, and I noticed she had rather remarkable eyelashes—brown at the tips, like her hair, but blonde near her eyelids, and it couldn't have been mascara, because we had both just emerged from the water. It was as if her eyelashes were replicating, in miniature and in reverse, her journey from a little girl with blondish hair to her adulthood as a brunette, and this tiny reminder of her child self—suddenly, she blinked, just once!—was almost too touching and intimate for me to bear.

After a while, Willa said, "Let's hope your girlfriend doesn't change her mind about the water."

"She won't. She's shopping. Willa, I've got a total of five performances here. That means three more days. Can I see you all three?"

She thought for a moment. Her lips moved infinitesimally, and then she said, "I've got to leave the day after tomorrow. But I promise you I'll meet you here again tomorrow at the same time."

"And tomorrow evening?"

She shook her head no. We both knew what my question, and her answer, really meant, though I didn't know if her "no" was because Alisa was here in Hawaii with me, or because Alisa was still nominally my girlfriend, or whether there was a deeper reason. In any event, it wasn't one of those definitive noes that shake you to the core.

As I walked back to the hotel with my towel, I realized, in fact, I had a smile on my face. I just couldn't wait until tomorrow so that I could kiss Willa some more. I stopped in a little shop and bought a pair of black wraparound sunglasses, finally, and when I tried them on in the mirror, that smile was still there. Suddenly that night's gig had become merely a task to accomplish on the way to something better.

That night in bed, after returning from the show (strong attendance, average performance) I got off on a weird mental tangent, maybe because I didn't feel right about lying next to a still-wide-awake Alisa while I was thinking about Willa. What I did, instead, was to try to force myself to have another unbidden vision of the light switch in Alisa's laundry room. Maybe I thought it would please her or something.

So I tried, and I tried, and the best analogy I could think of was trying to achieve an orgasm without being touched. I'd heard of some yogis who supposedly could do this, but I was no yogi. Alisa was switching back and forth between checking her mail on her iPad and reading *Harper's Bazaar,* and every time her finger swiped across the iPad screen, and every time a page flipped, I lost concentration. She and I weren't *not* speaking, but we didn't have a lot to say to each other either, and after a while she sighed, tossed her magazine onto the floor, and put her iPad on the bedside table. She said, "Wanna order a movie or something?" and I was about to answer when the image I'd been searching for suddenly flashed, once again, into my mind: a woman's bottom in a tiny white bikini, hovering above the laundry-room table. There was no question in my mind, at this moment, that this was Willa's round bottom and Willa's white bikini.

I became, suddenly, incredibly aroused and grabbed Alisa's longer and sleeker legs and butt. She didn't resist, and we made love really slowly and for an amazingly long time. There was something about it that was, for us, unusually tender and, I don't know, sweet. That was the best word for it; it was, very evidently to me and probably to Alisa as well, like we were saying goodbye to each other.

But of course I couldn't leave well enough alone, maybe because I wasn't really sure if I was merely cheating on Alisa with Willa, which I was, or had just, somehow, also cheated on Willa with Alisa. Somehow? Suddenly, in fact, I was certain—certain and unambiguously ashamed—that I had indeed been cheating on Willa. I felt flushed and jittery and uncomfortable; it was now close to an hour since I'd first grabbed Alisa's legs and, as we were both lying there naked, I said, "I had another mental image of the laundry room."

"Just now, you mean? While we were having sex?"

"No. Just before. I guess it turned me on. Except the weird thing was, I saw this girl in a white bikini hovering over the laundry table, but it wasn't you."

Alisa said, rather cautiously, "Well, who was it?"

I collected myself, and lied. "Nobody."

Alisa seemed oddly disappointed by this. "Nobody? You sure?" And then I knew with complete certainty that she was hoping it was someone else, though I didn't understand why she would want this to be the case.

"Not that it matters, because you're not back home to flip the switch anyway, and I didn't even see it. Anyway, I'm pretty sure it was nobody. Just a generic woman."

Alisa laughed. "I know you, Charlie. There are no 'generic women' for you, are there? I've never even caught you using porn." She was right—I didn't. "Every woman you know you either love or you fear, and whoever you just saw in your image, you love her." She paused. "And I know it isn't me, and I'm okay with that."

"And why are you okay with that? Is it because we're officially breaking up?"

"I don't know, *you* tell me, Charlie. Start by telling me who you were thinking of while we were having sex so intensely just now. I mean, we haven't had sex like that since we first started going out, so try to tell me that something or someone wasn't running through your mind the whole time, and I'll call you a fucking liar."

"So who was running through *your* mind just now? Frank?"

"I told you, Frank is in Cleveland." Frank was in Cleveland? Yeah, she'd told me that, but what the hell did his present location have to do with anything? I turned away from her and stared out the window of the Hotel Eva at the lights of another hotel across the street, trying to collect my thoughts.

After a moment, Alisa spoke again. "I told you on the beach that everything I said was true. And it *is* true. Frank talks to me about what he's going to do to me in the hotel room, except he really *does* do it, and I like it. And during the day, he rubs up against me just like I told you, and it just reminds me of what we did and what we're going to do, and I like that, too. So, yeah, just like I said, it was all true."

It didn't really hurt as much as I thought it would have, maybe because I had Willa waiting for me. I suddenly understood why Alisa had been trying to get me to identify the girl in the white bikini; she'd been looking for "permission" to talk about her own relationship, and moral justification, or at least a form of moral equivalency, that she could cite in justifying her own betrayal.

I pictured Alisa looking at me, my bony back and my hunched shoulders, and I shrugged those shoulders for Alisa to see, and I said, "We're not married. We're not even living together. We knew we were coming to an end. It's really fine."

"I'm sorry I had to be cruel about it just now, but I needed you to know."

"You weren't that cruel. I mean, I knew it was Frank, and I saw the two of you together at dinner with Diane, so I knew that whatever the hell was happening between the two of you, it wasn't harassment."

"I'm not even sure I'm going to keep going on with him. It's like he had me under a spell or something, and I don't like it."

"A spell?"

"He's just really weird, like a hypnotist. I mean, it's not like a sexual spell, if that's what you are thinking."

"Thank you for clarifying that." I meant that rather more sincerely than sarcastically. "Not that it makes that much difference at this stage."

She didn't say anything, and of course I couldn't see her face. Suddenly, I had a revelation. "Cleveland. I understand now about Cleveland."

"You do?"

"Yeah, your not wanting under pain of death to fly to Hawaii with me, and then suddenly changing your mind. You didn't want to go with me because you wanted to stay in Chicago and spend time with Frank without me around, am I right? And then, Frank found out he had to go to Cleveland on business, so you figured you might as well go with me after all since he wasn't going to be around. Or maybe, because he wouldn't be around anyway, that would give you an excuse to get as far away from him and his influence as possible, you know, his 'spell,' as you put it. Clear your mind."

Alisa actually laughed. "You are amazing, Charlie. I mean, I can't say you're wrong about any of that."

"I just feel badly for Diane in all this."

"Well, Diane's a piece of work in her own right. You don't know her as well as you think you do."

"Still."

"Still, I know. Don't go putting us in categories, okay? I hit you, but that doesn't make me evil, and you forced me to swim when you know that's my biggest fear, and that doesn't make you evil either. And Diane is no fucking Saint Teresa herself, by the way. Can we just leave it at that?"

*Yes,* I thought, *because of Willa, I can leave it at that.* But I just said, "Sure."

"So we can be civil?"

"Well, it's a long plane ride back to Chicago, so yeah. Let's actually be friends about it, Alisa. Can we do that? Not just civil, but you know, like the people in the row ahead of us won't even know we're 'ex' if they eavesdrop. Can we do that?"

"I'm fine with that, Charlie, if you are."

"I totally am."

"And I'll be zonked on Xanax and vodka anyway, don't forget."

I turned back around to face her. "Good point. Come to my show tomorrow night?"

She said, nicely, "I will. You're a good performer, Charlie, and I won't forget you."

And that was that. Except that, at that moment and again the next night as we were headed down to dinner before my show, I kind of mulled over what she meant when she said "performer." Alisa was good with words, and well understood their multiple meanings, even if I had to teach her some of them, and I wondered to what extent she was trying to tell me she knew that I wasn't telling the entire truth about who I'd been thinking about when we'd made love.

Willa and I did indeed meet one more time on the beach, and we kissed a bit more—not as much as I would have liked—and it felt a little strange to me for reasons I couldn't quite pin down. Maybe I couldn't quite make the connection between this young woman—who accepted me and was attracted to me even though I'd played an inadvertent role in her sister's death—and her mother, who'd excoriated me and, in some ways, destroyed me. I was no more at fault than Willa had been, but I somehow expected her to be angry with me. Instead, she kissed me and talked to me about her life in Seattle, and joked about her lousy boyfriends and why it was I still wasn't wearing my new sunglasses, and, as she packed up to head for the airport, even invited me to come and visit her.

# 4

My flight home was blessedly uneventful, and Alisa and I didn't argue a bit, not even at the baggage claim back at O'Hare when her bag had somehow wheeled itself over to the wrong carousel. In fact, I even stayed over at her condo that night because we didn't want the taxi driver to make two stops, albeit not for any more-compelling reasons than that. I wasn't sure where we'd be a week or a month from now, but it suddenly didn't seem urgent.

I caught up on my e-mail before work the next morning. There were seven messages from Gilbert hectoring me about work projects and none from my father, who in any event rarely e-mailed. None, either, from Willa, though e-mail would be a bit formal at this stage. There was one, however, from Dr. Nemerov. It read:

"Carlos, I hope you had a fine vacation. Hawaii is not quite my style. Please read the following snippet, from a French novel I read a few years back: '*Do you know what an involuntary act signifies? Psychoanalysts say that it reflects the insidious maneuvering of one's hidden unconscious. What a pointless theory, in fact. When we do something involuntarily, this is the most visible sign of the power of our conscious will, for our will, when opposed by emotion, makes use of all of its wiles to attain its ends.*' Reflect on this, if you would. Take care and keep in touch."

After I'd settled in at my desk a couple of hours later, Gilbert sauntered by and said, "How were the islands?"

"Island, actually. We never left Honolulu."

"Interesting story behind that, I'll bet. And your eye, interesting too."

"Nah, not as interesting as you might think. How're things here?"

"Hawaii's for beginners, you ought to try Sardinia sometime. Now *that's* an island. In any event, Charles, let me congratulate myself on my thoughtfulness for not ruining your vacation."

I wasn't too worried, because I had gone to Paris with my previous girlfriend a year or so before meeting Alisa, and Gilbert had called my cell at 10:45 P.M. Paris time to remind me to come up with a good name for a client's website, which was still in the wire frame stage and wouldn't need a name for another month or two. Really, he was just calling to make sure I wasn't defecting to another agency, which I figured out only after he'd insistently inquired on the view outside my hotel-room window, as if he were comparing it to what he could see on Google Street View. Maybe he thought I'd slip up and describe Third Avenue in Manhattan. But by the time I'd figured this out, my *sole meunière,* wine, and *tarte tatin* had done a complete wash and rinse cycle in my belly and what remained of my evening had been ruined. Point is, he hadn't placed a single call or sent a single e-mail while I'd been in Honolulu, so how bad could it be?

But instead of reminding him of all of this history, I just said, "Bad?"

"Depends on how you define bad. Our billings? Let's let that spin on its own axis for the moment. Let us focus, instead, on your own dire situation."

"Dire?"

"Do I speak too plainly? So be it. Dire. You're the only consultant in this firm who was directly responsible for losing a client in the past—"

"That wasn't my responsibility. I got no cooperation from anyone on the budget."

He held up his forefinger. "Let me finish. The only consultant directly responsible for losing a major client in the past six months. We cannot afford to lose even one client in this environment, and now ClickEver's making funny noises."

"Noises how?"

"How? Not clicking, that's for goddamn sure. Noises like, 'there're plenty of marketing firms in New York, so why should we continue to do the tango with a Chicago firm that charges New York prices?' "

"We're doing everything we laid out for them in the proposal."

"And who won't even sit down with us to explore some out-of-scope proposals, won't make us feel like we are front and center with them..."

"So you're saying I need to go to New York?"

"Are you being interrogative with me at this moment? I mean, really? Yes, you need to go to New York. In fact, they're expecting you. Spend the rest of the day today with the social team coming up with some fresh ideas and working off your tan under the fluorescents, and then get on a plane first thing tomorrow."

"I've got a dozen other projects..."

"You know what, Charlie? The amount of work expands to fill the available time."

There was no point in arguing at that juncture. He'd told me and Bowen and all of our colleagues that the amount of work expands to fill the available time several hundred times over the past few years, whenever we got overloaded or asked for some account help.

It was hopeless.

"Alright, I'll make my reservations." But knowing what I knew about ClickEver, and its imminent departure, and the manner in which it would queer the deal Gilbert had set up with Glennis, put me in an odd spot. Clearly, Gilbert was panicked that ClickEver would walk away before the deal with Glennis was consummated, and he'd be left holding the bag, and maybe he was even worried that Jason was planning to take the account away as soon as he wriggled out of his noncompete, because he was asking me, and not Jason, to make the New York trip.

No question, it was a sticky situation for both Gilbert and me. There was no chance that I could impress ClickEver so profoundly that they'd have second thoughts about going with Jason, but I owed it to Gilbert, who after all was still my employer, to serve the ClickEver account as effectively as I could—even though I was likelier to keep my job if the sale didn't go through, because Glennis didn't know or care who I was. But I knew the whole thing was pointless and the sale wouldn't go through regardless of what I did or didn't do, as Gilbert himself would discover in a couple of weeks.

He grabbed my left shoulder, just the way he knew I hated it. "March into the breach with head held high, soldier. Run your concepts by me before you leave tonight, and I'll sign off on them. I have confidence in you, Charlie boy."

I had scheduled three days in New York to present our proposals to ClickEver, to meet with a smaller client, and to stop by our small New York office down the street from the Flatiron Building to take care of some routine business and personnel matters. I planned to do the best I could in all of these tasks, I suppose—and that "I suppose" speaks volumes, doesn't it? I was thinking about Alisa a bit and Willa a lot. And I was thinking about how I knew, and how ClickEver knew—though ClickEver probably didn't know I knew—that they were going with Jason anyway, and that all I was doing was going through the motions.

ClickEver's offices were near the Bloomberg headquarters, and on my first day I had some free time after lunch before my afternoon meetings, so I took a long walk down Fifth Avenue to enjoy the summer weather. I was feeling good about the likelihood that I'd keep my job a bit longer while Gilbert scrambled to replace ClickEver, I had Willa's cell number and was going to call her later that evening, and I wasn't especially upset about Alisa and Frank, maybe because I'd suspected it at the very instant that the steak knife in Frank's hairy paw had hovered a millimeter above the bridge of Alisa's nose. *Her* hairs bristled? *She* felt something vestigial, animal, primitive? No, at that moment, *I* did.

And Diane? Did she know about Frank and Alisa when she watched them at dinner that night? I doubted it. Diane probably would have called me. But I knew. And the reason I knew was the same reason I'd had those two walk-in dreams. I was a psychic, I was certain of it, and that made everything easier, even the image of Frank's cock hovering just a millimeter away from Alisa's open legs.

# 5

*I got* out of my last meeting at about 5:45 and joined the throngs of New Yorkers headed to the Port Authority or Grand Central or Soho or the bars on Second Avenue. I was thinking of finding a good ramen spot downtown, so I headed in that direction, feeling a little light-headed from a long day that had started at 5:30 that morning when my taxi had picked me up at the rental house to take me to O'Hare.

As I walked along in the late afternoon sunshine, the light-headedness started getting more pronounced, but it wasn't an unpleasant feeling—it was more as if I'd had a couple of shots of Laphroaig before leaving ClickEver. I veered toward a frozen yogurt shop, thinking I needed a shot of sugar in my bloodstream, but instead of entering I veered back into the stream of people, helplessly. I was wandering, but with some sort of purpose I could not discern.

When you walk down a New York sidewalk, it is impossible to register, much less absorb, every face of every person coming at you from the other direction. But suddenly, in my abstractedness, I began to try. Corollary, somehow, to my experience in the parking lot where I had suddenly seen, or imagined I'd seen, the beauty of the brake lights, I began to absorb as deeply as if they were lovers the visages of everyone who passed, three or four abreast, seven or eight a second, a hundred and fifty a minute, and I let every face pierce me to my core as if I knew them, and then suddenly I slipped into an even more abstracted state and began to imagine that, for each face in each slice of a second that I glimpsed them, that I not only knew them, I *was* them. I tried on their souls, each for an instant, and saw the world through their eyes and then, horrified or bored, discarded each in turn.

A middle-aged man with a long upper lip and soft brown eyes like a hound dog? Melancholia and ahedonia. Gone. The woman with a nostril ring and glossy lips? A doomed sensualist, and gone. And her friend who also had a nostril ring and tight thin lips? A narrow mind, and gone. A very handsome young fellow in leggings? Laboring under a severe misconception about what life was likely to give him and, hence, gone. A grumpy bohunk whose jaw was grinding sideways? Gone. A man with a horrifying beard and mustache that joined in the middle and sprouted into his mouth? Gone, just as I recognized that his beard was ordinary and he was gripping a black cell phone for some reason between his teeth. A little toddler, holding his father's hand? I could hear him say, "In da morning I put on my *shoes* and den I put on my *pants.*" And then, he too, and his father as well, were gone along with all the rest, just as endless others took their place.

And what did I mean by gone? Not that I wished any of them ill, it was nothing like that. Rather, it was that they passed by me within a second or two, and thus were gone from my consideration, dismissed, even as there was always another someone behind them ready to take their place. I didn't hate myself, and never had, but ever since I'd remembered I'd had a fascination with the notion of being another person, or more to the point, with the impossibility of being anyone other than myself, and suddenly I found myself, on this narrow concrete chute in the middle of midtown Manhattan, vested with the power of being anyone I wanted for a split second. I could try each one on, toss away the shell, and then try on the next. The elderly woman with an old-fashioned wooden cane and a coat despite the heat? I was her, and then gone, and then I was a pretty woman with pineapple-colored hair and a cross expression on her face, worried about work but looking forward to a weekend of smoking pot and shopping and then she too was gone, and then an imperious, patrician-looking woman, and I suddenly felt her sadness and disappointment in life and her brittle attempts to maintain her dignity in the face of disdain and age and then she too disappeared down the concrete chute.

I sustained this mood for a good fifteen minutes, and, at the end—by the time I'd reached a restaurant—I was feeling less lightheaded and even less upset about my job and Alisa and everything, because I had for this little stretch of time not only not been myself but been, instead, countless interesting others.

And only then, after all of this, did I remember Frank's story about the embittered flight attendant and how she'd instantly communicated her essence to him, and I realized that I had wanted to make the same thing happen to me. While I was awake and conscious, and not dreaming, I wanted to be as powerful as Frank was, and as insightful, and as hypnotic.

After dinner, I called Willa, but she didn't pick up, so I tried Bowen, but he didn't pick up either, and he'd changed his outgoing phone message, which worried me for some indefinable reason. So then I just lay on my hotel bed and flipped through the channels, and as I did so, it suddenly struck me that what I'd just been doing on the street was a form of channel surfing with human souls, and in the end, the program I'd been left with was the one I'd been watching from the day I was born. As in the moments after my vision in the parking lot, I couldn't help but feel deflated and defeated. Just like the taillights on the cars, the faces had all bleared and run together, because there were too many to keep track of, much less inhabit. And I was just one of those too many people myself and I, to an insightful other that I passed, was equally evaluated and equally dismissed. Gone.

*Some fucking psychic*...that's what I was thinking.

I finally found a rerun of *The Sopranos* that I didn't mind watching, but I kept the volume low and placed my cell on the bed next to me in case Willa called me. About twenty minutes later, she did. I mouthed the words, "I love you" to the phone, though I wasn't sure if I was addressing these words to the phone or to Willa, and I answered.

"Hey, Willa, how are you?"

"Good! It was nice to hear from you!"

"Yeah, me too. I had a nice time in Hawaii. It was so cool reconnecting with you. Actually, I'm in New York now."

"I've never been to New York."

"I love it. A lot of job issues, I mean, it's work, you know. And I'm still kind of processing breaking up with Alisa. Kind of tough right now, but I'm definitely glad it happened, and anyway it's a beautiful day here."

"I'm sorry about your girlfriend. I mean, you know, if you want me to be sorry."

"It's okay. It was coming sooner or later. Anyway, reconnecting, right? How cool is this? And speaking of that, I was walking downtown to find a ramen place and New York is so crowded, you know, and I'm looking at everyone's faces, and I fell into this strange mood like I could actually fall into everyone's soul, one at a time, and try it on like a mask, and see the world from their perspective..."

"So you mean, you saw you?"

"Me?"

"Yeah, you're saying you were imagining you were every person who was passing in the opposite direction, the moment you saw them. So that would have been the same moment they saw you, and since you were them, you were seeing you."

"That's true, hadn't thought of that."

"So what did you see in them?"

"I don't know, every person, without exception, I thought I could feel what it was like to actually be them, to inhabit their souls, and I kept on rejecting each one, every single one, because..."

"Because they weren't you?"

"I guess you could say that. But I don't mean it in the sense that I thought I was better than all of them, just that..."

"Yeah, I understand. Just that they weren't you. But what was the common denominator? Everyone you saw was seen by you. And everyone you saw, *saw* you. So maybe because of what you were doing, trying to read their minds or whatever, they could tell you were doing that by looking at you, I mean, you were probably staring at them, and they didn't like it and looked a little sour, and that's why they all looked unappealing to you like you wouldn't want to be them, just like they wouldn't want to be you!" She laughed.

"You have a succinct way of putting things, Willa."

"I really understand what you were trying to do. As I got a little older, I would sometimes imagine what it would have been like for Elizabeth, I mean just before we found her, but it always comes right back to how I would feel if it were me, and it's unimaginable because I've never been in a situation like that, and it's also unimaginable because I can't be her. No one can be anyone but who they are, forever."

"Willa, not to change the subject, but something has been troubling me ever since—well, I was going to say ever since we talked on the beach, but really, ever since it all happened."

"Okay."

"I mean, I was too scared and too young to say anything to your mother at the time, or even to my own parents when we moved to Argentina, but what the hell were a couple of eight-year olds like us doing watching an infant baby? I mean, what was your mother thinking?"

"I can't testify to what she was thinking."

"I mean, couldn't she get a babysitter, is all I'm saying?"

"I guess, but I think it was just one of those having to run out for a few minutes situations. She was working two jobs, remember, and my parents' marriage was constantly on the rocks. And besides, we really didn't have babysitters. Usually it was just Bea who watched us."

"B?"

"Bea. As in Beatrice. My other sister."

"Wait a minute. What other sister are you talking about?"

"You knew I had an older sister, right? Oh, shit, I forgot. You completely lost track of me, didn't you? I mean, once you got back from Argentina. Elizabeth and I had an older sister. She would have been, let's see, twelve years old when it all happened."

"So why wasn't she sitting for Elizabeth, or for Elizabeth *and* us, that day?"

"I guess she would've in theory, but she'd left for summer camp the previous day. So that was another reason my mom was going crazy. She didn't have anyone to help."

"It's so funny that I don't even remember your sister. Beatrice? Is that what you said?"

"Yeah, Beatrice Baer. That's her married name. She lives in St. Louis so I hardly ever see her, and we kind of drifted apart pretty bad. Last time I talked to her was maybe two years ago."

"Because of Elizabeth?"

"Huh? Why because of Elizabeth? Just because. Sister stuff. Family stuff, is all. Listen, Charlie, I really meant what I said. Elizabeth, the past, whatever...we can talk about it or not talk about it, whatever we choose. But come see me in Seattle."

# 6

**Though** the two events were not, in my mind, directly connected, I drove over to Alisa's condo the Saturday after my conversation with Willa to pick up some of my things. As I was getting out of my car, Gilbert called.

"Catch you at a bad time?"

"No, I'm just at Alisa's. What's up?"

"It's never an easy thing to say, and it's never a good time to say it."

"What? What are you telling me, Gilbert?"

"You understand I have a business to run."

"Are you telling me I'm fired?"

"Children to feed. Two in college. You *know* that, Charlie."

"So, yeah, I understand, I know all about your kids, but what I'm asking you is, am I fired?"

"I don't think that's entirely accurate. That characterization. I would say that we are mutually and reasonably reaching a point where we're going to have make a decision about your future with the firm, fair enough?"

"I guess. So I'm fired?"

"Look, we can parse this seventeen ways to Sunday. We can do this all day if you'd like. You'll have two weeks, okay? You can come in, use your office, look for your next job, you can tell everyone that this was a mutually agreed upon decision, which has the added advantage of being the truth. You'll be locked out of our files, of course, but you can make phone calls, work on your résumé, whatever you would like."

"And after the two weeks?"

"You go with my blessings."

"But I mean, severance? I've been with the firm for seven years."

"Contractually, you understand that I'm not obligated to provide you with anything in that area. But I would be happy to set you up with a woman I know who runs an outplacement business."

"So you're telling me no severance?"

"Charlie, what I'm telling you is that I'm opening up your future for you. If you were wise, you would just take it and run with it."

"Is this because of ClickEver? Did we lose ClickEver?"

"I'm not at liberty to discuss that, Charlie." But at that moment, Gilbert sounded almost jubilant, as if, somehow, the sale had gone through. In some fashion, evidently, he'd managed to keep Jason from walking away with the business, and neither the new agency nor, apparently, Gilbert, had any further need of me.

"Okay, thanks." I mashed the little red button with the miniature red telephone on it to end the call and stepped into Alisa's place.

The front door was open; Alisa was lying on her side in front of the television, crying.

"What's the matter, baby?"

"Nothing. What are you doing here?"

"Well, it would appear that I've just gotten myself fired."

"I'm so sorry." She was still crying and sniffling from whatever other thing had been troubling her when I first walked in.

"So what's going on with you? I walk in, it's the middle of the day, you're lying on your couch crying, is it me?"

She looked surprised. "No, it's nothing. They're just back and I got upset, that's all."

"They're back? Who?"

Alisa motioned over to the corner of the living room, where the heating grate was. I suddenly became aware, for the first time, that under Alisa's crying there had been another sound, a rustling sound punctuated by a faint squeak.

There, next to the heating grate, was a chipmunk, on its side, on top of a glue trap—really, just a sheet of thick paper coated in a heavy glue. In its struggles to free itself, the chipmunk had partially ripped off its fur, and bits of fur and flesh, flecked with blood, spotted the trap.

The dab of peanut butter that Alisa had used for bait was still visible at one end of the trap.

"Holy fuck, Alisa! Why the hell did you use a glue trap? Are you insane? The poor guy's skinned himself alive trying to get off!"

"I don't know. I didn't know how to use one of those cage traps and this was cheaper, and besides someone told me about garlic powder repelling chipmunks so I sprinkled some down the heating grate, so I really wasn't expecting any anyway, but this guy must've gotten past it."

"When did you put out the glue trap?"

"Last night, before I went to bed."

So the chipmunk could have been suffering all night and through the morning. I saw, next to the heating grate, a plastic bottle of McCormick garlic powder. I looked at it and at the struggling chipmunk. And then I strode into the kitchen, pulled out a white garbage bag, and then picked up the glue trap by one corner, with the chipmunk dangling sidewise from it by a strip of ravaged skin, and dumped it into the bag, where—surrounded suddenly by a world of whiteness it couldn't understand or interpret—the chipmunk began to struggle even more. Then I marched out Alisa's back door into the condo's little backyard and dropped the bag onto the grass. I felt more horrified with every second the chipmunk suffered, but something came over me and I set my jaw in the same way I'd seen Alisa do so many times when she was angry, except I wasn't really angry, just, suddenly, decisive. I pried up a loose paving stone from the little walkway that led from the condo's back door out to the alley—the stone was a big one, at least five or six pounds—and I threw it, hard, at the scrambling shadow in the bag. Instantly, the animal exploded, and in place of what was a life a second ago now there was only what appeared to be a bright blotch of raspberry jam with little black flecks that could have been seeds. I tied up the bag at the neck and tossed the mess into the garbage and wondered if the chipmunk, seeing nothing but whiteness for its last moments, had understood that it was already dead.

I came back into the living room. Alisa was seated now.

"Thanks for taking care of that."

"No problem. You know, I can show you how to set the trap. It's really easy."

"Thanks. So did Gilbert let you know this morning?"

"Well, no, actually, I just found out on the curb outside your place. He called me and told me in a kind of roundabout way."

"Shit, that sucks, sweetie."

"And no severance or anything. He's just giving me two weeks to use my office and job hunt. Two paid weeks, I guess, so maybe that counts as severance, I don't know."

"Thanks for coming over."

"You mean the chipmunk?"

"Yeah, no, I mean, thanks for thinking of me when you're down. I mean, after Hawaii and everything, it's, I don't know, good to know that we've still got this connection when either one of us is in trouble."

"Well, no, I agree, it's just that as I mentioned, Gilbert called me just now when I was on your curb."

"Oh, so why did you come then?"

"Alisa, how long were you going to let that animal suffer? I mean, if I hadn't come?"

"Enough with the fucking chipmunk, okay? I've got my own problems. Frank."

"Yeah, what about him?"

"Your buddy Frank and I just split up."

"My buddy, huh? He was your buddy up until just about now."

"Yeah, well, Diane is all broken up about the whole thing. You should call her."

"You mean, comfort her because her husband was having an

affair with my girlfriend? I guess she should be comforting me, too. Seems like the only one who comes out ahead in this whole deal is the Professor himself."

"I thought we handled our situation without a lot of rancor, Charlie."

"Rancor? Ire? Is that how you'd describe it? I felt humiliated in Hawaii, but I kept the whole thing low-key because I didn't want to make the end of the trip awkward. And now I'm out of a job, and you're asking me to go and comfort Diane?" And yet, as I carefully omitted, I had lain on my turquoise beach towel with Willa within hours of my humiliation and kissed her on her soft pink lips, and I also had to acknowledge that talking to Diane was something I actually was looking forward to.

"Charlie, just stop. Okay? Just stop. You still haven't told me why you showed up here."

"I guess to pick up a few of my things."

"You guess? A few of your things? How about just 'picking up my things?' All of 'em? I was expecting you a few days ago. Look, no offense, but at this stage, I'd rather not have them around anyway."

"Then it's a deal," I said, and with the same abruptness as before, I marched into the kitchen and pulled another white trash bag out of its dispenser. I performed a little tour of the condo, retracing steps I had taken a thousand times before; picked up a cell phone charger, a couple of dirty shirts, a can of shaving cream, and a cylinder of deodorant; and tossed them into the bag.

Alisa called out from the couch, "You've got some clean laundry in the basement."

So I left the lumpy, bottom-heavy garbage bag on the floor of the kitchen and walked down to the basement. Sure enough, Alisa had washed and folded a big pile of my underwear, no doubt in anticipation of my imminent arrival and departure. With my arms in a forklift pose, I scooped up the fresh laundry and then noticed the light switch above the aluminum laundry table, the one that had only once and never again appeared in one of my dreams. It was in the down position. I didn't want to put the laundry back on the table, but I was just able to extend my forefinger enough from underneath the pile of fresh and fragrant laundry that my ex-girlfriend had cleaned for me as a parting gift, and I used it to flip the switch up and then down again, and then up and down several more times, and each time I said out loud, "Fuck. You. Fuck. You. Fuck. You."

Then I stomped back upstairs and stuffed my laundry into the garbage bag. I picked up the little plastic bottle of garlic powder and threw it in on top of everything else, and then I noticed the unused cage trap shoved behind a bookcase and kicked it over to the heating grate where it belonged. I went back into the living room, put the white garbage bag down, and kissed Alisa goodbye.

"Listen, I'm not quite sure if we're fighting or not, or if we hate each other or not right now, but I just lost my job and you just lost someone important to you. Or I don't know, maybe two people important to you."

This would have been the ideal moment for her to acknowledge that I was one of those two, but she only smiled weakly. I grabbed the garbage bag and walked out. As I left, she shouted out, "You know, I really didn't appreciate your calling me insane."

# 7

*I was* feeling a little bit shaky after that encounter, so I pulled into a Walgreen's to pick up a six-pack of beer. As I was waiting in line, I smelled, somewhere behind me, an odor that could best be described as roasted peanut butter with rodent hairs. So I turned around and there, in line behind me, was Dr. Nemerov.

He must have recognized me ahead of him in line, because he just smiled and said, "Hello, Charlie." He was carrying a hairnet, a can of shaving cream, a bag of sugar-free Australian licorice, a bottle of zinc supplements, and a collapsible rubber colander.

"Dr. Nemerov! What a funny thing to see you! Is it, you know, okay to talk to you in public?"

"It's your reputation, Carlos. All is well, I trust?"

"Well, I have some other issues..."

"Which, of course, I cannot discuss with you in line at a Walgreen's. Make an appointment with me."

"I will. I just feel kind of weird running into you because I just murdered a chipmunk."

"Murder, self-defense or euthanasia?"

"Actually, more like euthanasia."

"Glad to hear it. Make an appointment and we'll talk soon."

As I paid for my beer, I could hear Dr. Nemerov behind me murmuring, "Your honor, I didn't murder that chipmunk!"

Later that evening, I used 20,000 points from my United frequent flier program to buy a round-trip ticket to Seattle, departing Friday morning, returning Sunday evening. I figured I might as well; I had no job and no girlfriend and nothing else on my agenda except my next appointment with Dr. Nemerov, and those 20,000 points had been earned in the course of many long and exhausting business trips on behalf of Gilbert and his children's futures. I called Bowen before I left to see if he could book me a gig while I was there, but he just laughed and said, "Hey, man, we got lucky once. Let's keep it at that."

"Okay, sorry, I thought it wouldn't hurt to try."

"So spill about Hawaii."

"You know, I'm not sure what to say yet. I'll let you know when I get back from Seattle."

"Why?"

"I'll let you know why when I'm back from Seattle, too."

"Man, I don't know about you. Okay, I'll leave it alone. Anyway, I talked to Reese, the manager at Palmyra, and he said you kicked some serious ass there. You should e-mail him and maybe he'll invite you back, who knows? Anyway, you owe me a nice dinner."

"I will. I promise. Listen, have you gotten a call from Gilbert?"

"No, have you?"

"Yeah, I got fired. I think he's trying to cut overhead to make the agency more attractive to Glennis."

"Holy shit. You sure you don't want to talk before you leave?"

"Thanks, Bowen. But I wanna go to Seattle with a clear head, you know? I'm just glad you survived, I mean, unless Gilbert's doing it in waves or saving some people for Glennis to fire instead. Hang in there, and we'll talk when I get back."

So I went with nothing on my mind at all except for having a good time. I packed my double-handled, calfskin carry-on bag with three fresh shirts, an extra pair of slacks, my shaving kit, a couple of paperbacks, a small gift for Willa (an expensive snow globe, depicting North Michigan Avenue in Chicago, that ended up being confiscated at airport security), some socks, an extra pair of loafers, and some of the clean underwear that Alisa had laundered for me. Just before I left the house, I sent Reese "the Knack" Nakamura a brief e-mail telling him how much I'd enjoyed my gig and thanking Don and all the guys, and I asked if he'd be interested in having me back.

As the United flight rolled away from the gate, I started thinking, had Willa actually invited me? Well, of course she had, and before the flight attendant had told everyone to shut down their electronic devices, I had read through my text messages with her; she would be meeting me at the Seattle airport and driving us back to her apartment. Had Willa and I actually kissed on the beach in Honolulu, two days in a row? We must have; and we must have had some sort of connection, or I wouldn't be visiting her now—and I could still remember how soft her lips had been. But I had an odd feeling that I was forgetting something important, though I had no idea what it might be. I patted my back pocket for my wallet, which was there, then took the wallet out and checked to see if my driver's license was there, or if I had lost it as I'd wended my way through security.

It was, of course, there.

Whenever a plane takes off, the sudden change in angle creates in me a moment of light-headedness that forces me to put down whatever I'm reading and look at the far horizon. It lasts only three or four seconds, and then the feeling passes. But this time, I couldn't shake the light-headedness even an hour into the flight. It was like that walk I'd taken in midtown Manhattan, but now there were no faces, no other lives, to distract me, only the backs of people's heads.

There was something very wrong, but I might as well have been a chipmunk in a white plastic bag, for all the capacity I had to understand what it was.

When I arrived at baggage claim, where we'd agreed to meet, the feeling that I'd forgotten something important and that I wasn't supposed to be there began to throb like my eye had throbbed in Hawaii. Maybe it was just that I was jobless and had no business taking a pleasure trip, and that made me relax a little bit, because while being financially irresponsible was a stupid thing for me to do, at least it was humanly stupid, and hence, for me, a most familiar feeling, whereas the odd, light-headed sensation I'd had on the plane had been something I'd never felt before.

After about ten minutes or so, I saw Willa and, at first glance, my heart sank. She was so short and slight—on the beach the high-cut white bikini had created an illusion that she was taller and leggier than she actually was—and she was wearing her hair in a ponytail, emphasizing the puffy, childlike curvature of her cheeks. Her round, wide-set eyes made her look, even more than before, like an illustration from a fairy-tale book, especially because, like an illustration, she seemed not to blink. Who was this young woman, and why was I here with her now, except that we'd shared something dark once upon a time, and a much briefer moment of brightness on the beach?

But she immediately hooked her arm beneath mine and started chatting about the Seahawks and the Mariners, and how much trouble she always had finding her car in an airport parking lot. But she'd tied a bright green scarf to the antenna of her bug-green Kia, so we found it right away.

Instead of going back to her apartment, she took us directly to a Mexican restaurant called Fernando's, and I was a little puzzled because it was only 4:30 and I wasn't especially hungry. But the place was already half full, and it smelled pleasantly of steamed corn and salsa.

She called the waiter right over and said, "We'll have a couple of margaritas." Though drinking was, at that moment, the last thing on my mind, I decided to just go with the flow, but I somehow managed to assert myself by saying, "No salt on mine."

We ended up drinking two margaritas each and sharing a bowl of chips and guacamole, and by the time we got back to her tidy little apartment in the University District, I was feeling a little bit loopy, but on the other hand I'd forgotten whatever it was I'd forgotten, so that was good.

She directed me to my bed—a fold-out couch in the living room

—and had me park my double-handled leather bag behind the couch. And just as I was thinking that this would be a sexless visit (and feeling oddly relieved at this prospect), she backed me up against the front door and we began to kiss again, as if we had never left that turquoise towel in Hawaii.

She stepped back for a moment and I was expecting her to say "slow down," or words to that effect, but instead she pulled off her baby blue sweater and a silky-looking blue bra and kissed me some more as I groped for her breasts. Suddenly I understood that our two-margarita stopover at Fernando's had been solely for the purpose of lubricating this encounter, and I laughed to myself at how easily I could ignore the obvious.

I was tremendously excited by her compact little body and her eagerness and we kind of waddled together toward her bedroom where she frantically pulled at her jeans and my slacks at the same time, and within seconds, I was on top of her and then I was inside of her. I cried out with excitement and delight, because it was all so unexpected—and yet what else should I have been expecting when a woman invites me halfway across the country to visit her?—and my exclamation made her laugh, too.

I slowed down for a second and said, "I need to put on a condom, okay?"

"I've got an IUD. I want you to come inside of me."

"I can't do that, Willa. I just can't."

"You can trust me, Charlie, it's okay."

Her eyes were so calm that I started to feel my fear fading away, or rather that I was less afraid of that fear than ever before. I felt like a mountain climber eschewing ropes on the Matterhorn, both calm and excited. I began moving inside of her again slowly.

She repeated, "Come inside of me. But not for a long time."

She squirmed out from under me and stretched out on top, supporting herself with her arms, so that I could see the full length of her body. Suddenly, again, she seemed to me as she had in Hawaii, long and leggy, and it was her appearance at the airport that began to seem an illusion.

After a few minutes, she sat up on top of me, and I grabbed at her very round and bouncy little breasts. I pinched one of her nipples, and she seemed to like that because she moaned deeply, so I pinched a little bit harder and she leaned forward and murmured, "Oh, good, you like to play rough."

Well, actually, I didn't, so I felt a brief moment of panic because I wasn't sure exactly what she meant, but I reached around and grabbed her ponytail and pulled, and she reared back on me and moaned even more heavily. I guess it was the right thing to do, but there was something odd going on in my body. I didn't feel light-headed any more, as I'd felt on the flight, and I wasn't that drunk from the two margaritas, either. What I was feeling, instead, was a kind of numbness, almost as if there were a sheet of plastic wrap between Willa and me as we fucked. My cock was hard and that part of me felt good, but the rest of me felt nothing.

She said, "So I'm a 'bunny wabbit,' huh?"

"What?"

She ground her hips in a circular motion. "That's what you and the other kids used to call me."

"I remember Nilla."

"No, bunny wabbit. 'Cause of the way I'd twitch my lips." She leaned forward and kissed me. "Well this bunny likes to fuck." She leaned backward again. "Pinch my nipples again."

I did as instructed.

"No, harder."

So I pinched really, really hard, and she suddenly sprang off of me as if an electric current had just shot through her body. She actually rolled off the bed and onto the floor.

In an instant, she scrambled back onto the bed and had stuffed my cock inside of her again. Her lips moved for a split second and she said, "Hey, I'm mad at you."

"But you said to pinch hard!"

She smiled slowly. "Do it again."

We went on this way for a good thirty minutes or so, and she seemed to want to try me out in every position she could think of, and then, because I have always had good control, I waited until I sensed she was getting a little tired from her exertions and, as I'd promised, I came inside of her.

Did she know, as we lay there side by side, that I'd hardly felt anything, except in my cock, the entire time? How could she? And how could she understand why I hadn't felt anything if even I couldn't understand it?

# 8

We had a good weekend after that, exploring the Pike Place Market and drinking a lot, going to a Greek festival where we ate a great deal of spanakopita and gyros, and lying around her apartment and reminiscing about our teachers in grammar school. We had sex three other times that three-day weekend, and each time we went for at least a half an hour, and every time she moaned and she came and I felt like there had been a sheet of Saran Wrap between us the entire time, and whether this was because I feared she might become pregnant, or for some other reason entirely, I could not say.

On Sunday morning, we went out for an early brunch at a restaurant called Flipside and I ordered Eggs Benedict with something called peasant fries—really just rough-cut potatoes with the skin still on. But the chef had done something with them to make them really delicious, and that's what started the whole thing.

I offered Willa some of my fries and said, "I don't know if you remember this, but there was a Jewish smoked-fish place near our place. Remember?"

"Sure, I never went there, but I can remember those incredible smells. I always wanted to try one of those lox sandwiches they sold."

"So anyway, my buddies and I used to play football like all year round, even in the dead of winter, and then sometimes when it was really cold, we'd stop by the fish place because they also had fish and chips, and the French fries were served in these big brown paper bags, but they were so incredibly hot and greasy that the bags would turn semitranslucent. I never had any money, but my buddies would buy me one of the bags, and they'd get their own bags, and we'd shake about a ton of salt on them and then stick the bags in our coat pockets. And then all the way home from football, cause I never had any gloves either, I'd stick my frozen hand in the hot bag and eat fries and heat up my one hand, and it was like the most delicious thing I've ever tasted in my life."

Willa smiled one of her slow smiles.

"So you never had their fries?"

"No, my sister and I did a lot of cooking. We hardly ever went out to eat."

"Yeah, you guys were probably as poor as we were."

Willa shrugged. "Yeah, probably worse, actually."

Something suddenly occurred to me. "So how did your parents afford to send your older sister—what was her name again? Beatrice?"

"Yeah. Bea, we'd call her."

"Bea. How could they afford to send her off to summer camp?"

"Well, it was just that one summer when she was twelve."

"And you never went?"

Willa shook her head.

"So the one summer when we were eight, and Elizabeth dies" —this was the first time I'd mentioned this name the entire three-day weekend—"was also the one time your sister goes off to summer camp, meaning that she wasn't around to watch Elizabeth when your mother was gone? Willa, don't you find that a little bit odd?"

She looked at me with those unblinking round eyes. "Odd? I don't know. I honestly, genuinely never gave it any thought. Why? What're you thinking?"

"I don't know," I said. "It just seems strange, is all. To be honest, Willa, I've been feeling strange ever since, I don't know, I was going to say ever since I came to Seattle, but it was before that, and maybe even before Hawaii. I've been having strange dreams, for one thing, and then I didn't even tell you this, but I lost my job."

Willa gasped at this, and I felt a surge of affection for her.

"Oh my God, Charlie, are you okay?"

"Yeah, I'm fine. My boss was kind of an ass. A philosophical ass, but that's an even worse kind. Anyway, I'm here on frequent flier points and I've got some money saved up."

"But you paid for all our dinners! Can I please pay you back?"

"It's really not necessary at all. I'll be fine. And I've had a wonderful time with you here." And at that moment, I felt as if I really had.

"I did, too."

"So, your sister. Bea. What's her last name again?"

"Baer. Beatrice Baer."

"How do you spell that? B-A-E-R?"

Willa shrugged. "I suppose. It's her married name, obviously. I went to her wedding and she said something like, 'I'm not sure I like the whole B.B. thing. But sometimes she used to go by 'Billie'—that's B-I-L-L-I-E, I'm sure of that spelling."

"Sort of like you went by Nilla. Or Bunny Wabbit, I should say."

She laughed. "Actually, I barely remember Nilla at all. But anyway, like I said, we've really drifted apart, and I haven't seen her husband since the wedding, and I've only seen her like once or twice. So at this stage, all I know is she lives in or around St. Louis, and her last name is Baer, however it's spelled. I guess I could scrounge around for her wedding invitation or something, but I wouldn't even know where to begin."

Well, how many ways *could* it be spelled? A lot, as it turned out. When I got back to Chicago, summer was fading into autumn, and I spent far too much time taking long walks along the leafy sidewalks, and watching Netflix and Hulu (which made me think, every time I saw the icon on my computer, of Honolulu) and talking now and again to Bowen, one of my few remaining friends. I hadn't worked up the courage yet to contact Diane, in part because I didn't know if she knew yet about Frank and Alisa.

In fact, I probably wouldn't have talked to Bowen, either, except he called me unexpectedly with the news that the sale of our old agency to Glennis had indeed been consummated. I didn't know what to make of it; hadn't Jason been planning to take the ClickEver account away? "Sure," Bowen told me. "As soon as ClickEver's contract with Gilbert is up, they're history. But I heard through the mill that Gilbert told Glennis that ClickEver's already renewed and he somehow got them to swallow this even with Glennis's due diligence, don't ask me how, maybe he drew up a phony contract. So basically, Glennis is getting a pig in a poke." I could only laugh at Gilbert's audacity, but neither Bowen nor I could imagine Glennis, a big agency, standing for it when Jason walked away with the only part of Gilbert's business they'd wanted.

Once in a while I'd chat with Willa by text or Facebook, which was nice, though neither one of us alluded to the fact that we'd had sex, nor to the possibility of a future visit, nor to Elizabeth, nor to anything more consequential than whether it really added something to a homemade ground-chuck burger to top it with an organic fried egg with a nice runny yolk. "Yum," one of us would say, and that was about the depth our conversations would reach.

I also spent a lot of time job hunting, because even with unemployment my funds were running really low, and I picked up some dollars here and there at Berto's. There was a new waitress there named Kathleen, and she seemed really nice.

But I spent even more time at my kitchen table, staring out the window at some ash trees in the backyard and Googling and Facebook-stalking Alisa and Frank (without learning anything too startling, other than managing to confirm that Frank and Diane were still married, and that Alisa was going to a lot of networking events, and that she didn't seem to have a new boyfriend). I called my father twice, but he didn't answer; I couldn't decide whether I was relieved by this, or more worried than before.

And I also spent a lot of time on Google looking for various permutations of "Bea" and "Beatrice" and "Billie" and "Baer." With a little online research, I determined that Willa's sister's married name could be spelled in the following ways, among, perhaps, others:

| | | | |
|---|---|---|---|
| BAER | BAIRE | BEHR | BAYHR |
| BEAR | BAYRE | BEHER | BAYHIR |
| BARE | BAYHRE | BERE | BEIRE |
| BAIR | BAHRE | BEARE | BEAIR |
| BAYR | BAYER | BAYIR | BEHRE |

Combined with "Beatrice" and "Bea," I was forced to do many hundreds of Google searches. Still, even though the name wasn't at all in vogue when we were growing up, I came up with a dozen or so possibilities in the St. Louis area, even after I'd eliminated some because they were outside of Willa's sister's age range. Adding "Billie" gave me even more possibilities. If I looked long enough, I could find addresses for most of the names, but very few of the results had e-mail addresses or phone numbers, and I didn't like or trust the online snooping services that purported to supply this information in exchange for a hefty fee. After a week or so of playing around with this, I shrugged and moved on to another time-waster.

By October, I'd picked up some freelance work writing copy for a series of investor websites, and I'd settled back into a regular weekly gig at Berto's. The new waitress, Kathleen, hadn't lasted, and now there was still another waitress who was rude and brusque and whom I didn't like at all. One of the cooks told me that Kathleen had been fired because she'd complained about seeing some mealy worms in the kitchen, and that bothered me a bit. I e-mailed Diane and asked her whether or not Kathleen might have grounds for a lawsuit, but Diane never responded, and, although I know that labor attorneys are busy all of the time, that bothered me even more. Reese Nakamura, the manager at Palmyra's, also hadn't responded to my e-mail, and that made me brood about just how bad my performance must have been.

Glennis, as Bowen and I both predicted, was not at all happy about discovering, shortly after they'd purchased Gilbert's firm, that there was nothing much inside it except for a big, ClickEver-shaped hole. They filed a lawsuit, and both Bowen and I were asked to give depositions on what we knew. I wasn't concerned about it; Jason hadn't consulted with me about taking the account away from Gilbert, and neither had the people at ClickEver—when I was in New York or before or after that time. I had no culpability and very little to tell the lawyers other than my opinion, which is to say that I thought Gilbert perfectly capable of doing what he had done. Nonetheless, it was one more item to add to my list of worries.

On October 30, late in the evening in my silent house, I was fooling around on Facebook while I was supposed to be writing some web copy when for no apparent reason I clicked over to Travelocity and, as if something else other than my conscious mind was moving my right forefinger across the keys, made reservations for a flight to St. Louis. I had barely enough space on my credit card to purchase the ticket, so I made the reservation for December 3rd, when I'd have been paid for the second third of my web project and could afford a rental car and meals.

No apparent reason. And yet, of course, "no apparent reason" did not mean the same thing as "no reason," no, not at all. Because now, if not perhaps then, I understand "what an involuntary act signifies."

And so it was that on December 4th, after a good night's sleep at the St. Louis Airport Sheraton, I picked up my car from Budget and went off to visit all of the Beatrice or Billie "Baers" that I'd managed to find.

# 9

St. Louis in December was a bleak place, though a good bit warmer than Chicago. The downtown area, where the first of my Beas lived, was especially barren and seemed to have the whole inadvertently back-to-nature, "weeds growing through the sidewalk" aesthetic fully perfected. The first woman, last name Bayer, lived above an old-fashioned hardware store called New Market, at the corner of Laclede and Sarah Streets, and it understandably took me a lot of time to convince her to let me upstairs to her room. She was a very tall, slightly stooped woman who resembled a bit one of those Depression-era farm wives from a Walker Evans photograph, complete with the minuscule vertical furrows in the area above her upper lip that women get from smoking too much (if Alisa had been there, she would have "reminded" me, though I already knew, that the area between the upper lip and nose was called the philtrum). It took me no more than a couple of minutes to determine that she had never lived in Chicago and had no sister named Willa. But she was nice enough to offer me a cup of instant hot chocolate and asked, not unreasonably, "So this woman you're looking for, if you don't know which Beatrice it is, why not just call them? I mean, call all of the ones on your list that still have home phones? Or send out a bunch of e-mails? It'd at least be a start."

"I don't really have a solid answer for that. I guess I thought it would be better if I took all of the women who could be the one by surprise so they didn't have time to think about whether or not they wanted to talk to me. I just don't know if I could bear sitting around in my apartment for months waiting for these women to return my phone calls or e-mails, which they probably wouldn't, assuming I even could come up with them."

"Well, I understand what you're saying, I suppose, a little bit, if it's a sensitive matter for you. But if it is, it's a sensitive matter for her too, whoever she happens to be. I can see you're a decent guy, but not every woman would have opened the door to you and I almost didn't either. So do yourself a favor and call ahead next time, why don't you?"

The second address on my list, which turned out to be a neat little English cottage-style house in a suburb called Valley Park, was owned by a woman named Beatrice "Billie" Beher, who had a sister named Wilhelmina. I had taken the first woman's advice and called ahead, so this Beatrice, the right one, had a pot of coffee brewing by the time I showed up at her door. She offered me a cup, and I explained that I had irritable bowel syndrome, so she suggested hot chocolate instead, and after hanging my winter coat in the closet, I accepted it gratefully, pretending I hadn't already had one at her namesake's apartment above the hardware store. Beatrice was taller than Willa, and a little rounder, and a lot wearier looking. She had the same round eyes, but they were pouched, and her hair had stray touches of gray that drifted helplessly above the darker strands. Her lips were much thinner than Willa's, and they looked like they'd gotten that way from a lifetime of being pinched in disapproval. But she wore bright carmine-colored lipstick, and, unlike the first Beatrice, there were none of those vertical furrows above her lip, though I could see those coming in a few years.

After Beatrice served me my hot chocolate, she went back into the kitchen for some coffee for herself and came back looking like she was ready to get down to business, whatever business it might be. I looked at the time on my cell. After picking up the rental car, wasting my time at the first Beatrice's house, and eating a big lunch at a Chinese place, it was now nearly 3:00 in the afternoon. Knowing, now, that I had the right Beatrice, and standing in her living room under her minatory gaze, I suddenly felt extremely nervous. My gut suddenly cramped hard, no doubt the crappy Chinese food and all the tea I'd gulped conspiring with my irritable bowel, and then there was a second vicious kick and I realized with horror that I would have to use Beatrice's bathroom. She graciously pointed down the hallway, and I thanked her, but to me, it felt like she was my teacher handing me a hall pass.

I opened the toilet lid and saw that there was a single sheet of translucent toilet paper with a lipstick kiss mark floating on the surface of the water; Beatrice, apparently, had applied a fresh coat of lipstick in anticipation of my arrival. I left the paper where it was instead of flushing it and did my business as quickly and as quietly as I could. Then I flushed, and after washing my hands, quickly opened the medicine cabinet to see if there was any trace of a husband—aftershave, shaving cream, men's deodorant, condoms, prostate pills, anything. There was none. Just Monistat 7 and Prozac and Tylenol and Midol and face cream and cotton balls and Chapstick and a couple of old tubes of lipstick, one of which might very well have been the color that'd stained the tissue in the toilet.

The bathroom was decorated with antique floral prints—sweet pea and nasturtium and phlox and the like—and there was a tissue box covered with an ugly pink-and-yellow knitted holder, as if tissues were a shameful thing to display. And though there was a full roll of daisy-embossed toilet paper on the cylinder, there also was a toilet-paper holder that was covered in the same ugly knit, and for some reason I lifted the top off of the toilet-paper holder, and inside, instead of toilet paper with embossed daisies, there was a bottle of Ron Rico Rum.

By the time I'd gotten out, a good five minutes had passed, and I felt dirty and humiliated for having snooped around her bathroom. I felt like the same shamefaced eight-year-old that I had come into this house with the express purpose of shedding once and for all, and I walked very slowly back into her living room through a hallway decorated with framed family photos—Beatrice (apparently) as a child herself and as a teen; her mother, Isabelle, looking bigger and heavier than Beatrice and as fearsome as I remembered her, though to be honest it was mostly only her voice that I remembered; her father, not familiar-looking at all; a young woman with a very strange, squinched-together face; and some old photos of what appeared to be grandparents.

No wedding pictures, no husband, and no Willa.

Beatrice stood there in her living room with her arms crossed under her breasts.

"So, Charles, Charlie, tell me again why you're here? You wanted to know about Willa?"

"That's right. We're good friends again after all these years."

"Ah. How is Willa?"

"She's doing well. She told me the two of you haven't really kept up much."

"No, that's true."

"She said there wasn't any particular reason, or if there was, she wasn't saying."

Beatrice looked at me closely. "So anyway. Friends again, you two. You and Willa."

"Uh huh."

"I remember you hanging around our house sometimes. You were always shivering in the winter because your coat was too thin."

I laughed. "I'm still cold just thinking about it." I took a sip of my hot chocolate as if it could somehow retroactively warm me, though the five minutes I'd spent in the bathroom had rendered it lukewarm. "Anyway, I'm sorry, I guess I don't remember you at all."

"Yeah, well I was four years older than you and Willa. Is there something about her you need to know?"

"Not exactly. I mean, not directly. It's more about Elizabeth."

"Elizabeth? Ah. You know, I just assumed that, I don't know, maybe you're thinking of getting married to Willa, childhood sweethearts and all that. And you wanted to know if there were any old family skeletons you needed to be aware of. How is ol' Willa, anyway?"

"Well, like I said, she's doing well." Hadn't she just asked me that question? "She's a nurse now, in Seattle." I felt like adding, "And she likes long sex sessions and hates you for some reason, and it would appear you hate her too, and I'd be willing to bet you haven't had a 'sex session' in ten years." But of course I said none of these things.

"Seattle. Hmm. That's supposed to be a great city."

"Yeah, it is. I spent some time with her there."

"I'd be worried about earthquakes, though."

"Yeah. That's true. But anyway, Elizabeth."

"I get the impression you think I'm dodging the subject. Asking about Willa and Seattle and all that."

"Are you? Dodging the subject?"

"Look, Charlie, I know what happened. What my mother said to you wasn't right. It really wasn't. You've probably suffered a lot of guilt, and probably Willa has too, if I know her. It wasn't right, but I wasn't there to do anything about it."

"Because you were 'away' at summer camp."

"My mother, if you haven't figured it out by now, was an alcoholic. My father was too, along with having a thing for other women, so either he was out fooling around, or a woman he was chasing rejected him, and he'd get upset and take it out on his little girls by yelling at us for the slightest infraction, you know? No hitting, thank God. But he was an odd one, my Dad. He also loved his little girls more than anything, that's why he named us after queens, and when he wasn't upset he'd *treat* us like queens, wait on us hand and foot, but oh my God, then my mother'd get jealous and they'd fight and he'd take it out on us all over again. Christ. So a chance comes along to go to summer camp, I'm going to jump at it, you know, just to get away from that atmosphere."

"So what was the name of this summer camp you went to?"

"I'm not sure I understand why it matters, but it was called Seven Lakes, in Wisconsin."

"Seven Lakes."

"Is this name somehow significant?" She raised her cup of coffee to take a sip, and I noticed that her hand was trembling. This made me feel so much better, and it was starting to give me courage, that Beatrice, too, like her parents and mine (and, maybe a bit, Alisa), was an alcoholic. She was probably praying that I'd get the hell out of there so she could have a drink or three.

"Beatrice? Or do you prefer Bea?"

"To Bea or not to Bea. The kids used to say that. Bea is fine."

"So, Bea, the name of the camp itself isn't significant. What is, though, is the fact that Willa never went to summer camp."

"So this is a sibling rivalry thing? A little late in the day for that, wouldn't you say? And your little girlfriend sends you all the way from Seattle to deliver the message? I'd say that's pretty bizarre."

"Well, I'd agree if that were the point. But the point is that the reason Willa never went to summer camp is that your family was too poor, and so why did you go?"

"It's called scraping together money, buddy boy. I know you know what I mean because you were poor, too, but you still wore shoes, didn't you? Your parents drove a car, didn't they? I still remember that broken-down Dodge. They scraped the money together somehow and so did mine."

"Yeah, but I guess what I mean is, why just you and why just that summer in particular? And then why did your mother, alcoholic or otherwise, show the incredibly poor judgment of having a couple of eight-year-old kids watch Elizabeth?"

Beatrice made a small, dismissive snorting sound, but she was observing me closely. She went to pick up her cup of coffee, but drew her hand back rather suddenly, as if aware that the hand was going to tremble, and, more to the point, that I would observe this.

"Bea, try to understand. After Elizabeth died, my parents fled —literally *fled*—with me to Buenos Aires. We ran away, basically, is what it was. But from what I could tell there was no such reaction on the part of your own parents. Willa got off scot-free, and understand that I'm fine with that, because she was the same age as me and so she wasn't any more responsible than *I* should have been. And besides, I really, really like her."

"Good for you."

"But it just isn't plausible that your parents would suffer a loss like they did without some kind of reaction on their part, too. I don't mean in the mourning aspect of it, I'm sure there was plenty of that, I mean in the shame and anger part."

"So what are you saying? I'm struggling here, buddy boy."

"I'm saying that maybe you didn't go to summer camp before Elizabeth died. Maybe you went *after* she died. My parents don't like to talk about it either, but I vaguely recall my father saying to me once, years later, about Argentina, 'That's just the way it was arranged,' you know, in that passive way? '*It* was arranged' rather than 'we arranged it.' And there was even something about the word 'arranged' itself that suggested to me that the two families had agreed to something. We'd go back to Argentina, and you'd go away to 'summer camp,' like immediately, the very next day after Elizabeth died, and then your family would retroactively backdate the whole mess to suggest to Willa and me that we had been solely responsible for watching Elizabeth, whereas..."

"Whereas what, exactly?"

"Well, that your mother had asked *you,* not Willa and me, to watch Elizabeth. We were just hanging around the neighborhood. You put her on Willa's bed for whatever reason, I'm sure you didn't mean any harm by it, you left her alone, we came in later to find her suffocating, you were off who knows where doing who knows what."

"That's a pretty serious charge."

"So that's why I flew to St. Louis. That's why I couldn't do this by phone. I must've known that I would've had to look you in the eyes." I'd forgotten, for a second, that it was the first Beatrice, and not this one, who'd asked me why I hadn't merely called.

"And are you pleased with yourself, flying to St. Louis in the middle of the winter from Seattle, to engage in a bunch of idiotic speculations?"

"Chicago. Not Seattle. And I don't think it's so much speculation anymore, now that I can see your face. I think your parents wanted to protect your reputation because you were twelve and old enough to know better. And they didn't want the neighbors all talking, and then have to move themselves. Or I don't know, maybe I'm wrong, maybe they were actually punishing you, too. Either way, they probably probed a little bit first with Willa and me to see what we'd noticed, you know, if we had even been aware that you were supposed to be babysitting, but we were typical eight-year-olds, we weren't even paying attention—I mean, I didn't even have any memory that you *existed!* So it was pretty easy to get us to believe it was our fault. And no big deal, you know? Except a lifetime of guilt for Willa and me."

"Guilt, hah! Don't use that word again with me. Get out, or I'll call my husband and have you thrown out."

"You know, you haven't once denied any of this. So I'm feeling so much better all of a sudden, and even if your husband or ex-husband, or never-was husband from what I can tell, came by and tossed me into the snow, I'd still feel good because I learned the truth."

"You don't know shit, mister."

"Meaning what?"

"Meaning just that. Look, why don't you just leave? I don't know what the hell you're trying to accomplish here, and I don't think you know either."

"You want me to leave?"

"Isn't that what I just said?"

"Okay." I went to the closet and pulled my coat out roughly, causing the hanger to clatter to the floor, buttoned it slowly without looking at her, and then I walked out her front door and stepped into my rental car. I'd gotten what I needed.

Except that, as I drove slowly back to my hotel, I felt an indefinable itch that I hadn't. I *hadn't* gotten what I'd needed, though what that missing thing was, I couldn't say, and I had no way of knowing if Bea could say it either, and whether she would, to me of all people, even if she could.

I pulled into the remote parking lot of the Airport Sheraton, but instead of getting out of my car, I sat there, looking out of the windshield at the ground-floor lobby. The air was filling up with spots of darkness like little clods of dirt being shoveled into a limpid pond. Then, after about ten minutes or so, I started up my car and began the long drive back to Bea's house.

By the time I got there, the sky was completely bereft of light.

She took a good long while answering her door this time, but she didn't seem surprised to see me again.

I stood there awkwardly in her foyer and looked at her for a moment.

"Look," I said, "I'm really sorry to bother you like this, but I don't think our conversation from before is over, you know?"

To my surprise, she said, "No, I don't think so either. It isn't." Her eyes were very red, and a few of her gray hairs trembled and swayed in the air as her head shook almost imperceptibly. She hadn't moved from where she'd been when she first let me in. There was no coffee or hot chocolate this time around; she wasn't inviting me in, but on the other hand, she hadn't made a move yet to kick me out.

"So what else is there to say? I have to depend on you, Bea, to tell me what I don't know, and yet I understand that you don't really like me and have no real reason or motivation to tell me anything."

"Except..."

"Except what, Bea?"

"Nothing. Nothing. Why don't you take off your coat instead of standing there?"

I exulted at this invitation, because if she wanted me to stay, she probably wanted to talk. I flung my coat onto her couch instead of hanging it up as I had done last time.

"Okay, then. So we're making progress. And I really don't mind that you don't like me. It's okay. Just say whatever you need to say. Who else are you going to say it to? Tell me, Bea."

She sighed and motioned for me to sit down on her couch, in the space next to my winter coat. She sat down on the other side of the coat.

"The thing about you, buddy boy, is that you're easy to fool."

"You mean because I had to come all the way to St. Louis to figure this all out?"

"Well, yeah, yes, I guess I mean that, but I really meant you were easy to fool back then. You just weren't aware of my existence at all, so it wasn't a big deal for us. But think about it, Charlie boy, how could Willa not have noticed her own sister was there, or wasn't there, that day? I mean, how could you have ever thought otherwise? And now here in St. Louis, as a grown man, now that you know who I am? How could you think you and your little girlfriend were equally fooled? We just told her that we were going to blame you, and then that's exactly what my mother did. If Willa has any guilt, it's about that, not about Elizabeth."

"So she knew all along."

"Yes, I think that's roughly what I was driving at."

I waved my arms. "Okay, whatever, I get it. That's between me and Willa. But you're not focusing on the bigger issue."

"What's the bigger issue?"

"The fact that I didn't actually do anything wrong."

"And you didn't suffer for it, so what the hell difference does it make? Except for one little lecture. Me, unlike you, I really got punished. The 'camp' I went to, as you probably figured out, or I should say probably didn't, was my uncle's house. He was a Baptist preacher, and he spent the rest of that summer thundering down on me. And then the continuing punishment, every day, every day until today? You got off light, far as I'm concerned."

"Light? After a lifetime of hearing your mother's voice?"

"Yeah, but after that one time you only heard it in your head, so that's your own damn problem. My mother's been dead for fifteen years, get over it. I heard it for real, and my father's too, and my uncle's, and his second wife, and on and on and on—constantly, growing up. 'Elizabeth this, Elizabeth that, how could you have been so careless and stupid?' My father was the worst, because of the way he doted on us girls, he was so disappointed in me. God, it sickened me, I'd rather he'd've hit me. And when something else happened in my life, everyone else was like, 'Oh, that's just a pattern for Bea, that's the way she's always been.' Oh, and Willa? Your sweet little girlfriend with the chubby cheeks? You think she didn't hold it over me and make me feel like shit? The hell with her and the hell with both of you, and you know what? You're so stupid you still don't understand."

"I'm fucking trying, Bea."

"Okay, then pay attention to this part, because I don't even know why I should have to be telling you this. Charlie, c'mon, I mean, why would your parents possibly, conceivably have gone along with this scheme? This 'get out of Dodge' business?"

"Are you trying to tell me that my parents were in on this too? If they knew that it was you and not me..."

"No, no, they never questioned that it was you. They're as dim as you are, from what I can tell. Sorry, I shouldn't have said that. But what I'm saying is, why do you think they actually fled the country with you? Shame? They could nurse their shame and lick their wounds in another neighborhood just as easily. No, my father wanted your parents far away, because they were drunks too, and he didn't want them finding out there was more to the story, and he didn't want them blabbing to the neighborhood. For my father, being a big man in the neighborhood was everything, it's what got him laid, and it was one thing to be a victim with a...a suffocated child, and another to be the father of the other child who did it. So you know how I was talking before about scrapping together money, supposedly for that summer camp I didn't go to? It was for one-way tickets to Buenos Aires for the three of you. And believe me, your father was *delighted*. Your mom, I don't know about, but your father used to come over to our house while *my* dad was out chasing women and talk about the good old days in Buenos Aires and moan about how he'd never see it again. So this was a golden opportunity for him, and if you had to be a little bit misled in the process, well so be it."

I couldn't speak at all for a moment. My gut was twisting again, and I thought I might have to make another run for the toilet. But I held my ground. I would be damned if I ever went into that bathroom again with its carmine lipstick and knitted rum dispenser.

"So why are you admitting all this now?"

"Because you showed up in my home. And because why the hell not? I didn't commit any crime. I was careless. I was playing dress up with Elizabeth, and then I went over to a friend's house and forgot all about her, and unluckily for me, you and Willa were out, too. But lucky also, in a twisted way, because we couldn't have blamed you otherwise."

"You're forgetting 'unluckily for Elizabeth.' She's the one who had to die."

Bea shrugged. "What's done is done."

"You're good with the clichés when they let you off light. You don't feel any guilt at all for what you did? I mean, either to Elizabeth or to me? Or your parents, who lost their little girl? Or even to Willa, making her complicit? Any of us? Any of it at all?"

"Oh, Charlie. You grow stupider by the moment." She walked over to a bookcase, pulled out a hardcover book, and removed from the space behind it a small bottle of Johnnie Walker Red. She poured it into her coffee and took a long drink. "I try to pretend my friends don't know about this. Edgar Allen Poe," she said, indicating the book in her hand. "And Johnny Walker Red. I like the way they sound together, don't you?" She laughed briefly. "Charlie, I feel like dying every day of my life."

I let that sink in for a moment, for both of our sakes.

But then I said, "I'm sorry, Beatrice. And I'm also sorry that your mother died fifteen years ago. I keep on turning that around in my mind."

"Yeah, of cancer. So?"

"So one last item, and then I'll be out of your life forever, I promise. What I want to ask you, Beatrice, is this: Did you ever work at a medical supply warehouse?"

"No."

The way she answered—which is to say, without inquiring why on earth I would want to know something random like that—told me everything I needed to know about the question that had just a moment ago occurred to me, when Beatrice let it slip that her mother had already been long dead when I'd received my "gift."

I said, "So probably your ex-husband or one of your friends worked at some place like that, right?"

She said nothing.

"Beatrice, I just want you to know that whatever temporary expiation that gift gave to you was the worst moment of my life, but I buried it a long time ago and now it's fucking staying buried, but for you it never will be, so you're paid back tenfold, aren't you?"

"I am," she said simply. "But it was my ex who did it. I told him the whole story except for the little detail about me being responsible. He got outraged on my behalf, a lot more than I guess I was expecting, and decided to start a campaign against you. He was like that, about other things, too, which you can probably guess is why he's an ex. I'm very sorry about all this. And yeah, you're right. I've been paid back tenfold, just like you say."

# 10

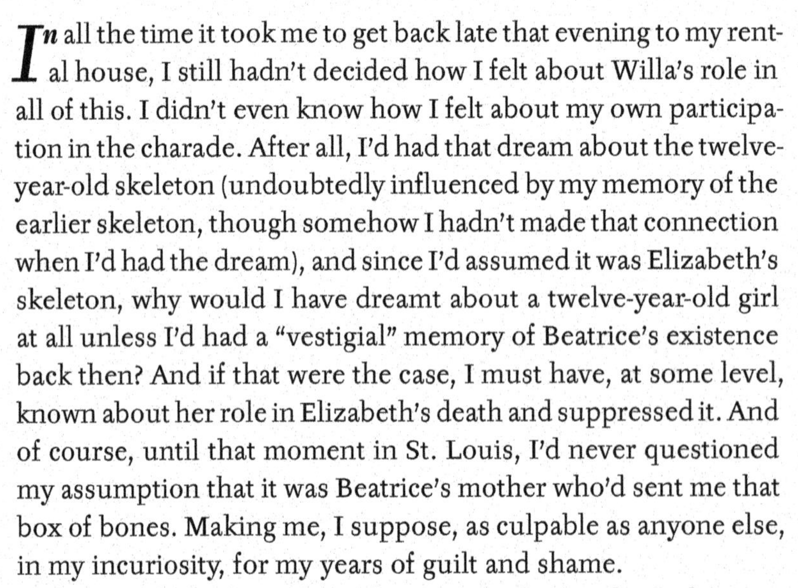

In all the time it took me to get back late that evening to my rental house, I still hadn't decided how I felt about Willa's role in all of this. I didn't even know how I felt about my own participation in the charade. After all, I'd had that dream about the twelve-year-old skeleton (undoubtedly influenced by my memory of the earlier skeleton, though somehow I hadn't made that connection when I'd had the dream), and since I'd assumed it was Elizabeth's skeleton, why would I have dreamt about a twelve-year-old girl at all unless I'd had a "vestigial" memory of Beatrice's existence back then? And if that were the case, I must have, at some level, known about her role in Elizabeth's death and suppressed it. And of course, until that moment in St. Louis, I'd never questioned my assumption that it was Beatrice's mother who'd sent me that box of bones. Making me, I suppose, as culpable as anyone else, in my incuriosity, for my years of guilt and shame.

I went to bed very early, and sometime during the night Mari-Angela walked again through the back of my skull, except this time, she wasn't walking, exactly. She was holding on to the insides of my skull for support, which caused the bones of my skull to creak and ache along the jigsaw lines where they were joined, and she pushed herself forward on rubbery arms until she'd reached my eyes. She was wearing denim overalls and a blue flannel shirt. Again, as in the other dreams, everything else was completely black. She looked at me with her orange eyes and said, "You haven't figured it out yet." And then she dropped to the floor of my skull and pulled her knees up against her chin, and, like a beach ball in a blustery wind, she flew away.

The end of the year was tough, but in January, as annual marketing budgets began to kick in, I started picking up more freelance copywriting and project management work. I paid off a few bills, took Bowen out to dinner as a belated thank-you for the Hawaii gig, and continued to send Willa messages on Facebook and her phone, though I never mentioned that I had met her sister. Finally, unable to determine to what extent, if at all, I was angry with Willa, I just said *What the hell* to myself and invited her to come visit me in Chicago. She responded to my text with the message "yes!!!! :)"

Late January is not the best time for an out-of-towner to get reintroduced to Chicago after so many years away, but Willa and I managed to have a good time. The night she arrived, a Thursday, we both had a drink at a clamorous neighborhood hangout called DeStrooper's ("When you drink at DeStrooper's, watch out for state troopers!") and then we went straight back home to my bed and we cuddled each other. We did not have sex that night, something that left both of us, I think, feeling relieved.

Friday morning, after she showered, was when I got up my nerve to confront her. She took a long, long time in the shower, maybe because she knew I was getting ready to talk to her and wanted to give me time, and maybe because she was getting ready to respond to whatever I might say. I made us a simple breakfast of English muffins and orange juice in my old, worn kitchen, and after we'd eaten, mostly in silence—I could barely choke down more than a bite or two—I finally broached the subject. By the time I did, twenty minutes had passed since her shower; her hair was dry, the room was quiet, and we both could hear, and were acutely conscious of, the sound of two dog owners out on the sidewalk, separating their bickering pups.

"Willa, I think you should know, I went and visited your sister back in December."

"Okay...?"

"You're wondering why."

"So you actually visited St. Louis? How was she? What kind of place was she in?"

"A nice house in a nice suburb. She was a little, I guess you could say 'tense.' Not entirely at her best. Though I wouldn't guess she often is lately."

"I guess I could see that."

"The visit itself was not the ideal way I would have liked to have spent my afternoon in one sense, but in another it was the best thing I ever did."

"Good."

"Good? Just good? Aren't you even going to ask why? I mean, why I was there in the first place, why it was bad, why it was good, whatever?"

"Well, I mean, I guess I can imagine why. You were a little surprised to discover I had another sister to begin with, so if I put two and two together..."

"Yes?"

"Well." She took a sip of her orange juice and I noted that her hands were steady. "You probably wondered why she wasn't there to babysit Elizabeth, and, based on our last conversation, you probably wondered why she and I don't speak and haven't spoken basically since her wedding, is that about it? Well, I'm not even going to ask you what Bea told you, if she told you anything at all."

"You can ask me."

"No, don't, it's okay, I want to talk, I mean I wanna tell you in my own terms. Was she drunk, by the way? Never mind. It doesn't matter." She paused. "I'll just tell you straight out. We had a very difficult relationship for years, basically ever since it happened, and the thing at the wedding was that I told her I was going to tell you the truth. And she did not want that, not at all.

So I backed off, I guess, but the damage was done between us."

"But why couldn't you have told me the truth a long time ago? I mean, even before her wedding?"

"When? When, Charlie? When we were eight years old? Do you think I understood the significance of my parents passing the blame along to you because they didn't want the stigma of the whole neighborhood on them? And then you were gone, just like that..."

"Yeah, gone because your parents had paid off my parents to go."

"I know. I understand that. That's what Bea told you, right?"

I nodded.

"I'm glad she's finally owned up to it. I guess you had a lot more influence over her than I ever did. But again, Charlie, I was eight years old, and so were you. I played no part in that decision. And then by the time you'd returned, you'd moved on to other things, and so had I. I mean, you didn't even have a memory of *knowing* me during that period. I didn't even exist for you. But I was in a fog all the time, too, it wasn't just you. If I passed you in the hallways in high school, I mean I was worrying about popularity and that my boobs weren't big enough and what college could I get into with no money and that my mother's a drunk and my father's all over the map, sometimes he loves us and sometimes he's an ass. Look, I'm not trying to make you feel sorry for me in the slightest. It's just that I had other things on my mind, and I'd put all that out of my memory because I felt guilty, to be honest, and c'mon, I mean, *you* had other things on your mind, too."

She paused. "Look, that isn't even the real reason. It was something I avoided talking about, and I rationalized to myself in high school that it wasn't important after all those years, it didn't matter anymore, and we could just sort of, you know, let it slide. Maybe that's the real reason why you didn't notice me in high school—I think I sort of just walked to the other side of the corridor and hunched my shoulders and slid by when I saw you coming."

"At least when you rationalize something, you're aware that it needs to be rationalized. You're aware that it exists."

"You didn't?"

"No, not consciously. I'm glad you came to Hawaii. And I don't just mean in a 'better late than never' way. You could have just slid by forever."

"I think it was just easier for me to get off the mainland and away from all of the memories and stuff."

"I'm glad you found me, but how *did* you find me? I mean, after the club?"

"Well, at first I tried some other clubs and bars and a few restaurants, but then I figured where else would you be but the beach, I mean it's Honolulu, right? I didn't picture you out shopping. And where else on the beach but somewhere near the hotel where the club was? So I walked around a good hour and got lucky and saw you on your towel."

"Willa, I have kind of a strange question. Did you come to Hawaii and talk to me to make you feel better or to make *me* feel better?"

"I don't know, Charlie. I guess I mean, I don't know, aren't they sort of one and the same?"

I started to feel overheated for some reason, and claustrophobic as well, in that old and worn missionaries' kitchen.

"And kissing me? Was that to make me feel 'all better?' "

"No, I don't know how..."

"Or to make *you* feel all better? Like, I'll have sex with the guy to make up for what my family did to his life, and then it'll all be even?"

"Oh God, no. How can you say such a contemptible thing!" And at that, Willa threw her English muffin, marmalade-side down, onto the floor, and began to cry.

"I'm sorry, Willa."

She looked up at me, her round eyes rounder than ever, like those of a terrified cat. "I'm telling you now, aren't I? Do you understand that I accepted your invitation to Chicago for two reasons? The first was to finally get up the fucking courage to tell you the truth. And the second was just to see you again."

"But the point is, you didn't tell me the truth. You didn't tell me the truth in Hawaii, you didn't tell me the truth when I called you from New York, and you didn't tell me the truth in Seattle. And you can't even say it now in Chicago, can you? It took your sister, your supposedly awful and alcoholic sister, to finally tell me the truth, that you'd known all along that she was the babysitter that day, and that I—you *and* I—were not responsible for Elizabeth. You told me half the truth, you told me about your sister and you gave me her name and city, and maybe you hoped I'd play detective and figure it out for myself, which is exactly what I did. But you didn't tell me the fucking truth."

"I know I didn't. I know. And I'm sorry. At first it was because I was too young and didn't understand, and then I figured it just didn't matter, and by the time I was old enough to understand that it *did* matter, I couldn't find the courage. You know that. And then on top of it all, once I saw you in Hawaii, it was even harder because I wanted to be with you."

"Be with me."

"Charlie, when I saw you on the beach, not so much at the club that night because you were playing a role, and I wasn't used to seeing you as a musician, and you looked so different and everything, but on the beach, it was like I remembered I loved you when we were little kids and I loved you again."

It was exactly what I had thought about Willa, in almost exactly the same words. It made me not want to continue my line of attack.

Willa continued. "I know, now, that the combination of the two was completely impossible, I mean both being with you and telling you the truth, and I guess I'm just really naive. Because if I lied to you, we could keep on being with each other, like, you know, a real couple, and if I told you the truth, you would never want to touch me again because I'm a liar and I'm horrible, am I right? So I made my choice—I mean this one, right now, here in Chicago, not the one I made in Seattle—and it was the right one, but I'm fucking miserable about it. Okay? If you want, I'll stay at a hotel tonight. But first, as long as we're headed down this way, I'm going to tell you the whole truth."

"I know the whole truth already, Willa."

"I don't think you really do."

"And I think you're wrong about that."

Willa looked steadily at me. I took a moment to force my heart to stop hammering and said it.

"Elizabeth is still alive, isn't she?"

Willa nodded. "How did you know?"

"I'm shocked. I mean, she's alive? She's actually alive? I *didn't* know. I was just, I had this feeling, I thought I'd chance it, but I just...I'm just glad, that's all."

"You have to understand, by the time we found her, it was pretty much too late. She was more or less clinically dead. They took her to the hospital and they'd managed to resuscitate her, but her brain had been deprived of oxygen for way too long."

"So, that means..."

"Yeah, that means she never really developed mentally. She's almost twenty-four now, but she has the mental capacity of a four-year old. She can go to the bathroom by herself and say some phrases, but it's really mostly echolalia. So if I say, 'You want some candy?', she'll say back, 'Some candy!' But oh my God, she's so loving and sweet, Charlie."

"Where is she now?"

"I still don't get how you knew."

"I don't really know myself. I mean, I didn't. It was just some kind of intuition, like something I heard in your voice when you first referred to Bea as your 'other sister' instead of just your sister, and how you kept on saying 'what happened' instead of 'when she died.' And Beatrice too, she kept on saying I was stupid and I still didn't get it, and I don't know, it was just a feeling."

"You're amazing, Charlie."

"I'm not quite sure if you mean that in a good way, or a bad way."

"Well, kind of both."

I hadn't actually expected that answer; I was expecting her to say, simply, "In a good way." But she didn't, so I said, "What do you mean by that?"

"I just mean, I don't know, you're so oblivious that you don't remember we went to high school together, you don't remember my sister, but you intuit stuff that you have no way of knowing. Anyway, you asked me where she is now."

"Yeah."

"Well, obviously, she's been institutionalized her whole life. I don't know if you know this, because you didn't really know him, but my father, I know I called him an ass, but he really worshiped us kids."

"I know. Beatrice said that's why he named you after queens."

"Uh huh. He wasn't the greatest father, because he liked to go out at night, and he'd drink sometimes, but when he was home, he was super-sweet, and the whole thing just broke him up big time. My mother, too, but in her case it was anger. My dad, it was more like, he became so super-attached to us girls, he couldn't let us out of his sight, and he'd go visit Elizabeth with me and say, 'This is your little sister, Willa.' And he'd bring her treats, oh my God, he spoiled her rotten. Then, when he died, and then my mom died, there was never any question about it, I went through bureaucratic hell to move her out to Seattle where there are better facilities, and now she lives where I work, and I get to see her every single workday."

"Did Beatrice fight you?"

"Fight me? Are you kidding? The whole thing tormented her. She was glad when I moved away after college, and even more so when I brought Elizabeth out with me. But at the same time, glad and all that, it just twisted the guilt and she felt even worse. Like I was supposed to feel bad about that, but Bea started blaming me for her own guilt and for being the caring one, and it was all over for us way before the wedding thing. Human beings are fucked, aren't they?"

I laughed. I thought, for some reason, of the deeply disappointed flight attendant that Frank had once encountered on an airport escalator.

"And I'm fucked too, aren't I? On top of everything else, not telling you about Bea to begin with, I had you thinking all the time that Elizabeth was dead."

"That began with your mother."

"Uh huh. She wasn't about to let you off the hook, and the decree came down to us kids not to either. We didn't question it, what did we know, she was our mother, but I think she never could forgive you for not having done it."

"That's so messed up. But if you hadn't told me the rest of the truth and had only said she was, you know..."

"Brain damaged. You can say it. It's what she is."

"Brain damaged. I would've felt probably just as bad. I mean, don't misunderstand me..."

"No, I understand. You don't want me to think that you'd think being brain damaged was just as bad as being dead. But I couldn't possibly think that, and you couldn't possibly think that either, if you ever met her. She's so loving, and obviously she's eternally a child, and that's wonderful in its own way. There's a nice little library at the facility with books that the families donate, and she loves to take the books out and build forts with them, and then she knocks them all over and puts them all away! I mean, they're all out of order and everything, but she tries so hard to be good. Anyway, Charlie, that's all I can tell you, and with all of this between us now, I'm really glad it's all out finally, and I hope you are too, but I'll repeat my offer to stay in a hotel."

But I wouldn't hear of it. She stayed with me. We managed to see all the sites that were new since Willa's long-ago life in the city: the modern wing of the Art Institute, "the Bean," and what had become of Bucktown. And she stayed with me all three nights, in my bed, and we had breakfast together every morning. After our conversation, there was a little awkwardness, but not as much as I might have expected, I suppose because she had willingly told me everything and because, until that point, her only real transgression had been that she had withheld this "everything," but for reasons that were, to some degree, understandable. And yes, we had sex again, and it was much as it was in Seattle. I think she felt a little restrained because of everything that had passed between us, as children and then again during that difficult conversation at Friday's breakfast, so the sex was more hurried and conducted with less abandon than before. Still, it was warm and loving in its own way, and she seemed to crave it, and I enjoyed it in exactly the same way, and to the same extent, that I had when we were in Seattle—in other words, as if there were a thin film of cellophane between us.

MariAngela—if indeed that was her that night inside my head—was right, and so too, perhaps, was Beatrice. There was something that I still hadn't figured out.

I drove Willa to the airport and stayed with her until security. Just before she stepped into the winding line, we hugged for a long time but kissed only very briefly—a "peck." Infinite are the permutations of emotion between men and women, and no doubt the feelings between us were more complex than most, and utterly un-locatable, probably, on any linear scale between loathing and love. We were somewhere else entirely off the charts that mapped what most human beings felt and did with each other, and I doubted that Willa and I would have another chance ever again, or the energy, or the intelligence, to determine exactly where that was.

But as I walked away, she shouted out, "Charlie, I'm starved. Can you run and get me something at the newsstand?" Shit, I thought, of course, those skimpy little breakfasts I'd served her were really rude of me. There was a small newsstand on the visitor's side of the security line, so I walked over there—a good thirty feet from where Willa was now standing and inching her way forward to the backscatter machines and metal detectors—and I held up a bag of M&Ms (she shook her head no) and then a soft pretzel (an enthusiastic nod). Then I grabbed a big bag of

Gummi strawberries (lovingly shaped like flat cartoon strawberries with little green "stems") and waved it in the air for her to see and shouted, "For Elizabeth," and Willa jumped up and down delightedly. After paying, I walked back to the security line and reached over a couple of winding lines of passengers to the spot where Willa and her carry-on had now advanced, and she gave me that slow smile of hers and said, "Bitty."

I said, "What?"

"Not Elizabeth. It's Bitty now. She'll love these."

# 11

By the time I drove home, it was barely lunchtime, and I had a whole day of nothingness ahead of me, so finally, for the first time since our steak house dinner, I called Diane.

She picked up on the first ring. "Charlie! Dear, dear Charlie! You couldn't have timed this call better!"

"Diane, I am so sorry I haven't been in touch. How are you doing?"

"I'm wonderful, Charlie. I'm actually, literally, better than I've ever been." And would this be because she'd found out about Frank and Alisa and forgiven him; or found out about Frank and Alisa and dumped him; or was living in blissful ignorance? I had no idea, but I decided to test the waters.

"That's really good. I'm pretty good, too. Did you know about me and Alisa?"

"Yeah, Alisa called me. I'm sorry that it all happened, and I should have called you at the time, but I thought you might want to work some things out on your own. But I think it's going to be a wonderful thing for both of you."

"You haven't asked me why we broke up, which would suggest that Alisa told you everything you need to know."

"Charlie, would you like to meet for coffee?"

"Sure. Where?"

"Our place?"

"Yours and Frank's? I suppose... How about a Starbucks or something?"

"That works."

"Look, I know you want to talk about this over coffee, but since Alisa clearly told you everything, and you seem to be upbeat, but don't want to talk about it on the phone, clearly the implications, or repercussions, or whatever, for you, are not entirely positive and not entirely negative."

"Charlie, you've turned into quite the detective since the last time we've talked! But you don't have to tiptoe, Poirot! I know all about Frank and Alisa, and I knew about it a long time before you did, and don't you dare get mad, because I was gonna tell you soon enough anyway. But at this point, Frank and I are doing pretty well. We're working it out. And he's not home today, so you can definitely come over."

I laughed. "I'll stick with the Starbucks. The one on Clybourn by your house, okay?"

Diane 2.0, as I came to think of her, was beautiful. She'd gotten her braces off, finally, and she'd added some subtle red highlights to her hair, which she'd grown out to shoulder length. She was wearing a beautiful pale green, raw-silk blouse, by far the nicest piece of clothing I'd ever seen her wear, and the top button was unbuttoned to show a bit of cleavage. She saw me as I came in and smiled, dazzlingly.

"Charlie!" She bounded up from one of those cracked-leather Starbucks easy chairs that approximately one million other people have sat in and raced over to me and gave me a big, long hug —the kind that women sometimes do where they rock you from side to side and then pull back and look at you and then hug you some more. "I'm so, so happy to see you!"

"Me, too," I said. "You look fabulous."

"I know, I know! But wasn't I horrible that night in the steak house? All that talk about death!"

"I know, it didn't seem like the Diane I knew."

"Charlie, I'm a whole new me! And I think it must've started around that night!"

"Well, it wasn't a very..."

"What, auspicious start? I know, it totally wasn't. I was such a downer, but it was something I had to get through, I guess, to get where I am now!"

"I just thought you were in a gloomy mood."

"Well, I was, but I think it was because I knew I was losing Frank."

"I didn't really pick up that you were angry with him that night, or even with Alisa, for that matter."

"Well, I wasn't! Not at all! I just felt like everything was changing so fast that I couldn't even hold on. But you know what? Corny alert, but I've really come to embrace change. I have! I got my braces off, did my hair...." She did a little feminine, flirtatious sweep with her hand, flipping her hair back and smiling.

"Your hair looks fantastic. That kind of red color really suits you."

"I know! I know! And I had a good, long discussion with Frank." Her voice dropped to a whisper. "This isn't the first time this has happened, you know. Frank has a way of coming on strong. That's what made me like totally jump into his arms the very first time I met him!"

"And so some other women were jumping into his arms, too, you're saying."

"Yeah, but you know the good thing? They all dump *him,* not the other way around. I mean, Alisa too, right? Isn't that what she told you?"

"She said she felt hypnotized by him."

"I know! Exactly! And then, at some point, the spell is broken. Same thing with me, but I'm sticking around, and you know why? Because I'm the only one who can handle him."

"And you're the only one who *will* stick around."

"Well, don't make it sound like I'm settling, Charlie! Or some martyr. I'm sticking around because I love him! All this," she pointed to her hair and teeth and to her new blouse and the bit of lacy bra peeking out from underneath, "is for him." She laughed. "I have a role to play too, you know."

"And you're playing it to the hilt," I said, casting an exaggerated, Groucho-like leer at her cleavage.

She gave me a little slap on the cheek and laughed. "Oh, Charlie. So tell me, what happened after Alisa? She told me all about Hawaii, but that's where the story ends."

"Let's order first."

We got our drinks and sat down on a couch, and then I took a deep breath and started.

"Well, here's the story. I ran into a childhood friend in Hawaii, this girl named Willa, and I sort of took up with her. Well actually, she flew to Hawaii to seek me out."

"Wow, Charlie, romantic!"

"Yeah, well, kind of. She'd Googled me and saw I was doing a gig there."

"Yes, Alisa told me all about that, trans-oceanic musical superstar! How did it go?"

"The gig? Fine. Five shows, some better than others. Anyway, I sort of took up with her, the old friend, like I said, but it was complicated, and now I think that's over too, but not in any way you could define, exactly."

"Well, why? How complicated could it be?"

"Her family did something terrible to me. And Willa, back then, well, she didn't cooperate, exactly, but she acquiesced. I mean, to the extent that an eight-year-old can acquiesce."

"My dear, if you're not old enough to know the word, you're not old enough to do it."

"Hah, I suppose. That was kind of her defense. Mine, too, I guess, come to think of it. Anyway, in an odd way I loved her and I still love her, but that's over. And then I didn't even mention, but I lost my job, so I've been doing web design instead."

"Oh, Charlie! I'm so sorry! Did you at least go see Dr. Nemerov?"

"Yeah, but Diane, you should've warned me!"

"Oh, no! Did I steer you wrong? Are you telling me that you don't like him?"

"No, no, he's really interesting. It's just that his place stinks to high heaven."

"Yeah, I know! Doesn't it? Frank claimed he hardly noticed, and that's how full of shit *he* is. But he's really good, I mean Dr. Nemerov, because he's the first and only person I've ever met in my life who's actually decided to live his life *exactly* the way he wants to and then goes out and actually does it, and if you don't like a little cat shit, you can go soak yourself. So Charlie, if I might ask, how are you paying for the good doctor? Is the web design paying the bills?"

"Yeah, I'm making decent bucks and picking up unemployment and I'm still doing some gigs at Berto's."

"Oh, that reminds me, how is that girl at Berto's doing?"

"Oh, you mean Kathleen? I haven't spoken to her."

"Kathleen? Is that her name?"

"Yeah, I think so. Why? Do you think she has grounds for a suit?"

"A suit? Against whom? Did Berto's fire her?"

"Yeah, that was in my e-mail, remember? I sent it to you a while ago."

"Your e-mail? I don't remember getting an e-mail from you."

"Yeah, I mean I thought I sent it to the right address, didn't I? She was fired because she was complaining about mealy worms in the kitchen. I've stopped eating there after my gigs."

"Well, it might have gotten caught in my spam filter. Sorry. But I thought just now you were going to say she was fired because of her illness."

"What illness?"

"Charlie. This is the girl who came down with that horrible neurological disorder, right? Isn't that who we're talking about? Not mealy worms, the one from our dinner, who you had that dream about."

And indeed she had come back into my brain again just recently, to remind me that I didn't yet fully understand. But somehow I had forgotten all about her now, while talking to Diane, and before, and before that, and every moment before *that,* since I had last seen her on the sidewalk outside of Berto's and, in the setting sun, she had said "no" to me, and then in our last phone conversation shortly thereafter, when I had described the second dream to her and she had dismissed me yet again.

I had completely forgotten her.

At the airport, on the way to Seattle, when I'd had the odd, light-headed feeling that I'd forgotten something?

It was her.

"MariAngela," I said. "Her name is MariAngela. Sorry, I don't know what just happened. I don't know what's wrong with me."

"Well, I certainly haven't forgotten her," Diane said. "I had chills all that night thinking about that dream."

"To be honest, there were two more dreams."

"You mean the same kind where she came into your brain?"

"Yeah. The first one was not long after our dinner and she came to me and asked me to wake up Alisa because she had something to say to her. That didn't really make any sense to me. And then again just a few nights ago, when she said something like 'You still haven't figured it out.' "

"Figured what out?"

"I don't know. Willa, or what her family'd done to me, or maybe something left over with Alisa, I guess."

"So let me review your story. You go to Hawaii for your big concerts and you break up with Alisa. Right? And then you meet another woman in Hawaii whose family apparently did something to you when you were a child that was bad enough that you still think about it to this day, and then you go and have a relationship with her and then you break up with her, too?"

I laughed a bit. "That's about right."

"And then you get fired."

"Actually, I got fired between breaking up with Alisa and Willa."

"Okay. Anyway. So then you keep on having these very disturbing dreams about yet another woman, MariAngela. Man, Charlie, that's a lot of women."

I was glad I hadn't mentioned Beatrice.

"And," she added, "your irritable bowel is acting up again."

"How do you know that?"

She indicated the iced green tea I had ordered. "No coffee. I've got some detective skills too, you know! So Charlie, I know that in most or maybe all of these cases you were just a victim of circumstance or whatever, so I'm totally not blaming you or implying anything when I say this, but clearly you're quite depressed or confused or whatever. Are you still seeing Dr. Nemerov?"

"Yeah, I need to make another appointment."

"Do. He's really helped me and Frank. His domineering issues, my need-to-be-domineered issues, stuff like that. And Charlie, MariAngela? That's her name, right? Maybe you should, you know, call her or visit her, don't you think?"

"I promise I'll see both of them, really."

She flipped her hair again, so that the red highlights shone in the winter sun streaming in through the windows. "See," she said, "now we'll both be fixed up!"

Not a lot of Americans know this, but Buenos Aires is the world capital of old-fashioned Freudian analysis. They love their psychiatrists in Argentina, and I guess I must have inherited some of that predilection, because I didn't hesitate to make a new appointment with Dr. Nemerov; indeed, I was intensely curious to learn what he might discover about me.

The apartment smelled worse than the last time, although I would not have thought that possible. When I came in, Dr. Nemerov was sharing a can of pineapple chunks with an orange tabby. He'd give the cat a chunk, which the tabby would chew thoughtfully, and then he would pop one into his own mouth.

"You want some?"

"No thanks. I'll pass." He looked disappointed, so I added, "I guess I'm kind of tired of Hawaiian food."

"Murdered any chipmunks lately?"

"No."

"Nor cats, I trust."

"No cats."

"You've probably seen the James Bond movies where Blofeld is always excessively polite and strokes a cat in his lap while adumbrating his plans to destroy the world. But I stroke kittens for entirely unironic reasons. So don't let me hear any stories about you killing cats, okay?"

"Don't worry, I don't. And does that mean you're not planning to destroy the world?"

"No, although I could if I wanted to." He laughed. "So let's pick up where we left off. How's your friend?"

"She's doing as well as can be expected."

"Which means with ALS, poorly. And how are you doing? You look alarmingly thin."

"Not great. I feel completely turned inside out. And yeah, I'm not eating very well. I stopped eating at Berto's, the club I perform at, because they had some mealy worms in the kitchen, and just in general I don't feel much like eating anyway. I keep on thinking about those mealy worms."

"And you're not eating very well because you're upset. And also because you're not entirely sure what you're upset about. Right? That would seem to be characteristic of you."

"Yeah, I guess. I'm not sure if I'm upset because my girlfriend broke up with me, or two of them actually, or because I lost my job, or because MariAngela keeps on appearing inside my head."

"My answer would be yes."

"To all of the above?"

"To all of the above." As if to mock my lack of appetite, he pulled out a long black-licorice whip and began chewing on it meditatively.

"There's more. I didn't even talk about this in my first meeting, but I discovered recently that my parents, and one of my childhood friends who also was one of the girls I just broke up with, were lying to me for many years and making me believe I was responsible for the death of a baby girl when I was not responsible, and she wasn't even actually dead. And the baby girl's mother said some horrible things to me at the time that I guess I've never really come to terms with."

"Well, I suppose that could be a reason to be upset and not eat, too. Why didn't you mention this at our first visit?"

"Well, you said you thought there'd be plenty of time to get into stuff from my childhood..."

"But you said you just found out recently that you were lied to for all these years..."

"And also because it's the opposite of finding out I *was* responsible for someone's death, you know, so it wasn't ultimately that big of a deal."

"Oh, clearly not," he said dryly.

"OK, I think I got your point."

"Do you, Charlie? Do you understand the reason you're not eating is that you're too full of shit? Charlie. *Look* at me. Look at me, Charlie! Explain just this one thing to me. OK? Why are you not angry?"

"Who said I'm not?"

"I take that back. Of course you are angry. It's just that you're pretending that you're not. You've got quite a lot of things swirling around in your mental cesspool, young man."

"I suppose. The little girl, Elizabeth, was left alone by her mother, and she nearly suffocated. She survived, but she was brain-damaged, and the mother blamed me and said I was crazy."

"Is the mother still living?"

"No, both parents passed away."

"How about your parents? Are they still with us in this vale of tears?"

"Yeah, both. I talk to my mother fairly regularly. It's harder with my father, they both drink a lot, but he's driving his taxi all the time or at his kiln or out gambling, and she's a bit more in touch with reality, you know?"

"Okay, Charlie. We'll get into what happened with your parents and your childhood friend a little later. But I'm a man of action." He actually flexed his left bicep when he said this, and one sleeve of his partially unsnapped overalls flopped down. "I'm going to do two things with you today, give you two assignments that'll have you feeling much better and eating your Wheaties again. Are you with me? Okay, first, girlfriends, eh, not that important. People break up all of the time, although I think we should get into more detail about why you would choose as a girlfriend a childhood friend who lied to you about a supposed death in your past. That's a little bit odd, young man. But let's put that aside, alright? The number one thing that's plaguing you, I think, is that, quite understandably, it's upsetting that someone is entering into your head without your permission. And why is this plaguing you? Because you don't know whether this is your doing or hers, and why it's happening at all. So talk to her in your next dream. Ask her what she wants. Ask her, Charlie. See what she has to say."

"And how am I supposed to strike up a conversation in my dreams if my dreams are out of my control?"

"Partially out of your control. But—and listen to me carefully, Charlie, because this is very important—the whole problem with you is that you're too much *in* control. The state of semi-consciousness that we experience when we dream is the only time when you're unable to engage in active acts of suppression. It's true that while asleep you have a predominant lack of awareness of your environment, but you clearly have some level of consciousness. Have you ever heard a police siren, out on the street in the real world, while you were asleep, and managed to incorporate that into your dreams? I'm sure you've done something like this, everyone has. And have you ever had a terribly upsetting dream where you've forced yourself to wake up? These are examples of volition. So just do as I say, and don't ask how. In your next dream, just *ask* her."

"I'll try my best. But I don't know if that's gonna work."

He sighed heavily. "Alright, before we get to your objections, I want to make a couple of observations. We are never so alone as when we sleep. Would you agree?"

"Yes. I mean, sure."

He took a last bite of licorice, reached into another pocket, pulled out a thin black cigar, and lit it. "To state the obvious, we are unconscious and thus unaware of our surroundings and of those we love. Except to the very minor degree that we are perhaps entangled with someone, cuddling them, and the tactile sensations exist somewhere at a very low level of awareness. But you are not sleeping with anyone now, since your breakups with your girlfriends, plural, correct?"

"Correct."

"Okay. So to take it one step further, what strikes me about you is that you are not only alone when you sleep, but alone, and indeed asleep, when you are awake. You seem to be in a sleepwalking state, where the isolation and unconsciousness you experience when actually asleep is being replicated in your waking existence. Okay?"

"I can accept that."

"Of course you can. Which leads me to my second observation. You accept everything. I won't say that you are suggestible, in so many words, but you are very open to the feelings and opinions and moods of others, which may be why you're not eating and wasting away at the very same time MariAngela is. Now how do we reconcile this empathetic capability and your easygoing willingness to engage with a psychiatrist like me with the paradoxical fact that you are sleepwalking through your existence and seemingly oblivious?"

"I don't know."

"Of course you don't. But I do. That's why I'm me and you're you!" He laughed at this. "It is because you have developed these sympathies in lieu of normal, everyday ones, in the same way that, when one portion of the brain is damaged in an accident, another portion adapts itself and takes over. This is why you have the dreams where you are visited. This is why the mealy worms —which are in my opinion another way for you to think about what is happening to MariAngela's nervous system. But this is unusual for you, for you to have waking disturbances like this, right? Because we have agreed that you are a very rigid person, most of your 'worms' arrive from underneath, from the black soil of your sleep. Okay?"

"Okay."

"So. In our dreams, we have exceptionally low standards, wouldn't you agree? Very low. We'll believe any kind of bullshit we make up. We'll believe that we can pump our legs like we're on a bicycle and suddenly we're walking in the air. And so on. So these low standards, so to speak, and I don't mean this in a pejorative way, have seeped into your waking life as well. You are a rigid person, but like a weed that is covered up with a heavy layer of concrete...."

"If I'm following all of this..."

"Then I'm merely suggesting that your emotions are no different than anyone else's, but because you have suppressed them in order to work in advertising and have pretty girlfriends and live a seemingly normal life, these emotions have had to find softer soil from which to sprout, and that would mean your dreaming, unconscious self."

"Don't weeds eventually just grow through the concrete?"

"Of course they do, eventually. That's precisely why you feel as if you're cracking up. That's why the worms are coming to the surface."

"And if I ask MariAngela if it's her inside my brain or me and she answers that it's her, how will I know for sure if it's her and not me being 'her'?"

"I'm not sure that it's even a question of 'know' or 'don't know.' It's not like a switch you flick on or off, where it's either one thing or the other, in other words that it's either something that is clairvoyant in nature or merely a form of intuition. Your connection with MariAngela may be at a level so deep that you don't recognize, that it would be impossible, either in your waking self or your dreaming self, to separate whether she is speaking to you or you are taking on her persona to speak to yourself, or if indeed there is really that much difference between the two. What I'm telling you is, you may never know. "

"It's funny you should say there's no simple on or off switch. I tried an experiment with my girlfriend where I tried to dream whether a light switch in her basement was flicked on or off."

"And it failed, I would assume, because the experiment was purely mechanical. No, the point is not definitive answers. The point is just that you gain greater insight. Ask her. Do what you want with her. Have sex with her if you want, temporarily 'cure' her of her illness, fly with her to a resort—it's your dream."

"Okay, so that's my first assignment. Talk to her. What's my second?"

"Eat a goddamn sandwich."

"Seriously?"

"Yes, Charlie, seriously. But no, that's not the second assignment. The second assignment is to call her. Confront her."

"MariAngela?"

"Oh, please, Charlie, of course you should call MariAngela. That would be the decent thing to do, how could you even ask? But no, I deliberately didn't make clear who the 'her' was to evaluate just how dense you possibly could be. I'm talking, in this case, about your mother."

"I don't understand. It was Elizabeth's mother who said those things to me."

"Yeah, but she's gone. She's dead. Out of your life. No, your mother. And your father, too, if he's sober enough. Call her, call them, and find out why they fled the country with you. And now we have to wrap up. Call your mother tomorrow. Then you can report back to me with something interesting, and hopefully with a few BLTs under your belt."

I frittered away my Monday night juggling bills, watching TV, and learning how to play Skyrim. It seemed like the perfect pastime for an unemployed, depressed, and confused person like me. I couldn't bring myself to call my mother, nor to acknowledge that the reason I couldn't call was because I was afraid. By the end of the evening, I'd decided to visit MariAngela the following night. It had been too long, and possibly too late as well.

THREE

# *Everything Solid has a Shadow*

## (MariAngela)

# 1

The very next day, I called MariAngela's cell.

After MariAngela answered, I said, "Hey. How are you?"

There was a short silence at the other end of the line, but it was long enough that it made me contort my face into a horrible grimace of anxiety and embarrassment as I waited.

Finally, I heard, "Long time no see, Charlie."

"Listen, I was wondering if I could stop by your apartment this afternoon and say hi, see how you're doing and catch up and stuff."

"You could stop by my apartment, but I wouldn't be there."

"Oh, where did I catch you?"

"I'm at a place called the Rehabilitation Institute of Illinois. They stuck me here temporarily until they can figure out where to put me, even though there's no 're' to 'hab,' or no 'hab' to 're.' Well, you know what I mean. Most of the people here are recovering from something or other, and I'm kind of declining a bit at this point and was having a little trouble cooking for myself and stuff, but I don't have what you'd really call a 'hospital' type illness right now, so I was sort of caught in the middle. But you're welcome to visit me here. You know where it is, right? On Pearson. Near that tourist-trap, deep-dish pizza place with the lines out front."

"Yeah, I know where it is. Are you doing okay?"

"I'm okay. Yeah. Maybe a little bit of a headache. So I can expect you this afternoon?"

"Of course."

"Good. I look forward to seeing you."

She met me in one of the family waiting rooms. I don't know what I was expecting—nothing much at all, I suppose—but I was surprised to see her, as I entered the sunny and odorless waiting room, waiting for me while leaning on one of those three-pronged canes and wearing a big pair of dark sunglasses. Surprised? Maybe that's not quite the right term—horrified would be better.

Did ALS cause blindness?

I hugged her, gingerly, on her left side, the side that wasn't leaning on the three-pronged cane.

"MariAngela. I'm sorry it's been a while."

"A while."

She was a bit upset, clearly, but the way in which she'd repeated 'a while' got me thinking about Elizabeth, or Bitty, whom I'd never again meet, and how in her own permanently reduced state she'd repeat the last few words of things that people would say to her.

But MariAngela wasn't Bitty.

"I'm sorry I haven't visited you or called or anything. Things have been kind of complicated lately, but that's no excuse, and I'm so sorry, but MariAngela, your vision? I mean, can you see?"

"The cane and glasses? I know, looks like I'm blind!"

"But...?"

"I can see just fine, it's just a migraine. Can we go to my room? It's starting to get worse, and I have this like insane over-sensitivity to light."

"So what are you doing out here?" I indicated the windows, with the late-winter sun streaming in.

"I know, I don't know, I wanted to greet you and make sure you found me." She hobbled toward the corridor, and I saw for the first time, as I walked behind her, that the parenthetical posture was now reversed, and instead of that sexy little swayback she now walked with a slight, forward-leaning hunch, not like that of an old lady, but like someone hobbling determinedly in that direction.

Her room—semiprivate, though the other bed was unoccupied—was completely dark, the lights off and the curtains drawn, and I realized the sacrifice she'd made by heading out into the lighted reception area to greet me or to ensure that I'd actually show up. She propped her cane against the wall, took off her sunglasses and tossed them carelessly on the floor as if lacking the last strength to place them on a table, and rolled under the comforter on her bed, whereupon she placed a pillow over her eyes and pressed it down with her raised forearms.

"Is it bad? The migraine?"

"It wasn't really bad at all this morning, but it's taken a turn for the worse."

"Is migraine one of the side effects of ALS?"

"Not to my knowledge. It's on my list of questions for mister doctor-man. He's the expert, though I keep telling him that a few months from now, I'll know a hell of a lot more than he ever will."

"How've the doctors been treating you?"

"Pretty good. They mostly tell me the truth, which is there really isn't much they can do for me, and that itself is doing something for me. Anyway, I'd rather die without a bunch of bullshit that I have to hack through first. They told me there's one drug that sorta works for like three months for some patients, but then, eh, you're just back where you started, delaying the inevitable a bit. They'll send me back to my apartment at some point with around-the-clock nurses so I can die at home, and that's fine."

The room was so dark that all I could see of MariAngela, in the bit of light leaking through the heavy curtains, were her pale forearms and the white pillow she was pressing over her eyes.

"Did you have migraines before?"

"Not really, headaches around my period, tension headaches, stuff like that, but no real migraines. I think God just thought it'd be fucking hilarious to throw something else in the hopper, you know, ALS is about your body dying around you while your brain functions perfectly, so why not give you pain in the one part you have left that's healthy?"

"I'm so sorry."

"And I'm so bitter. Though why the fuck should I apologize for that? You know, if you read the *New York Times* or something, and they've got a feature on bad diseases like ALS or whatever, it's always like, 'I refuse to become a victim' and 'I'm not going to feel sorry for myself' and shit like that. And this guide to 'caregivers' I read was all about, 'always be positive,' but I always wondered, what the hell is the matter with being bitter when the time comes? Isn't bitter an emotion like any other? Didn't God give us bitter just like he gave us joy or forgiveness or compassion and all the other official, culturally approved emotions? If I wanna to feel bitter, if I'm gonna feel sorry for myself, and then society is telling me, 'oh, feeling sorry for yourself isn't going to help anything,' well fuck 'em, you know? If I get pleasure out of self-pity, with all the other things I've got to deal with I'll be damned if someone tells me I can't."

"Do you want me to get a nurse or something? Do you need some painkillers?"

"No, I've already taken something. Don't listen to me, Charlie, I'm just ranting a little 'cause it feels good and you're so great to rant to, the way your eyes get all wide like you're scared or something."

"How can you see my eyes now?"

"Oh, they were always that way, any time you'd get chastised. But I mean, if I can't rant in front of a friend, who can I rant in front of?"

"I know."

"We're still friends, aren't we, Charlie?"

"Of course. I mean, I know you're mad that I haven't visited before now."

She made a dismissive waving motion with her hand that looked like a flickering flame in the darkened room. I interpreted it to mean not "don't worry about it," but rather, "I don't have the energy to be angry right now." And that must have been how she meant it, because she placed her hand back over the pillow and said, in a changing-the-subject kind of tone, "So how was Hawaii?"

But I still wasn't sure how she felt, so I said, "Are you sure you want to talk about that right now?"

"Given the choice between Hawaii or death as the topic of conversation, which one would you choose?"

I laughed a little at that. "OK, I got you. So Hawaii was weird. Definitely weird. I broke up with Alisa, and she punched me in the eye, and then I got together with this old childhood friend who sort of stalked me there and we sort of broke up too, and I got fired, and I figured out something from my past that had kinda wrecked me for years, and oh my God, you remember my boss Gilbert? He's in trouble, so I guess I'm glad I got fired, but now I'm testifying in this lawsuit..."

"Charlie, I kind of hate to say it, but I'm really sick to my stomach. Can you come to see me again another time?"

"Sure."

"And tell me in detail about Hawaii and all that other stuff."

"I mean, you're not mad at me? Do you want me to?"

"You'd better leave now." She rolled out of bed and limped over to her cane and then began to hobble toward the bathroom. "God, I hate throwing up." I grabbed her around the waist to steady her as she staggered into the bathroom, and suddenly I found myself on my knees with her, holding her as she vomited in the darkness.

I was very glad that I had waited instead of leaving when she had asked me to. I moistened a washcloth and wiped her mouth, gave her a sip of water—she and I fumbled a little bit in the pitch-black bathroom until I could guide the glass to her hand—and then I walked her back to her bed and tucked her in. She replaced the pillow over her eyes and took a deep, ragged breath.

"Do you feel another wave?"

"No, I think it's okay for now. On the way out, you can stop at the nurses' station if you wouldn't mind and tell them I need another painkiller. Thanks for coming."

I leaned over to kiss her on the cheek, but of course the pillow was in the way. I wanted to see her eyes in the deep darkness, to see them as she saw me, but I couldn't, and she couldn't. So I squeezed her shoulder and departed. She was what I had forgotten. And those other two women, the one in Galena who was so damaged and the one on the train who kept on taking out and putting back in those little objects, had reminded me of the one I could not remember because they, too, like MariAngela, were trying to reassemble themselves even as they fell to pieces.

But now that I'd remembered—not quite too late—I promised myself I would not forget again.

# 2

*I came* back again that Saturday, and this time I brought with me a big fruit basket filled with shiny Fuji apples and Honey Belle pears and little jars of jam and marmalade and fancy packages of dates and dried apricots. I thought it'd be a nice late-winter treat.

Once again, MariAngela met me in the family waiting area. This time, she wasn't wearing sunglasses.

"You feeling better?"

"Head-wise, yeah. I actually feel fine. Now that I've had one for real, I'm actually kind of grateful that I never had 'em when I was younger. It would've sucked to have lived through all that kind of pain and puking in my twenties when I was out partying, but I guess I got off scot-free in that department. But now I'm paying for it, huh? That roller-coaster ride? I'm starting on the swoosh, down, piss-in-your-pants part."

And indeed, as I accompanied her back to her room, her rolling gait was more pronounced than just a couple of days ago, and she seemed to be leaning more heavily than before on her cane. As we entered her room, I happened to glance at the doorframe, where there were two small horizontal aluminum slots for the patients' name cards. One, for her missing roommate, was empty. The other one read "M. Halloran."

I hadn't known her last name was Halloran. As an occasional performer, I didn't clock in like the regular employees at Berto's and so I wouldn't have seen her time card, but I still wasn't quite sure how I hadn't known.

This time she sat down in the easy chair at the foot of her bed, and I dragged over the other easy chair from the foot of her absent roommate's bed. I sat with my back to the window—the curtains were open today—and that allowed me to look into Mari-Angela's eyes for the first time since that time on the street when they'd been tinted orange with the sunset.

"It's funny," she said. "When I was a kid, I literally could not *stand* roller coasters, and when someone'd talk me into going on one at Great America or something, I'd immediately regret it and kind of pray that I could turn back time and not get on or I'd think about yelling to get off, and then I'd just grit my teeth until it was over. And that's my only choice now, too. So, Hawaii. You were just starting to tell me about it."

"Are you still okay with that?"

"I told you, Charlie, what else are we gonna talk about? You have to understand, from here on in, if I don't live, whaddya call it, viscerally, I won't live at all."

"Do you mean vicariously?"

"I guess, yeah."

"Because, I don't know, I kind of hesitate to bring this up, but you could have actually *come* to Hawaii this past summer when I asked you."

"I'd rather not talk about that."

"Why?"

"Because I don't want to talk about it."

"I mean, *why* don't you want to talk about it?"

"Because I don't want to talk about it, Charlie. Drop it, okay? Besides, if I had gone, you probably wouldn't have had your little adventure with your childhood friend and all that other cool stuff like getting socked in the eye."

"I keep picking up on this hostility you have, and I don't understand why. Okay, I understand about the not visiting you part, and I'm sorry, but I didn't cause your illness, you know."

MariAngela laughed. "You just hate it when women are mad at you, don't you?"

"Yeah, I suppose."

"And why is that, do you suppose?"

"I'm not sure, but I think it's because I was once accused of being responsible for the death of an infant, and her mother said some negative things to me that I didn't really realize but they've stuck with me all this time."

"Because you made it seem the other day like my being upset with you for not coming to visit me was a reason why I didn't want you to come visit me again, whereas it was just the opposite, I mean, why would I be upset at all about your not visiting to begin with unless, you know, I *wanted* you to visit?"

"Well, I'm here, aren't I?"

"Yeah, you're here. But you need to see beneath the surface of what people say. Sometimes people say things because they're under the influence of something or other, or they have a migraine, or a stupid fucking illness, you know?"

"And then, what, if the lights are turned back on and the migraine is over, that's when the real person is speaking? Or is it the other way around? Is the real person the one who's speaking in the dark?"

"God, Charlie, you just have to accept that people go through moods. Especially if they're fucking dying, you know? Ask me, I've been doing pretty well, considering. God knows that a lot of my friends are freaked out and won't even visit me. Like my I-guess-former girlfriend, Dani, when we first started going out, she told me this story about a friend of hers who'd been in a terrible accident, stepped out of a taxi in the middle of Michigan Avenue and a car swerved into him and he ended up losing both legs. So he's sitting in the hospital with no legs anymore at age twenty-six, can you imagine, Dani says, 'You know, I just couldn't bring myself to visit him.' " She shook her head. "And guess who hasn't visited *me* either?"

"But weren't you saying you just have to accept?"

"Yeah, but in her case it isn't just a mood, she's an unfeeling bitch. I've adjusted alright. I've been reading a ton, all these books I'd never had a chance to read before. You wanna hear my favorite new quote? It's from Emily Dickinson. Let me see if I remember this:

Either the Darkness alters—
Or something in the sight
Adjusts itself to Midnight—
And Life steps almost straight.

"Not bad, huh? So that's my thing, Charlie: I've adjusted myself to midnight."

"I'm not sure if that's a good thing or not, but anyway, I guess that's what you have to do."

"So this woman, the mother, back when you were a kid, she'd just lost a baby, right?"

"More or less, yeah."

"And I assume you weren't actually responsible for the death, right?"

"No, not really. I wasn't."

"Well, maybe she was just operating under the influence of extreme emotions, have you thought about that? Maybe you should just forgive her."

"You say I need to see beneath the surface of what people say, and yet I'm the one who had those weird dreams about you that are true."

"My point precisely. Why did you have those two dreams? Because you were like utterly oblivious and that was the only way for a thought to get past your defenses."

"I know, that's what everyone says. I actually had a third dream about you. Not that long ago. You said something like 'you still haven't figured it out,' and then you curled up into a ball and blew away in the wind."

"Well, you got the curling up in a ball and blowing away part right. I feel like an orange that rolls under the refrigerator or something and you find it six months later."

"I'm sorry."

"Stop with the fucking sorrys. My illness is not your fault, and I never said it was."

"Yeah, but somehow it is my fault that I had dreams about you."

"I never said that either."

"Sure you did. You did, you blamed me, and that's why you didn't want to go to Hawaii with me."

"You don't understand."

"And that's exactly what you told me in my dream."

"I know."

"You know? You mean you know because I just told you that's what you said, or you know because you were actually trying to communicate with me?"

"Because you *told* me, Charlie."

"Because just a minute ago, you said something like it was just a way of getting past my defenses."

"I meant that in a figurative way, Charlie. More like in the sense of you getting past your *own* defenses. No, I'm not actually walking into your brain and consciously delivering messages to you, I thought I'd explained that to you before." She paused and took a deep breath. "But I think what I said, or I should say what you *imagined* I'd said, is right—that you just don't understand. I mean, I *agree* with what my dream version of me is telling you. Maybe you should just listen to what you're telling yourself, so you don't have to have dreams with other people telling you or people having to tell you in person."

"Yeah, God forbid someone should tell me straight out in person. To be honest, I'm sick of understanding, or trying to understand, especially when women won't communicate directly with me and tell me what they're actually thinking. So, let's say I leave now and ask you if it's okay if I come and visit you again, and you say, 'Don't bother.' Am I supposed to know if that really means 'don't bother' because it's not that important to you, or whether it's just you being petulant because you're a woman, or angry because of your illness, or what?"

She laughed. "I don't think other guys in my experience, or other chicks for that matter, have as much trouble as you do figuring out that kind of stuff, but whatever. Please come again. I kind of enjoy our wrangling, and I want you to come again, okay?"

"Okay, I will."

"And thanks for the fruit basket. Next time bring me a chocolate malt instead, okay? I love those."

"Shit."

"No, that's okay. I'm just getting to the point where an apple or a pear is kind of a challenge. Malt's not gonna last long either. Few months from now, it'll be juice and water."

# 3

*The* basement of my rental house, unlike Alisa's basement, is a dank, crowded, spiky, and tangled cave. The house was once a farmhouse, after all. On one side of the basement, with its sloping, water- and iron-stained floor, was an old coal chute and bin; a 1920s-era, octopus-style, gravity-fed Holland coal furnace with multiple, massive, silver-duct-tape-covered pipe arms that plunged upward into the ceiling; a white mangle and an ancient icebox; a Federal Brand mechanical washing machine and, bolted into the top of it, an Anchor Brand (Pat. May 1, 1928) hand-cranked wringer; and a couple of shoulder-height crawl spaces that led to the area underneath the covered porches that abutted the house, with glass windows that swung up and out to reveal impossible clumps of rusted barbed wire, harrows, hoes, oxidized and raggedly perforated cans of rat and ant poison, lengths of lumber, jelly jars filled with screws, watering cans, spades, ice picks, encrusted paint rollers, rusted hose fittings, and other dark things that covered the dirt floor and were too far back in the space to discern. And everywhere in the dirt and among the objects that rested on the dirt were earthworms and other grubby pale things that squirmed and slithered and crawled.

To an outsider, it might seem much more of the sort of place for subterranean discoveries than Alisa's sterile laundry room. The other side of the basement was more contemporary—a modern hot-water heater; cabinets filled with painting supplies and cans of paint that had dried to solid lumps; a big box filled with Star Trek: The Next Generation action figurines; a gigantic carton holding old, warped and waterlogged board games from the '60s and '70s; and many other cartons filled with flaking, water-stained magazines—*Christian Century, Sports Illustrated, Harper's.* Here, too, there were papery little moths and minuscule worms. I felt sick.

Is that why I went down there after visiting MariAngela? Was I hoping to discover something, seeing as how Alisa and I had discovered exactly nothing in her laundry room? And yet Alisa's laundry room had served its purpose, because those visions I'd had about the laundry-folding table had led me away from Alisa and, later, to Willa, if only for a short time. Maybe I was hoping to find something in this wormy, rusted, entangled mess, on a clammy winter day, no less, when the basement was cold and gloomy, that would bring me closer to MariAngela before she died, or at least help me to understand what she was hinting at but could not say. But I came upstairs feeling as if the rental house's basement and its crawl spaces were not even as complicated as my own brain, and when I stepped into the bathroom to take a hot shower, I looked in the mirror and discovered long, undulant strands of gray and white cobwebs festooning my hair and ears.

But as I showered off that basement dust and rust and cold and mess, I started to think: Hadn't I already discovered everything I needed in my house? The Felix cartoon, with that sweater that was unraveling the way MariAngela's nerve endings were unraveling, and, as in Felix's universe, her whole world would unravel soon enough? And the dollhouse, with its little shutters that opened out into the street and let in a tiny puff of frigid air?

That night I had another walk-in dream, though this one was a little different: I, myself, walked into a version of the dormer room—which then shifted into something resembling one of the basement crawl spaces and then back into a version of the dormer room—and opened up the tiny shutters.

There was a gigantic eye staring back at me.

It was MariAngela's eye.

It didn't blink at all. It looked at me steadily. I shouted, "Leave me alone!" in my dream, and then I woke up and realized I had actually shouted those words in my sleep, though no one was around to hear.

It was 3:30 A.M. I shuffled downstairs, took a Xanax from a bottle that Alisa had left in my medicine cabinet, and managed, after another hour or so, to fall asleep.

The next morning, at 9:00, I phoned Dr. Nemerov.

His next available appointment was not for three weeks. I was starting to feel like I was on the edge of losing my mind, and, somehow, that losing my mind was the direction I was meant to go in, like MariAngela's roller coaster screaming downhill.

I buried myself in freelance work for the next three weeks and visited MariAngela every third day or so. I went to the movies in the evening to distract myself, and I ate hardly anything, either at lunch with MariAngela or before the movie started. I'd gone hunting in the cabinets one day for the old bottle of McCormick black pepper the missionaries had left behind for me and had discovered that some of their boxes of leftover pancake mix and bags of flour were infested with the same mealy worms Kathleen had discovered at Berto's. So I cleaned out everything that wasn't canned, and when I looked a few days later, the mealy worms were all gone, but so was my appetite. Skinny to begin with, I now looked at myself in the mirror and saw with horror that my ribs were visible. This I could not stand, and yet the thought of choking down a bowl of chili, with or without mealy worms, was just as repellent to me. I looked ahead to my next appointment with Dr. Nemerov as if he would be some sort of lifesaving savant.

My Glennis deposition took an entire afternoon at a law firm on Monroe. Gilbert was there, with his attorney, and so was the owner of Glennis and two of her attorneys. Jason wasn't there, probably because Glennis was suing Gilbert, and Gilbert was suing Jason, so the two were separate cases. I kept my head down, figuratively, and just plowed through what I knew to be the truth—

that the ClickEver account had been hanging by a thread by the time I'd been fired, that the people at ClickEver had been sticking with us only because of Jason, and that once he decided to walk, there would have been no way that Gilbert, whether with me or with anyone else at the agency, would have been able to salvage the account. I told them this, and I told them that Gilbert must have known this when he sold the agency to Glennis. I knew that Bowen, and a couple of my other colleagues, would be telling the lawyers pretty much the same thing when their turns came. Gilbert refused to look at me while I was giving my deposition, which I could tell because I looked at *him* more than I looked at the lawyers as I spoke. His jaw muscles rippled the entire time, as if he were rehearsing the act of ripping out and masticating my esophagus. Afterward, as we were walking out, he said, with clenched teeth, "You'll find out that I don't take betrayal lightly."

I tried mightily to say something devastating in response, but all I could come up with was, "So what?"

But that was okay; by the time I'd gotten out of there, I felt like a tiny bit of the pressure that had built up in my "pipe" (I refused, out of what remained of my pride, to call it a sewage pipe) had been alleviated.

When I hit Monroe Street I remembered that Diane worked nearby on LaSalle Street, so on impulse, I called her cell. I was actually astonished when she answered.

"Diane, can I meet you at Starbucks again?"

"I would love to! But I'm working."

"I know, I know. I mean a Starbucks downtown or something. There must be one right by your office, right? Just fifteen minutes? Please?"

"Charlie, you don't sound great."

"Just came out of a deposition. You know, lawyers."

She laughed. "Hah! Lawyers! We're the worst! Okay, you remember my office building, right? There's a big old-fashioned Greek coffee shop in the lobby. I'll meet you there in fifteen minutes *for* fifteen minutes, but that's all I have. Maybe twenty. But only for you, Charlie!"

I was so relieved and happy to see Diane that I could hardly speak. We got a booth in the back of the coffee shop, and I ordered a Greek salad to pay the "rent" for the space, and Diane ordered a cup of tea. I told her a little bit about the deposition and about Gilbert's parting words.

"Ah," she said, "those are the words of a loser. Go on with your life and forget him."

"I have, I have."

She balled up her fists in a comical way and spoke out of the corner of her mouth like a movie tough guy. She sounded more like Cyndi Lauper. "Gives you any trouble, I'll take care of him, that's what I do for my daily bread!"

"I sometimes forget what a tough broad you are!"

"Still playing music?"

"Nah, not really. I'm just too distracted. And Nemerov's going to help me with this dream stuff. And I keep on thinking about what you said at dinner, about how everything shifts, and I have a question for you."

"Shoot."

"Well, in general, my dreams are exactly like what you were talking about, where nothing is ever the same. But MariAngela? When I have one of my dreams about her, she looks exactly like she does in the real world. What do you think that means, Diane?"

"You know, I once had a dream where I was looking at tulips, and I noticed that they didn't cast any shadows on the sidewalk, and then some voice said to me, 'That's how you know this is a dream, because the flowers have no shadows.' That creeped me out for some reason when I woke up, but I guess I would have been totally freaked if the flowers *did* have shadows. Then I would have felt like, you know, if the real world was invading my dream world, then the dream world could invade my real world, too. So maybe, is that how you're feeling? Like when you're seeing MariAngela, you know, exactly like in real life, that it's really her inside of you?"

"I don't know, I was hoping you'd answer that question."

"It's really her, Charlie. I haven't met her and *I'm* not inside your head, but I think it's really her. And you know why?"

"Of course I don't."

"Well, if everything shifts in your dreams because you fear death, maybe you no longer fear *her* death, or at least you've come to accept it. She's fixed in your mind in a certain way. There's a whole other aspect to dreams that I didn't even talk about at the steak house with you guys, anyway. Not only are things always changing, like I said, but you almost never see anything clearly and directly, like the flowers that don't have shadows. You sort of have a *suggestion* that you're talking to a certain person, 'cause you know who they are and you've seen them before, but you can't really see their features, it's like when you play with your peripheral vision"—and here Diane rolled her eyeballs all the way to the right side—"and you can barely see some things, and then there's a spot right after that that's kind of ragged where you can't really see anything at all, but you can sense it. Right?" I rolled my eyeballs the same way she did, and saw the counter and, beyond it, as she'd said, the fuzzy suggestion of something else that was solid. I turned my head in that direction and saw that it was a gleaming silver coffee urn. "So the interesting thing is not only that you're seeing the actual MariAngela, but that you're seeing her straight on, and not peripherally. That's why I think she's real."

"Diane, I know my fifteen minutes are ticking away, but I have to use the facilities. I'll be back in just a second."

I walked into the bathroom, used the urinal, and then, as I was washing my hands, I looked at myself in the mirror. I stared and stared until the sight of me looked strange, and then I turned my head away from the mirror and turned my eyes back in the mirror's direction. I could just barely sense that someone was there, in the mirror, and then I had to swivel my head really quickly to confirm that it was me, and for the split second it'd taken me to do that, I'd felt terrified, as if my own face might have changed.

When I got back, I saw Diane thumbing her iPhone.

"I'm really sorry, I know you're busy. It's just I think I might be cracking up."

"Charlie, you don't have to worry. You're too strong for that. And besides, the kind of people who crack up for real are the ones who it never even occurs to them that they're cracking up."

"Well, I definitely don't want to. I just want to be normal, just like I was when Alisa and I first met you and Frank. Or maybe I was never normal, I don't know, and it's all just coming out now. But I want to have a happy life, I really do. I am the one I have been given to live my life with, and it's a shitty deal, but I'm all I've got. So I have no choice except to live it with the tools I have at hand."

"Do you wish you were someone else?"

"No, not exactly. I'm okay with being me, but I sometimes want to be other people at the same time. To me, you know what's the biggest mystery of existence? Of all? It's not what everyone else says, where do we come from and where do we go, and why are we born and why do we die, and what happens when we die. No, to me the biggest mystery is that there are billions of us, but every one of us, without exception, can always and forever only be the one person we were born as and never anyone else. It seems so incredibly, I don't know, *limited.*"

Diane thought about this. "Charlie, every ghost in history that I know of has come of its own accord. Except for yours. It's like you *want* to be haunted. Maybe it's because you're lonely, maybe it's because of Alisa, or maybe like you said you want to be someone else too. I don't know. But now with MariAngela, I think you've got what you wanted, and she's going to be living inside of you now."

# 4

***When*** I got back to my house, I went up to the dormer room and laid down with my head facing the dollhouse and my feet sticking out, just as the one-armed man had done in the video. I played a bit with the shutters, opening and shutting them, and then I peered through the little hole in the wall at the street. From my angle, I could see a fragment of concrete stoop, a metal handrail, a piece of lumpy tree root, and, fleetingly, a girl's foot shod in some sort of black shoe or boot. I knew the house; the family that lived there had five children, all girls. I waited for the boot to reappear, but it never did; the little girl had moved on. One isolated spot on my cheek was icy from the winter wind, and the rest of me was getting chilled, so I wriggled out of the dormer room and went downstairs to watch television.

But there was an idea forming in my head, less tangible even than a dream, but there nonetheless, that had come to me while I'd peered through those tiny shutters. I could feel it forming on the horizon like wisps of clouds coalescing into something I could not name.

The next day, I went to see MariAngela in the morning, a couple of hours earlier than my usual lunchtime visits. I was true to my word and brought her a big chocolate malt, which she sipped at decorously throughout the visit. Decorously? It was pleasant to use this term, with its implications of femininity and politesse, but the truth, as I well knew, was that her swallowing problems had just begun, and taking too large a sip, or, worse, swallowing a big lump of ice cream, could have resulted in a team of nurses rushing to her room. I found myself wishing she would just use a goddamn straw.

She tilted the cup toward me. "Want some?"

I looked at the sloping milkshake and I felt awful—there actually were little lumps inside, and I wasn't sure they were ice cream. It looked disgusting; I couldn't believe I'd bought it for her.

"No, thanks. Are you sure you're okay with those lumps of ice cream or whatever in it?"

She looked puzzled. "There aren't any lumps. It's really good."

We talked for a few moments of this and that, and then I said, "MariAngela, I know you're the one who's dealing with a terrible situation, but I need your help with something."

She smiled in an uncomplicated way. "Sure."

"I really need to understand for my own mental health if the dreams I've had about you are actually psychic."

"I have no way of knowing, do I? And if you don't mind my saying it, that's not even what you really want to know."

"Really? You know what I want to know?"

"Yes, Charlie, I do. You want me to tell you if you're going crazy or not. I don't think you are, but you're under tremendous strain, obviously."

She placed the milkshake cup on the table next to her chair, but she had trouble placing the bottom squarely on the table's surface—the cup reeled a bit on its cardboard circumference, a little bit like the way she herself had reeled when she had walked into the room.

She smiled. "Remember that night we drank Mississippi Mudslides?"

"The malted makes you think of that?"

"Yeah. That was fun, wasn't it?"

"It was."

"So tell me about it, Charlie."

"You don't remember? I'd stayed late one night at Berto's after my set two summers ago, drinking with the old manager, Jack, and with you and a couple of the other waitresses. By 1:00 A.M., this waitress named Erika, I think her name was, the one with the big hair, had whipped up some Mississippi Mudslides with Baileys, Kahlua, well vodka, and I think it was a carton of whipping cream. The air conditioning had been turned off, so the cool drinks had been a real treat, remember? By 1:45, we'd finished the drinks and placed the glasses at our feet, and everyone but you and I had gone home. By, I don't know, maybe 2:15, you and I stepped out into the alley to clear our heads just as it started to rain. It rained really hard for a while. But instead of heading back inside, we stayed under the eaves enjoying the cool air, and it really felt good, remember, the way the wind would whip little splashes of rain in our faces."

"Anything else?"

"Are you having trouble remembering things?"

"No, Charlie, you are."

"Like what?"

"I said something about how it's a 'palatial downpour,' and you laughed and said, 'No, it's torrential, not palatial.' "

"I don't remember that, but it sounds like something you would have said."

"Still would say," she said, and laughed. "And then you kissed me."

"Wait, what? I did?"

"You did. It was really nice."

"Must've been because with Alisa, it was always her making fun of *my* word choices."

She smiled. "I was a change of pace, wasn't I? And then when we were talking about how I get words wrong, I told you I have reverse dyslexia, remember?"

"No, what's that?"

"It's just something I made up, but I can read writing upside down just as easily as right side up, like if I'm sitting across from someone at a desk, it's like my own personal WikiLeaks, and I've always been incredibly fast at unscrambling, whaddya call them, those backwards words...?"

"Please don't say pachyderm. Palindrome."

"Yeah, palindromes. And I have a touch of synesthesia, too—remember how when I got back from Australia I told you all of the accents were colored blue?"

"Yeah."

"And so anyway, you'd kissed me, and like I said it was nice, but I said something like 'Don't you find it weird that I mix up words so easily but I can unscramble them like this?' " And then Mari-Angela attempted to snap her fingers, but missed, and there was the faint, disconcerting sound of flesh and bone damply flapping against flesh and bone. She flushed. "And then I said to you, and I remember this as clear as day, I said to you, 'Yeah, I guess I have a weird brain.' "

She looked at me, hard.

"So you said you had a weird brain."

"And has this occurred to you, Charlie, that this was the reason I 'came' to you in your dream less than a year later and said that there was something wrong with my brain?"

"And you're telling me that your coming to me the very night of the day you were diagnosed with a brain disease was just a coincidence?"

"That's not the point, Charlie."

"Quit saying my name, it sounds like my mother when she was mad at me."

"The point is that..."

"What about *your* parents?"

"Huh?"

"Do they know about your illness?"

"Yeah, I told them. My father. My mother hasn't spoken to me in years."

"Why?"

"Don't try to change the subject, Charlie. I'll give my parents this, they bought me great health insurance. And my dad and brothers and sisters are deeply upset, and as far as I know my mother is too, at least from what my dad tells me. But let me get back to my point. The point is that, there in the alley, drinking those Mississippi Mudslides, we stayed up until, I don't know, it was probably close to dawn, and then we went to Golden Nugget and had eggs over easy with hash browns and a huge plate of greasy corned beef hash, remember? It was delicious."

"Yeah, I remember that."

"And that whole night, it was like we shared some kind of intimacy, I told you all kinds of things about myself, but now in retrospect it was like talking to Colonel Data—"

"Commander Data."

"For all the effect it had on you. It was humiliating. A couple of nights later when you came in for your gig it was like nothing had even passed between us, do you remember? Except of course you went back to your usual half-assed flirting. I'd rather it'd been just sex and you not calling me, instead of what we had, and what happened afterward."

"I remember the night, yeah, but I don't remember acting unusually the next few days."

"Well, that's the point. You *didn't* act unusually the next few days. You acted like nothing had happened, I sent you some texts and you didn't even respond."

"Look, MariAngela, I'm sorry. I didn't know you were holding this over me. I guess I should've responded."

"You don't even understand my point."

"Do *I* get to have a point? I mean, *do* I? Because I know you're facing something far, far worse than I am, but I'm falling apart here, MariAngela. I even went to a psychiatrist and he told me—"

"I don't care what your psychiatrist told you."

"But this part of it is about me, because it's happening inside *my* head, not yours."

"It's *not* about you."

"What, you're gonna tell me it's about you, when you've been denying all along that you're doing or thinking anything to make yourself appear inside of my head?"

She appeared to think about this for a minute. "I guess what I'm saying is it's about us. Look, I mentioned my mother. She's a very brittle personality. Borderline personality is the technical term. She not only isn't speaking to me, she went for a long time not speaking to a few of my sisters, and some of my brothers, and my dad, and my dad's sister, and I guess this has given me this tremendous sensitivity to being ignored. And the more sensitive I am about it, the more it seems to happen to me. It's one thing for me to have sex with a guy or a girl and then I don't get a call afterward, I'll admit that's happened to me a few times, and it crushed me. My own fault, I should've known better. But you were worse."

"Because kissing is somehow more a commitment than fucking?"

"That shows just how totally you don't understand. You and your songwriter sensitivity, you faked me out. I thought we'd shared something. I thought that that kiss was a lot deeper than any sex I'd ever had. But it's just so fucking par for the course."

She stopped for a moment, as if she were out of breath. "I mean, in a sick way, I feel like I'm lucky, incredibly lucky, even to be having this argument with you right now, instead of being brushed off in a text message..."

"That's what Willa said."

"Refresh my memory. Who is this Willa?"

"Oh, this girl I met in Hawaii, after I broke up, well sort of during while I was breaking up with Alisa. It doesn't matter."

"No, it doesn't. Or worse, being brushed off *without* even a text message, the person just never responds at all. No one fucking notices me because they think all I am is a waitress so I don't matter, and that's why I didn't want to go to Hawaii with you, because after Alisa said no, I was a fucking afterthought."

"You were my very first thought after Alisa said no. That's not so bad, is it?"

"What, that Hawaii is a consolation prize to me for dying? That you, here, now, us, having this discussion finally, for the first time when we should have had it a long time ago, is also my consolation prize for dying, because you fucking know damn well that if I wasn't dying we wouldn't be having this conversation at all?"

"You have to understand that I've always had trouble confronting or dealing with angry women."

"Yeah, well I've had a similar problem, so maybe that's why we hit it off that one time in the alley. I get ignored, I just curl up in a ball and lick my wounds. But no more. No more." She laughed bitterly. "Now that it's too late, of course, I'm turning over a new leaf."

"I'm glad at least we're talking now. I had no idea."

"And then worst of all is that I'll be gone soon and I won't have anyone to talk to ever again. I'll just be fucking alone forever."

"But your brothers and sisters. I don't get it, MariAngela. You just made a reference to your mother not speaking to 'some' of your brothers and 'several' of your sisters. Just how many siblings do you have?"

"Twelve. I mean eleven. I'm the twelfth. Second to last in the birth order, so I guess that means I'm the eleventh *and* twelfth, if you know what I mean."

"Wow, how Catholic can you get!"

"Yeah, we were old school that way." She curled her right arm in front of her as if she were guarding an imaginary object. "This is how I had to eat at our family meals. All my brothers and sisters were always picking off my plate!" She laughed. "If I didn't protect my food, I would've starved."

"So where are they all now? I don't get it, aren't they visiting you?"

She uncurled her arm, stiffly, as if it cost her a great effort, and let it drop down by her side. "Not really. They have their own lives, they're scattered all over the country, kids of their own, I don't know. When there are so many people, I guess it's just the odds that someone or other might slip through the cracks, and that someone was me. And maybe I said some things to some of them when I was a teenager that I regret now, rebellious stuff, you know, to try to get noticed. So the good news is, I have my food all to myself now. Can I tell you something, Charlie? Do you know I gave myself a nickname years ago? I have to warn you that it's going to sound self-pitying, but like I said before, I really don't care, it's just what I feel so I'm gonna say it."

"So what was it?"

"I called myself 'the Great Exception.' Since I was one of the last kids, I was an afterthought with them, just like I was with you. School, I wasn't bullied, I was just a nobody—average grades, average everything. And then when I got out of the house, it was the strangest feeling, I don't know, it was like I'd talk to someone and they wouldn't even hear me, like I wasn't even there. Everyone has close friends, but I was the Great Exception. I don't know, if there was a big party or camping trip, for some reason they'd always forget to invite me until the last minute. Everyone who's halfway decent-looking has boyfriends, but I was the Great Exception. I knew for pretty damn sure that I was pretty, but they looked right through me. Sure, some of them would fuck me, but that was pretty much the beginning and the end. So at some point, I sort of switched to girls, but they weren't really any better. Everyone gets told by someone in their life that they love them. Everyone but me, Charlie."

"That's the title of one of my songs."

"Oh, I'm very aware of that, Charlie. Very aware. Do you understand what it is like to have never heard, not from your father, not from your mother, not from anyone, the words, 'I love you'? And now, this..." She indicated her own body with a laboriously slow sweep of her right arm. The Great Exception.

I was feeling hot and uncomfortable, so I took off my sweater.

MariAngela raised her eyebrows. "Wow, Charlie, you look skinnier than me. Are you trying to keep me company while I waste away?"

"I am." I had intended to say something light, but that was the way it came out, a simple and declarative "I am."

"I guess you've been really active," she said a little bitterly. "So this Willa you mentioned from Hawaii. You had a little thing with her, too?"

"Yeah, well she was this childhood friend, and she ended up reconnecting with me in Hawaii, but it's complicated, because she could have told me the truth about something that's plagued me all my life, and I only found out because I ran into her in Hawaii, and so could her mother—"

"This is the one who yelled at you once?"

"Yeah, and then my own mother didn't tell me the truth either, I just found out."

"One thing after another, huh? I mean, I'm like totally sympathetic, 'cause I'm not speaking to my own mother, or I should say she's not speaking to me, so I know how it can be. But..."

"I know, I know, Willa kind of overlapped with Alisa a little, so I guess I cheated, too."

"Whatever."

"I'm sorry, now's not the time to be talking about me."

"No, it isn't. And I'll tell you something else. You feel cheated? You feel betrayed? Huh? What about your betrayal of me?"

"Oh, c'mon."

"What, am I harping on this? Is that it? I get to harp, Charlie. This is my last chance, so I get to say what's on my mind finally, for the first time. And you? What did you do? Did you call this grade-school sweetheart yourself? Did you call the mother? No, you waited until this Willa tracked you down. In Hawaii! What was stopping you years before from asking her whatever it was that was troubling you? Why is your passivity my problem?"

"Yeah, why is it your problem? I mean, it's mine. I shouldn't have brought any of this up."

"Your passivity is my problem, too, because whether you like it or not we're connected. Look, one thing I've learned from all of this back and forth with you ever since that first time in Berto's is that, for whatever reason, we're stuck with each other. Would this have been my choice? Was this something I wanted? I don't know, if you had asked me when we had that night behind Berto's,

I would've said yeah, but after that, no way. But sometimes you just can't choose, you know? You had a fling with your childhood friend, okay, that's fine, whatever, you do what you have to do. But here you are, aren't you? Fight it all you want, we're together."

"MariAngela, are you trying to tell me you love me?"

She shrugged. "I know, fucked up, isn't it?" She closed her eyes, opened them again. "Like I said, sometimes you can't choose."

At this moment, a young Filipino nurse brought in MariAngela's lunch, and it distressed me to see that her meal consisted mostly of soup, vanilla pudding, and several glass dishes of orange and lemon Jello. It was no meal for an adult.

She looked at the food blankly for a moment. "Hold on, Charlie, before I eat, I have something for you."

There was a small tower of paperback books next to her bedside table. With great difficulty, she extracted a slim paperback from near the bottom of the pile, causing, in the process, all of the other books to slide in various directions—some behind the bedside table, some in front, and some under the bed. Of course I thought of Elizabeth—Bitty—knocking down her piles of books at Willa's facility.

"Shit. Fuck. It's like they all got together and said 'next time she knocks us over, let's all scatter in different directions to piss her off.' Anyway, I've been reading a lot of this guy." She handed me a paperback book. "Open it to where the second Post-it note is, okay? Thanks." She took the book back from me and recited. "Now listen: 'Take it that you have died today, and your life's story is ended; and henceforward regard what further time may be given you as an uncovenanted surplus, and live it out in harmony with nature.' "

"That's pretty nice."

"Yeah, 'nice' if you're just reading it because you happened to pick up his book or someone like me reads it to you, right? But it means something else entirely to me, now that I understand what it means in my bones."

"Who wrote it?"

"A Roman general, believe it or not. But that isn't even the part I wanted to read to you. That first quote? That was for me. Turn to the other Post-it note now." I complied.

"Okay, this one is for you, Charlie: 'Come back now to your sober senses; recall your true self; awake from slumber and recognize that they were only dreams that troubled you; and as you looked on them, so look now on what meets your waking eyes.' "

And with that she let the slender paperback slide out of her fingers, where it joined its slippery fellows on the floor. She smiled at me. "If you want to be nice to me, Charlie, you can start by getting me a new iPad."

# 5

*When* I got back to the rental house, I climbed up to the dormer and stooped down for a moment and checked out the dollhouse. The house was quieter than I'd ever heard it, and I missed, in an odd way, the family of missionaries off doing God knows what in the Philippines; I wished they were there with me, or that I was there with them, in the warmth and the sun. I looked at the yellow scribbles on the opposite wall and saw for the first time, in a child's hand, the words "Sweet Maggie," and I wondered if that was the name of the little girl who'd thrown the egg roll, or the name of a friend of hers, and I saw a crude green caterpillar and a few stick figures and tic-tac-toe games in yellow and orange, all of it covered in a swirl of concentric, complex yellow circles. I spent a good fifteen minutes considering this canvas as if it were a Cy Twombly or a cave painting from Lascaux.

That wisp of a thought I'd had the previous night was starting to form into something, but I still couldn't say what it was.

When I woke up the next morning, I ducked briefly into the dormer room and saw that the shutters, oddly enough, were now open, and there was a splash of orangey light on the opposite wall. It looked like the sun as seen through a slice of tangerine. It hadn't been an especially windy night, but it seemed possible that a gust of wind had popped the shutters open. It was also the case that the intricate hinging mechanism was affixed to a drywall anchor that was beginning to crumble, and perhaps the tiny doors were loosening, or on the verge of becoming detached. But I didn't spend a lot of time thinking about this. I got into the Lexus and ran some errands and picked up my unemployment check, because it was a Friday and I didn't want to be without my check over the weekend. And then late in the afternoon, I drove back to the South Side of Chicago, although this time not for the purpose of consulting with Dr. Nemerov.

Armed with Google Maps, and the knowledge that her last name was Halloran, I headed to a neighborhood called Beverly and, after a bit of trouble finding the place, I drove up to the house where MariAngela had spent her childhood.

It was a little cottagey place on a very typical South Side Irish street—neat, trim homes with neat, trim lawns. No butterflies, no sidewalk cracks, no chalk marks on the sidewalk, and no children to be seen. I noticed a sodden, rolled-up newspaper on the roof, lying diagonally half in and half out of the rain gutter, full of news that no one would ever read.

The trees in front of MariAngela's house looked nothing like the trees Willa and I had played under, nor the trees in front of my rental house that the missionaries' children must have played under, but as the sun began to set and all the colors started to run together, the trees, and the sidewalk, became indistinguishable from all of the ones I'd known in my life up until that point.

The windows in her house were dark, but I closed my eyes and tried to imagine MariAngela, in the half-awake, half-asleep stumbling state that is childhood, where we accept everything and understand nothing, playing with the multitude of brothers and sisters that would one day see her as less than even a stranger. I could almost see her, in there in the darkness, playing with a plastic train set that snapped together neatly, and I suppose that if she could have known what awaited her as an adult, she would have screamed out in horror. Thank God that she did not, and instead innocently played and unknowingly drifted to her fate.

I woke up very late the next morning, a Saturday, feeling more exhausted than if I had never slept at all. I lay in bed staring at the ceiling, feeling like a failure, until I had to urinate so urgently that I knew I had to get up and turn on the overhead light. But still I lay there and stared at the big, bare, old-fashioned light bulb and pretended that I really did have the power to turn light switches on and off. But then, as I imagined doing so, I started thinking that if I flipped the switch, the bulb would fill up with mud instead of light, and that even if I flipped the switch off again, the mud would keep on flowing, and then I suddenly realized that it wasn't mud at all but liquid shit, and I was terrified that the bulb was about to explode.

After I finally urinated and took a long shower, I felt a bit braced. I had a bit to eat and then I texted Willa. "U wanna talk? How's Bitty? She like the candy?? :)"

I stared at my phone, expecting an instantaneous response, but there was none.

I walked down the street to buy some orange juice for Sunday's breakfast and deliberately left my phone on the kitchen counter. When I came back, I ran to the phone to check for Willa's response, but there was still nothing.

That evening, I got on Facebook and sent Willa a message. "Hi Willa, I hope you're well. How's Elizabeth? How's everything with you? I've been thinking about you, and us, and everything that happened, and I guess I've come to the conclusion that maybe you could have handled things a little bit better. I'm sure I could have, too. But I mean specifically about letting me know about your sister and what happened to Elizabeth. Hope you don't see this as unreasonable. Send me a message when you get a chance and tell me what you think about all this."

After I sent this message, I went on Amazon and purchased an iPad for MariAngela that I had shipped straight to the Rehab Institute. Then I went back on Facebook and fooled around for a while longer, and a red "1" popped up in the "Messages" column, so I clicked through excitedly, but it was only a message from Bowen checking in on me. I reread my Facebook message to Willa, and my text message, and as I looked at the little smiley face I'd appended to my text, it suddenly occurred to me that the reason I'd intuited that Bitty was still alive was that, when I was in Beatrice's house in St. Louis, I'd seen in her hallway several photographs of a young woman with an odd, scrunched-up face, and I had known instinctively that her face was scrunched-up because she was brain-damaged, and that she was brain-damaged because she had fallen between a bed and a wall when she was an infant.

On Sunday evening, I blocked out some time to call my mother so that I could report to Dr. Nemerov the successful completion of at least one of my two tasks, but I kept on putting it off, and by 9:00, I found myself getting into my Lexus to take a little ride to the sports club where MariAngela had once been rumored to work.

This time, I didn't turn around in the parking lot of a Burger King, though I didn't have much more of an idea than I did in the last go-round why exactly I was there.

The club, which was called the ManCave, was rather handsome, I thought, dominated by blond wood walls; darker rosewood-looking, round, high-top tables; and, like every other sports bar I'd ever been to, twenty or so gargantuan flat-screen TVs, all of them tuned to either basketball, football, or mixed martial arts. I sat at one of the rosewood tables for about twenty minutes sipping a ginger ale and watching two MMA fighters involved in a complex entanglement on the mat that I had trouble following; I couldn't, at times, determine whose arms and legs were whose.

My waitress, who like all of the other waitresses was wearing a lavender polka-dotted halter top tied tightly under her breasts and a pair of white short-shorts, seemed faintly distant to me, no doubt annoyed that I hadn't ordered any wings or drinks. She was a leonine redhead with fine features but slightly flattened cheekbones that gave her a faintly bruised or offended look. There also were two other young women with trays of brightly colored tubes of liquor shots around their necks, wandering around the tables looking for takers. Though rather noisy, the place was mostly empty, possibly because there were no major games that evening and the MMA fight was a rerun, and most likely neither the shot girls nor the waitresses were making very much money at all. So after the match was over—I thought the guy on top was the winner, but it turned out that it was his hand, and not his opponent's on the bottom, which had frantically slapped the mat to indicate that his other arm was caught in an inextricable trap and about to be hyperextended or broken—I called the waitress over and ordered a Heineken draft. I drank it very slowly, and then more slowly still, as if it were a glass of pitch or darkest tar, and at one point, I saw the waitress eyeing me curiously, and then at some later juncture I thought I saw MariAngela at the back of the bar, so I got up to go to the washroom, but when I got back there, the young woman I'd seen looked nothing at all like her.

I went back to my table and resumed drinking my warm beer, and after finishing it, I merely sat. I reflected on the fact that I had never self-medicated; I drank rarely, never used illegal drugs, didn't gamble or indulge in pornography. Instead, I did nothing, and for some reason consciously imagined that my irritated waitress had just come up to me and said, with some considerable tartness, "You're a good little boy, aren't you, Charlie?" The remark stung, even though I had merely imagined it. I had never quite felt the way I felt at that moment, as if I were alive and of this Earth merely by dint of my breathing. It was a form of meditation, I think, though who meditates in a clamorous sports bar besides me, I don't know. I envied those two exhausted and flattened-out fighters I'd just seen, though I couldn't figure out why until I had driven halfway home. It was because they were engaged in something difficult and demanding that carried with it a definitive result; they were striving after something they and those who watched them deemed worthwhile and exciting; they were contending, battling, hammering, grappling, jabbing, and breathing very hard; they were doing something bloody and visceral, as MariAngela would say, and all too real; and they were fully and painfully alive.

It took me another week to finally call my mother. Or, to be more precise, it took me three days to finally dial her number and another four days of dialing for her to pick up. When she finally did, she sounded awful—croaky and weak.

"Mom, you okay?"

*"Lo siento, me hagarras en un mal momento."*

"Mom, can we please speak English here?"

*"Realmene no me siento bien. Tu crees que podemos hablar en otro momento?"*

"Mom? English?"

"English?" She said this like she had never heard the term.

"English. Please, Mom. My Spanish is pretty much gone."

"Okay. You okay?"

"I hope you remember more than the word 'okay.' Yeah, Mom, I'm basically fine. How about you?"

"I told you I'm not feeling well."

"What's wrong?"

"Nothing, who said anything was wrong?"

"Well, you did. In two languages."

"Oh, you know, it's the usual stuff. Your dad drives the taxi all of the time, so I have no one to help me."

"So how is Dad? How are his kneecaps?"

"His kneecaps are fine, as far as I know. Why would you ask this?"

"Oh, he was drunk and said they were shot off, and then he said they were going to *be* shot off, you know Dad."

"I know better than I would wish to. Yes, my dear, I know. He's had some trouble with some money he owes, but so far there's no shooting."

"Good. So what're you doing with your time?"

"Oh, this and that."

"Specifically which this and that?"

"Hah, hah, don't be so smart with me. How's your job?"

"My job is fine. I just don't happen to personally occupy it anymore."

"I'm not sure I understand what this means."

"Never mind. Listen, Mom, do you mind if I ask you something?"

"I mind. I mean, I *don't* mind, that kind of a saying always made me confused in English. So? What?"

"You and Dad, when we moved from Chicago to Buenos Aires for a few years, remember?"

"Of course I remember."

"So why? Why did we move there?"

"Why are you asking me this question now? I couldn't possibly remember this if you paid me a million dollars, why we moved back. Anyway, is this really a thing you want to talk about at this time in your life?"

"Not really, no. But I sort of feel like I need to know anyway."

"Well, I don't know what this means, this difference between you-don't-want-to but you-need-to business."

"Just trust me on this, okay?"

"Okay. Well, your father missed Argentina, that's all."

"What about what happened with Elizabeth?"

"Who?"

"The little girl down the street that I was supposedly babysitting."

"What about her?"

"You don't remember?"

"Honestly, I don't even know what you're talking about. Babysitting? So you were a babysitter, all the kids in the neighborhood did that, even the boys back then."

"Yes, but this was a special kind of babysitting. I wasn't old enough to do it, for one thing. And for another, the girl we're talking about, Elizabeth, fell behind the bed."

"Oh, her. I don't think I ever would've remembered that name. That was a sad thing."

"And her mom blamed me. Did you know that Elizabeth never actually died?"

"Of course, sweetheart. Who said she did?"

"A lot of people implied it."

"Silly, if she had died, there would have been a funeral. She was taken to a hospital, that's the last your father and I heard."

"But you never actually told me that she didn't die."

"Didn't I? Then your father must have."

"No, and if he were on the phone now, he'd probably say that *you* must've."

"Well, I'm not sure what difference it makes."

"The fucking difference is that I spent my entire adult life thinking that I'd been responsible for the death of a baby! And it turns out she didn't die, and it wasn't even my responsibility anyway!"

"I never said it was your responsibility."

"And *why* wasn't it? Did you tell me *why* it wasn't my responsibility? Did you tell me that Elizabeth and Willa had an older sister who was supposed to be watching Elizabeth?"

"I don't remember. It's possible I told you, and it's possible I didn't. Anyway, I repeat this to you, what difference does it make?"

"The difference it makes is that we moved away to Argentina, the place where old Nazi war criminals go to die, we *slunk* away, out of shame for what I supposedly did but in fact did not do. How do you think that's affected me growing up?"

"We most certainly didn't slunk away."

"Slink. The word is slink."

"Sorry, it sounds funny. I don't speak much English these days. We didn't *shlink.*"

"You're slurring, Mother. But let's accept that this is true. That leaves the other possibility, which is that Willa and Elizabeth's father, whatever his name was, paid you with one-way tickets to Buenos Aires to get you out of the neighborhood."

"I think his name was Herbert. And why would he have"—she searched for the right word—"supposedly done this?"

"To get the neighborhood to think it was me and not Beatrice who was responsible for Elizabeth's accident."

"Be-a-trish?"

"That's the older sister of Willa and Elizabeth. She was the one who was supposed to be watching Elizabeth."

"Darling, it's true that Herbert bought us tickets back to Buenos Aires. And it's also true that we left right after the accident with their baby. But back in those days, before, what do you call those computer travel agencies?"

"You mean like Orbitz or Travelocity?"

"Yeah, back then it took a while to buy airline tickets, and it took weeks of planning to travel internationally. We were still Argentine citizens, yes, but do you think we could have just packed up and moved in a day or two? The incident with the baby was just the final straw after the camel's back."

"What were the other straws? Mom? What else are you referring to?"

"Let me get a glass of water first." I knew she meant another glass of wine. There was a bit of clattering on the line, and then she returned.

"Okay, so what were we talking about?"

"Oh, come on, Mother. You know. Why did we move? If it wasn't Elizabeth, why did we move?"

"He broke a window."

"Who broke what window?"

"Your father. He threw one of his sculptures through the kitchen window of the Dunleavys and it landed right in the sink that was full of dirty dishes and broke some dishes, too."

"Why did he do that?"

"And the funny thing was, the sculpture broke, too. At least I thought it was funny. Enough with his goddamn sculptures, naturally with those stupid holes they're fragile, of course they'll break, though there's more of them than ever now. It's like they breed while I'm not looking, though how they do that with no 'thingies' I don't get."

"Okay. Mother. So why did he throw one of his sculptures through Isabelle Dunleavy's kitchen window? He was drunk, I assume?"

"Well, of course he was drunk. Herbert said some things to him he didn't appreciate."

"Hah, you mean criticizing his artistic talent?"

"You're joking, but that was part of it, too. He basically told your father that he sculpted 'lumps.' That was the word he used, lumps."

"Okay, so that was part of it. What was the other part?"

My mother sighed. "Oh, you know, just the jealousy."

"Which jealousy? What?" I suddenly was seized with a terrifying thought—that my father had had an affair with Isabelle Dunleavy, that he had gotten her pregnant, and that Elizabeth was my sister. That would explain so much—Beatrice's inattention, the sudden flight to Buenos Aires. I said, shakily, "Do you mean Father and Isabelle?"

My mother laughed. "No, your father had no interest in such matters. You're too young to remember, but he'd retire every evening to the backroom to work on his lumps with the holes and drink. Women? Hah. He also had a hole where that was. And with *me?* Hah!"

"So you mean..."

"Look, sweetie, all I mean is that Herbert was lonely and maybe doing without a lot of affection because the pregnance, the pregnancy, of Elizabeth was unplanned. And maybe Isabelle didn't have a lot of time for him. So he made a little, I forget the expression...an attempt, you know?"

"He made a play for you?"

"Yes, he went after me so to speak. He kissed me a couple of times."

"And you kissed him back?"

"Yes. You're an adult now, I can be honest with you. I was very, very interested in Herbert, he was a handsome man if you remember."

"How would I remember that? I can't even picture what he looked like."

"And he was an insurance executive." She slurred and etiolated the word "insurance" so alarmingly that I was afraid she was about to drop the phone and pass out. "I felt he was doing something with his life. He was very, very attractive, and he dressed beautifully, not like most American men. So we kissed a few times, and your father found out and he broke the window."

"So why would this lead to Herbert paying for a flight back to Argentina? Wouldn't he have wanted you around?"

"Well, the problem was that when your father smashed the window with the sculpture, Isabelle asked, 'Well, why is this man's broken sculpture in my sink?' " And one thing led to another, and she found out about the affair..."

"Affair? What affair? I thought you said it was just kissing."

"It was, I swear. That's all it ever was. But you kiss another woman's husband and that's an affair, don't you think? So she threatened to leave Herbert and take the girls with her, and he loved those little girls, and he couldn't bear the, you know, the *humiliation,* so he begged with her and said he'd never see me again, and she insisted that they move out of the neighborhood, and that's when he came up with the idea of moving *us* out instead. It was easy, your father was unhappy and had wanted for a long time anyway to move, and so for the price of a few plane tickets, I was out of his hair, the expression is, and then when the accident happened with the baby, well, the timing couldn't have been better, if you know what I mean."

"Oh, I know what you mean. Better for everyone, except for me. So it all came down to something I supposedly did and that covered up the affair and everything else."

"I wish I could put a better way of saying on it, but that's what happened."

I remembered very little about Buenos Aires. I remembered my father, back when he looked more like a matador than a bull, taking me for walks along an endless avenue of antiques and glassware and beaded purses and little brass Buddhas and bric-a-brac where, on weekends, he would sometimes set up a table to sell his sculptures. I used to stoop low in front of the table and peek at him through the holes in the sexless reclining figures, and he'd wink wearily back. And I remember an outdoor café—really just a raised concrete platform with a rough metal grill and a dozen or so metal tables—where my father bought us a couple of steak sandwiches, soaked with a green-flecked spicy sauce that I didn't like, and a beer for him and a Coke for me. He tore off hunks of bread and meat from both sandwiches, focusing on the parts that hadn't been befouled by the spicy sauce, and fed them to me one at a time, as if I were four years old and not eight. I loved him a little bit, I think, but it all is very hazy.

And I remember the Catholic elementary school for English speakers I'd attended. All of my classmates, like me, were the children of expatriates, but none, as far as my eight-year-old brain could comprehend it, were the children of exiles nor exiles themselves. The nuns weren't too bad, and in fact this particular order had a real fondness for animals, so I remembered with pleasure the guinea pigs in our classroom and the small flock of peafowl in the concrete play yard that was fenced in by an elaborate black ironwork gate. For reasons I can't remember, I would fight my male classmates constantly, stalking them into the corners and throwing punches from every angle or wrestling them to the ground. The peacocks would scuttle around self-consciously and act a little nervous, but my classmates, even the ones who were bigger than me, seemed at once terrified and impressed. I broke one boy's collarbone when I threw him to the ground, and never heard a word about it from him or his parents. I broke my own collarbone twice, both times in bicycling accidents when I was much older, and never regarded either break as a form of retribution. I wasn't the least bit ashamed of being the skinny little bully that I was.

If I had told all this to Alisa, especially after she'd punched me out in Hawaii, she would have simply snorted in disbelief.

And I remember most of all a miniature city of crumbling concrete tombs that I wandered around in one sunny early-autumn day, and I must have been there with either my mother or my father, but I remember neither one, only how immense this aboveground cemetery complex was, and how rectilinear and claustrophobic were the narrow, indistinguishable avenues. Most of the tombs were fashioned like miniature churches, chapels, and homes, and at one time had been extravagant, a way for the wealthy to compete even after death. The one- or two-story tombs were far too tall for an eight-year-old, and in fact were more confusing than an actual skyline filled with skyscrapers, because they were all pretty much the same height so there were no reference points on the horizon, and the grid never varied, so there were no reference points on the ground either, except for the feral cats that sunned themselves in the middle of one walk or another.

It was impossible not to get lost.

Once I did lose my bearings, I discovered that while the avenues were identical, each tomb was as idiosyncratic as the souls that resided within, though this was something I only felt and was far too young to actually understand. The tiny cathedrals and stage-set homes, which looked like narrow slices of real rooms, had been decorated as the reliquaries they were, with elaborate iron grilles that reminded me of the black iron fence that protected the peacocks, and behind the grilles, cracked glass windows and double doors that were padlocked but sometimes swung partway open anyway, and behind the windows small altars and empty candlesticks and artificial flowers in green glass vases and elaborate filigreed crosses and terrifying crucifixes and ornately framed, hand-colored photographs of the doomed individuals within, and, in the center of each display, an elaborate coffin with lion's head handles and the like, splashed with orange and yellow light from the small panels of stained glass on the sides and back of the tombs. And over all of this original decoration in memory of the dead was a second layer of decoration that replicated the process of dying itself, crumbled leaves from that autumn and the one before, and concrete dust and flaking rust from the tombs themselves, and shattered glass where the windows had been broken by stones or gusts of wind, and bits of dried paint, all of it connected in random fashion by trembling bits of cobweb, and then a third layer that replicated the resurrection, ivy and blue-green moss that carpeted the concrete and skinny weeds that sprouted out of the cracked and crumbling mausoleums, around the iron globes, through the glass, and into the coffins themselves.

After what seemed like an hour of wandering and worrying among the dusty avenues, but probably was no more than fifteen minutes, I finally figured out where I was. I'd realized that, by looking at the decorations on top of many of the tombs, the Pietàs and the saints in the stone robes, I could triangulate my way, through trial and error, back to one particular tomb near the entrance that had a thick, rusted iron spigot on the side and, underneath the spigot, a particular striped tabby I remembered from when I first arrived.

I probably would have found my way out long before if I hadn't kept my eyes nervously averted for much of the time from the mausoleums, having discovered that some of them had lower levels that could be glimpsed through the shattered glass and half-open iron doors. These levels were incomplete ur-basements and cellars that ended in darkness after a single half-turn of a spiral staircase, at the end of which rested a casket that had been placed there on purpose or slid down over the years from its original ground-level resting place. One of these lower-level tombs, I'd fleetingly thought, must have held the bones of Elizabeth.

And that was why, I concluded as I'd stroked the warm fur of the striped tabby, I'd been left there to find my own way out.

# 6

"So, did you call your mother?" Dr. Nemerov asked at my next visit.

"Yeah, I did. Just the other day. She claimed we left for Argentina because she was having some kind of half-assed affair with Willa's father, not because of Elizabeth."

"And what about MariAngela? Have you seen her?"

"Yes, but don't you want to talk about my mother and Elizabeth?"

"I want to talk about what you want to talk about. But the dreams you keep on having are about this MariAngela, so I think we should stay on that. Have you had any new ones?"

"No."

"So what else have you been up to?"

"Not much. Went to a sports bar and watched some guys rolling around punching each other in the face."

"Ha, sounds like something I'd enjoy if that was something I'd enjoy."

"And I took a little drive and saw the street where MariAngela grew up."

"Good. That could help. Have you asked her yet?"

"This time you mean MariAngela, right?"

"Yes, of course, who else would I mean?"

"Well, yes, in real life, I have. Just not in a dream."

"Charlie, you know the moments when you first fall asleep? I'm referring to that instant where you're still technically awake, but your thoughts go from being solid eggs to suddenly cracking and then all of a sudden you've got a swirl of gloppy yolk and sticky white and once it's out of the shell you can't put it back in, and that's your dream, you're asleep? If you follow the metaphor, what I'm asking you to imagine is the instant the shell cracks. Okay?"

"Okay." I closed my eyes and actually imagined the egg swirling around, and Dr. Nemerov's voice was so soothing that I kept them closed.

"This moment, when the egg cracks, this is called a fugue state, a brief instant during which you can acknowledge that things are not making sense and that you're about to be asleep. Now normally, when we make a point of acknowledging this, that conscious acknowledgment snaps us back to a waking state for just a moment. But some people are able to recognize that they're dreaming and go ahead and slip into a dreaming state with the knowledge that this is precisely what they are doing. I have heard of one patient of one of my colleagues who says, 'As soon as the people I see in my mind start looking like old, worn-out silk scarves with holes in them, I know I'm dreaming.' "

I couldn't help but think of my father's dream objects with their holes in them. I opened my eyes, and there was Dr. Nemerov. He was wearing a green-and-blue plaid pair of overalls over a pink T-shirt.

"So I would like you to try for the next couple of weeks, as you feel yourself slipping into a dream state, to tell yourself to keep on dreaming but to summon MariAngela and to speak with her in your dreams."

"But even if I do this, how will I remember the next morning?"

"Simple. Every night when you're ready to go to sleep, set your cell phone alarm for a half an hour after you lay your head on the pillow. Is that about how much time it usually takes you to fall asleep? Twenty minutes? Okay, twenty minutes. Then, every night, focus on summoning her to one location. Make it the same location every time, your house, a park, whatever."

"I have a location."

"Okay. So you wake up after twenty minutes, and either you remember MariAngela in your dream or you do not. If you remember it, scribble down what happened on a sheet of paper by your bed. If you don't, no big deal, just go back to sleep—or try the experiment again that same night if you want, and set your alarm for another twenty minutes."

"If MariAngela comes to me and I wake up after twenty minutes, I don't think I'll need to write it down. I think I'll definitely remember."

"Good. And then you come and tell me, and we'll figure this out together. Are you ready to set up a regular schedule of visits?"

"Yeah, but I don't have my calendar on my phone. Can I just call you in a couple of days?"

He nodded. "Go in peace, my boy."

I felt as if I were skinny enough at this point to slither down the shower drain, and I was terrified, so I did exactly as Dr. Nemerov suggested. Every night, I went to bed with my cell phone in my right hand, and as I felt myself drifting off to sleep—usually at the moment when my cell phone started to slip from my hand—I struggled to bestir myself and set the alarm for twenty minutes later. Sometimes the effort of setting the alarm would so disturb my sleeping patterns that the effort was a waste, and I would suffer insomnia for an hour or two. Sometimes I would stumble out of bed and shuffle downstairs to the couch and read an old book for a while, uncomprehendingly. Just as often, the alarm would go off, and I would automatically mash the button to shut it off in my half-sleep without giving it a second thought.

But one night, when the alarm went off, I awakened and lay there in the silent bedroom where once Alisa and I had shared a bed, and I kept my eyes closed, though I was fully awake, and remembered the dream I'd had when I'd first slipped into sleep: It had been of Felix the Cat in all of his flat, black-and-white glory, swimming about in great circles in a blue-green sea of pleasantly slippery, little white eggs, like tapioca or milky caviar, and I knew, though there was no "narrator" to tell me so, that these were the eggs of a young female human being, waiting to be fertilized. Felix had been grinning like an old roué as he'd done his little flips and dives among the shiny white eggs. I scribbled it down in my bedside notebook: "Felix swimming eggs."

Interesting, but it told me nothing—except, perhaps, that I'd been influenced by Dr. Nemerov's description of the very earliest moments of dreaming as resembling a runny egg escaping from an eggshell.

A few days passed, and then I had a second memorable dream at the twenty-minute mark. In this one, there were no human beings at all, just a sidewalk, but it kept on shifting, so that at first it was at the height of my feet and then, like a magic carpet, at eye level and then at the level of the treetops. And as the ribbonlike pavement rose and fell, it gathered to itself encrustations of objects that I must have been recalling from my childhood: black tar and Black Jack gum; the little wooden sticks called "punks" we used to burn for their sweet smell, and the red and green "caps" filled with minuscule pinches of gunpowder that we'd put in our toy guns or strike with rocks for the tiny bang and satisfying gun-smoke smell; spittle and blood from banged-up noses; crushed bits of limestone and ancient seashells from the last visit of the glaciers; an oyster-shell-shaped chip in the cement; twigs and leaves; little square red and green, jewel-like Charms, and white peppermint Lifesavers; squashed fireflies and water bugs; wadded-up Fruit Stripe and Chum Gum; potbellied, meat-eating robins hopping around for worms; little black ants swarming a chunk of chocolate-covered coconut candy; and, in a sidewalk crack, a single, much-larger brown ant, struggling with crumbs amidst crumbling leaves.

The Felix dream and the sidewalk dream seemed to be two steps along a path that was taking me somewhere I needed to go. I thought of Bea, using her Johnnie Walker Red and Edgar Allan Poe to take her someplace dark and far away; I was doing something similar, I thought, but headed, I hoped, in a different direction, closer instead of farther away, and toward something that might actually do me or someone some good for once.

I finally heard back from Willa at about this time. It was a chatty text about Bitty and her job and some new restaurants in Seattle. She didn't in any way address the issues I'd raised in my previous text, and for this I felt, oddly, relieved, as if I'd dodged some sort of bullet. From that moment forward, we continued from time to time to text and to message each other on Facebook, but we never again talked about what had happened between us.

I guess I didn't care too much one way or another anymore because "what had happened" got lost in the shuffle of what was currently happening; I had received some very good news. The owner of Glennis, whom I'd met at the deposition, had taken a liking to me and called about possibly bringing me "back into the fold," as she'd put it, and so I became excited at the prospect and put aside my dream work and assorted other spelunking for a few days to research the agency and prepare for my interview in two weeks' time. But I felt worried, as well, because I was indeed a "good boy" and was horrified when I contemplated the prospect that people who saw me on the street, skeletal and unshaven, would think I was a bum, or mentally ill, or homeless. I wanted a new job, and I wanted to be "in the fold" like everyone else, but I couldn't accomplish either if I wasn't able to eat.

So I plucked my cell phone out of my pocket to make another appointment with Dr. Nemerov, but just as I did so, my phone buzzed.

It was Dr. Nemerov.

"Oh, my God, I was just about to call you."

"Hi, Charlie. I'd like to pretend I knew that, but you were just on a list of patients I wanted to check up on. You were on the top of the list."

"Really, why?"

"Because you're so mentally sick."

I don't know why, but I just laughed, and Dr. Nemerov laughed too. "Nah, just kidding. You told me you'd call me in a couple of days so you could check your calendar and we could set up a regular schedule, remember?"

"Oh, shit, yeah, I forgot. I'm kind of panicked because I got a possible job offer, and I need to get healthy before then. I can't walk in for an interview looking like a wraith. I don't know what to do, and I'm really upset."

"Well, it helps not to flail. Force yourself to eat something, even if it's only a bag of pistachios, and I'll squeeze you in tomorrow night. In the meantime, I want you to think about the image of a tree reflected in a lake, as Maugham discusses somewhere in one of his writings. Okay? Maugham says the reflected tree cannot exist without the actual tree, but the actual tree, needless to say, is not in any way affected by its reflection. So the question is, do you agree that the same applies to your human consciousness?"

"I'm not even sure what you mean."

"That's exactly why I want you to think about it."

I came early for the appointment but wasted much of the time evading what was really on my mind. I complained that I'd never heard back from Reese "the Knack" Nakamura about another gig at the Palmyra; I told old stories about Gilbert and his callous cluelessness; I reported, truthfully, that I'd eaten a bag of pistachios and drunk some orange juice; I told Dr. Nemerov that I was ashamed that I'd not picked up my guitar in months. After about a half hour of this, he made a waving motion with his hand and said, "I told you on the phone not to flail, but I didn't mean you should go all the way to the other extreme and just drift."

And then he said something interesting.

"You know, Charlie, when I called you yesterday, it was purely coincidence that you were about to call me. But at the risk of stating the obvious, there's something about our miraculous communications tools that makes it easier than it's ever been to dodge people. The more tools we have, the more means of telling people to 'fuck off' we have, right? So I'm going to step out of my psychiatrist role for just a moment and be a human being, and admit to you that I picked up the phone to call you because I'd put a lot of effort into our first few sessions and I was frankly hurt and pissed off that you hadn't called me back like you said you would to set up a regular schedule of appointments."

"I'm sorry, that really wasn't my intention. I just feel scattered."

"I know, don't worry about it. You're not the only one who's scattered. We're not going to be around to see if I'm right, but I think in a couple of hundred years, the intuitions that we call 'vestigial' that we once all possessed when we were still half-animals and lacked the powers of speech to communicate with each other verbally will have returned in full force to become part of our daily lives, because we'll have walled ourselves off with so many devices that make ordinary face-to-face communication unnecessary that we're going to devolve ourselves back into that half-animal way of communicating in order to make ourselves understood. Every time I see a robin on the lawn, cocking his head at the grub beneath the grass, I think of you and me and all of us after the power goes out."

During the nearly two weeks before my Glennis interview, I resumed my dream work. One night, long after I'd shut off the twenty-minute alarm with no results, I felt a cold sensation in the middle of my forehead, and I awakened and checked my cell; it was 3:45 A.M. I thought, improbably, that the tiny shutters had popped open again and that the cold air had somehow wended its way into my room and chilled me. But it was only my forehead, or rather one tiny patch just north of my nose, that was cold. And then it came back to me: I had just dreamed that my one-armed predecessor, or some version of him, for the face in my dream was predictably vague and distorted, had placed his hook hand against the spot where the bridge of my nose touched my forehead.

It hadn't been a threatening gesture, but rather an admonitory one, it seemed to me.

I knew exactly why he had appeared. I rolled out of bed, right then and there instead of going back to sleep, and popped open the miniature shutters, and then I went back to sleep and waited for my next dream. And as I lay there, I decided that I understood—well, more or less—Dr. Nemerov's question about the tree. A tree is not affected by its reflection, no, of course not, but a human being is, in whatever form that "reflection" might manifest itself.

The next dream came a few mornings later. I awakened at the moment the alarm went off and lay there in the dark, staring at the ceiling, and I could remember my dream with perfect clarity. I was walking through a multilevel shopping center in the form of a gigantic full-service gas station (which is to say that the garage where the cars were repaired contained dozens of interesting shops on either side, and the gas station's office contained still more) and it made me think of a gigantic indoor antiques mall that had been located somewhere along that long avenue where my father used to exhibit his sculptures and where he'd bought me the steak sandwich once and torn off the little bits that weren't contaminated by the spicy sauce.

Somewhere in this gas-station-cum-mall, there was a shop that sold "bumper pool" tables, the kinds with knobby obstacles scattered among the holes, and a gaucho type with a green scarf around his neck was demonstrating his mastery of the sport, which morphed into a kind of Skee-Ball game, except that at the very top of the game, where the smallest hole was, another man stuck his head through and caught the cue balls in his mouth and spit them back at the gaucho. I was merely an observer in the dream, and heeding Dr. Nemerov's instructions, I managed to become minimally conscious, enough so that I could look past the absurd physical details and focus instead on my feelings, which, as I recalled them the following morning, were akin to those I experienced when watching, say, professional golf: a kind of abstracted admiration for a specialized skill that was far greater than mine.

Then an efficient-looking American man in a short-sleeved

white shirt and tie came around, and he made it clear to everyone involved in this game that he was a "bumper pool professional," and in my dream, I found it exciting to anticipate him "showing up" the Argentine players. But large heaps of wrinkled laundry had suddenly appeared at the base of the table, and there were dirty socks and other odds and ends hanging from the Skee-Ball holes, and he became engaged in an irritated effort to clear all of the clothes away.

Then the American turned to me and said, "Why is it that cats and dogs get to eat such savory foods but all horses get is straw and oats?"

I didn't know what this meant.

The next day when I visited MariAngela, she was wearing sunglasses again.

"Do you want me to shut the curtains?"

"No, keep them open, please. I'm feeling okay."

"Really?"

"Yeah, headache-wise."

"And otherwise-wise?"

"The same. Maybe worse. I don't know." She sounded irritated. "What did you want to talk about today?"

"The usual, I guess, if that's ok with you."

"That's fine, but I think you want to actually *talk* about something, Charlie."

"How do you know that?"

"Don't ask me, I just know."

"Okay. I mean, if you're sure. There *is* something, MariAngela. I've been discovering a lot of things over the past few months, and as far as I'm concerned, one of the most important is to ask follow-up questions. Okay? Well, there's a follow-up question I've been needing to ask you for a long time. When you came into my head and told me to wake up Alisa to tell her something, what was it? Don't bother telling me that you don't know what I mean, because you and I talked about it on the phone, you were out with your girlfriend, and you said, yeah, you wanted to talk to Alisa, 'but it was nothing important.' Well, I call bullshit on that one. So tell me what it was that you wanted to tell her, would you please?"

She was silent for a moment. "Charlie, I just wanted to tell her to be nicer to you."

I thought about this for a moment. "Did you think she wasn't very nice to me?"

"C'mon, Charlie, she was a bitch on wheels, you know that."

"She had a lot of facets, like anyone else."

"Yeah, well one of those facets kept on saying demented things to you. Is that the right word? Where someone puts you down?"

"Demeaning."

"That's it. Demeaning. Insulting. Why did you put up with it?"

"Well, obviously I didn't, at least not much longer, because I'm not with her anymore. But why didn't you just tell me?"

"I did, Charlie. That night in the alley. That should've been enough for you, and now it's too late."

Fortunately, my interview at Glennis went well, and they offered me a position as an account manager—a bit of a demotion from junior partner, but I was happy to take it.

I had spent far too long with Gilbert and had become used to the contingent, churn-and-burn uncertainty of it all; the ugly, putty-colored cubicles; the low-level dread; the way that clients would come and go seemingly overnight, usually because we were understaffed, or because Gilbert engaged in highly theoretical "strategic" cogitations about "disintermediation" and "securitization" and "monetization" instead of focusing on building his clients' revenues, or, just as often, because Gilbert would invite a client out for a "friendly" lunch and then bill the client $350 an hour for his time, not neglecting the fifteen-minute increment when they retrieved their coats from the coat-check and stood on the sidewalk saying goodbye. It wasn't all that much better at Alisa's agency—if indeed she were still working there.

But Glennis was a revelation. Their Chicago offices were in a converted loft building, formerly a cannery, in the River North area, and the whole enterprise reeked of confidence and professionalism. I was assigned three accounts in my first hour of my first day of business, and by the end of my second day, I knew what their needs were, what our strategic goals on their behalf were, who my partners were in achieving these strategic goals, and, most important, that all three had been clients for a minimum of three years each.

What all this meant was that I had very little time for either wakeful dreaming or sleeping dreaming, and no particular interest in fishing for pork on the Volga or playing bumper pool in an Argentine gas station. I stopped visiting Dr. Nemerov and had no time, either, for Bowen, or Diane, or for anyone but MariAngela, whom I'd started visiting every day after work. And I started eating again—lunch with my new colleagues at first, because I didn't want them to think anything was wrong, and then, after I'd forced a few Thai curries and Italian subs down, I found myself eating dinner again, and breakfast too, and actually enjoying it.

My irritable bowel symptoms had disappeared.

About a month after I'd begun the new job, MariAngela walked into my brain again for the last time as a living person. This time, for the first time, there was an actual background: Instead of appearing out of darkness, she walked down the sidewalk. (Which sidewalk? I couldn't say—it could have been the one outside the rental house, or the one where I once gave the green gumball-machine ring to Willa, or the one outside of MariAngela's childhood home, or another one entirely. More likely—and needless to say—it was all of them at various instants.)

MariAngela joined me where I was sitting with my back against the old elm tree with the fantastically gnarled exposed roots that looked like the knobby knees of a kneeling person perched atop another kneeling person. There was just enough space among the complicated roots for a child's body to squeeze in, back against the broad trunk, and though I was already seated there, Mari-

Angela magically slid in next to me, and we snuggled together for a moment.

Once again, as with the sidewalk itself, the figure next to me shifted from MariAngela to Willa, and then from Willa to the little girl who actually lived across the street from the rental house, and then to the little girl who'd thrown the eggroll, and finally back to MariAngela herself. As if to prove who she was, MariAngela lifted her light shirt and displayed for me four small moles, or, as we used to call them, "beauty marks," in a diagonal line on her ribs. They looked like an excerpted portion of a constellation. At this point, she "settled" into MariAngela and did not change again.

She pulled her shirt back down and said, "I want to remind you of the things we did under this tree. One time when we were really little, we got ahold of a teaspoon, and we each took turns tasting dirt. Remember? It was cold and sweet, but gross, and we decided that that was the flavor of earthworm poop. And then we got a package of Charms candies and buried some of them under the tree, who knows why, maybe we thought it would make the soil even sweeter, but then we ate the rest, and we were talking about if we would be willing to endure the worst possible pain any human being could feel for just one second if it meant we then could eat the most delicious candy ever invented, and we both agreed we would. And then on a different day, we also buried one of your mom's teapots. And there was another time when I asked you why there had to be money and why everything in the world couldn't just be free, and you tried to explain it to me."

And then she looked at me very intently in my dream.

And she said, "I need you to stop fighting this."

I said, "What?"

And she said, "The earthworms."

And then we found ourselves in the backyard of my childhood home, and it was completely filled, trunk to trunk to trunk, with elm trees. MariAngela lifted her arm, and all of the complicated roots suddenly disentangled from the earth and shot like rockets up to the sky, raining down clumps of sweet (for now we knew that it was sweet) black dirt.

MariAngela lifted her arm upward again, and I followed her gaze up into the sky, where all of the uprooted trees were floating there, branches and roots trailing in the gentle breeze. And then she said, "Look for me."

As I thought about this dream the next day, I realized that all of the memories that MariAngela had related—the tasting of the dirt with teaspoons, the burying of the Charms candies, the naive discussion of money—had been things that occurred between Willa and me when we were very little. And yet, for the first time, I didn't automatically think that the knowledge and the memory of these events were mine alone, but rather that MariAngela herself had somehow, in her repeated entries into my brain, made these memories hers.

Our roots were entangled.

Not long after this last dream, MariAngela was transferred to a different and much-smaller room. She was no longer able to use a three-pronged cane for more than brief trips to the bathroom and now spent her days in a small wheelchair, though not yet one of the high-tech ones that would be coming later. Along with the new room and new seating arrangements came a new nurse, whom MariAngela was chatting with when I arrived. She seemed to be chipper, and I told her this. She and the nurse laughed.

"What's so funny?"

"Hey, Charlie, sorry. This is my new friend Ludmilla."

The nurse nodded and said in a lugubrious voice, "Hello, Mr. Alessandro. MariAngela has told me all about you."

MariAngela added, "Ludmilla is going to be pretty much my constant companion during the day. She'll help me eat and go to the bathroom and stuff. Sometime beginning in the next couple of weeks probably, she's gonna have to start siphoning my spit too." She laughed. "Sorry about that, Ludmilla! By the way Charlie, did you know I almost was a nurse myself?"

"You? No."

"Yeah, that's why I first started waitressing at Berto's and working at the sports bar. I took a year off, before I knew you, to build up some tuition. I was thinking about neonatal intensive care, but I couldn't handle all that chemistry stuff in my first year, and I just ran out of time and money and energy and everything, so I went back to being a, you know, 'professional waitress.' Anyway, we were laughing because we were just talking about 'doctor talk,' like 'sharp as a tack' means just on the edge of full-blown Alzheimer's, and 'out and about' means shuffling along the corridor attached to an aluminum pole, and 'chipper' means you should be suicidally depressed but somehow you manage to be in a good mood anyway."

Ludmilla said, "Actually, I don't think we discussed this word 'chipper.' " She was a tall, middle-aged, rather dour woman with a slight Russian accent. She had a gray knitted shawl wrapped around her even though it was a warm day for March. She cast a worried glance at MariAngela. "We weren't really talking about it in terms of MariAngela."

MariAngela said, "Don't worry, I'm really fine. And that's another one, by the way, 'fine.' 'Oh, I'm fine,' or 'it's perfectly fine.' It just means it's one step away from being shit."

Ludmilla looked slightly stricken, and it was clear that she and MariAngela had been talking about these terms in the context of other patients, not MariAngela. I said to her, "Listen, it's just fine. I mean, *really* fine. Listen, would it be okay if MariAngela and I talked privately for a little while?"

Ludmilla said, "This would be okay. Just ring if you need anything."

After she left, I said, "So is the wheelchair...I mean, is it OK?"

"Yeah, I'm just, you know, rolling with it. So to speak."

"I had another one of those dreams last night, and you told me to stop fighting it."

MariAngela smiled. "It's funny. I have a therapist now, along with the new nurse and all the other cool stuff. I mean, a mental-type therapist. And he told me the same thing. Given the nature of my disease and its course and outcome, he said more or less to stop fighting it too. Just to go with the flow and accept what's coming, because the panic comes from fighting it, like when you're drowning and your arms are all flailing and you're trying to grab the water or the air with your hands but there's nothing to hold on to, eventually you just realize it's pointless, and you let the water flow in and then you die. So that's what I'm going to do, and that reminds me of a favor."

"Okay. I have a favor for you too, speaking of coincidences."

"Okay, you tell me yours first."

"MariAngela, could you lift your shirt for me?"

She smiled. "You could have had plenty of opportunities to see me naked after our alley encounter. Too late now, Charlie."

I knew she meant this more or less lightheartedly, and I tried to answer in the same vein. "Oh man, I never even got to see you in a halter top at the sports club!"

MariAngela looked puzzled. "ManCave? No, I was never a waitress there. I worked there sometimes as one of the shots girls to pick up some extra cash when I was short on rent." She shrugged. "So why do you want me to take off my shirt now?"

"Not off. Just lift it up, halfway. I want to look at your ribcage."

She shrugged again and lifted her blue cotton shirt. There, on the left side of her body, were four little moles arrayed diagonally across her ribs like an excerpted portion of a constellation.

"I saw those marks last night in my dream. You were a little girl at the time, and I wasn't 100 percent sure if it was you or another little girl, but then you told me it was you and you lifted your shirt to show me those exact same beauty marks, in exactly the same pattern."

MariAngela just stared at me.

Then, after a moment, she said, "Even if you ever came to the sports bar, you couldn't have seen this there. We shots girls wore these spangly T-shirts. I'm not the bare-belly type anyway, too much, in public."

Of course, she was right. The shots girls wore midriff-covering

T-shirts to distinguish them from the waitresses in their halter tops. I remembered that quite clearly from the night I'd been there, and I recalled the segmented trays of rattling test tubes they carried in front of them with straps around their shoulders. The tubes were filled with brightly colored schnapps and liqueurs and vodkas that looked like fluorescent lime and cherry Fla-Vor-Ices. When a patron called one of the shots girls over, she'd do a little "shimmy" and then tilt the guy's head back and pour the test tube full of alcohol down his throat. This was what MariAngela had done—a moderately humiliating job, I suppose, but whether more so for the patron or the server, I couldn't say.

We were both silent for a long time. I wished for a moment that I was one of those clueless tourists freezing in the winter wind as they waited to get into the deep-dish pizza place down the street, but then I pushed that out of my mind and focused on MariAngela.

"So what happens now?"

"Look, I'm on thin water here, and I need you to help me."

"Thin ice."

"No, I meant exactly what I said. I'm in desperate need, and whether you asked for it or not, and whether I asked for it or not, I need something from you."

"And what is that?"

"Well, before I get to that, let me tell how it's going to happen. I'm moving back to my apartment soon, but not for a particularly good reason. Basically, as long as I have nursing care, there's nothing more they can do for me in a 'facility,' for lack of a better term, so I might as well be comfortable for the next eight months or a year or however long it takes."

"Well, at least you'll be at home."

"Yeah, and with Ludmilla. So anyway, at some point later this year, after the suctioning-the-spit part gets underway, I'm not going to be able to talk to you anymore, not with actual words. And I'll be in a high-tech wheelchair, and what they'll do is, they implant a chip in my forehead so I can tell the computer where I want to move and stuff. Okay? But then later, even the high-tech shit isn't going to help, because I won't be able to breathe any more. That's the point where I gotta make the decision if I wanna be put on a ventilator, which really does nothing but allow me to exist, period. I'll never be off it again and I'll die soon enough anyway. So let's say I don't want the ventilator, I'm gonna start having trouble breathing at night, and then trouble sleeping at night because I'm gasping for air, and then I probably have only a few weeks to live at that point, and Ludmilla's great and all, but at some point I'm gonna swallow something into my lungs, they call it 'aspirate,' and then I'll get pneumonia and die anyway."

"Can't you get antibiotics for the pneumonia?"

"Of course, but antibiotics"—she pronounced it *auntie-bee-otics*—"and ventilators will just put it off for a few days or weeks, and then I'll be right back where I started from, and then the next go-round will be even worse with the choking."

"So once you're in the wheelchair and you have the chip implanted, there's no real treatment?"

"Well, there's one. At some point, after the first or second bout of pneumonia, or when I am gasping for breath in my sleep and shit, the doctor slips me a nice, healthy dose of morphine. But that's only if I decide to go the hospital and time it right, it won't really work if I want to die at home."

"Shit. I don't know what to say."

"Charlie, I want you to help me to die. I'm sorry, I didn't mean that. I don't 'want' you to help me to die. You will. At this point, you will help me die. You have no choice because I have no one else and you have no one else, and I promise you I'll haunt you for real this time if you don't."

I went over to her narrow wheelchair, and she managed to shift her body to one side so that I could get my arms around her upper thighs and waist and I lifted her up and then I collapsed into her chair with her seated on my lap. It had taken a lot of work; there wasn't really room for two people, even two people as skinny as us, in that one chair, so I had to do a lot of twisting and arranging of her legs to get her to face me. We were as crammed together as we were in my dream, in the roots of that ancient tree.

I held MariAngela around the waist, and then around her buttocks, and I could feel how terribly frail she was by how sharply the bones stuck out. They stuck out as much as my collarbones did, and that made me feel that we were brother and sister under the skin.

I had never told Alisa that what I was afraid of was bones, and I didn't tell MariAngela now, because I wasn't afraid anymore.

MariAngela's skin was warm, like the skin of someone very much healthy and alive. There was no thin film of cellophane between us, nothing between us at all except, here and there at various points of our bodies, the pulsing of my blood pressed against the pulsing of hers.

I stroked her hair a bit and said, "You know, I've always been fascinated by the fact that we can only be one person. I used to say to myself, 'I am the person I have been given to live my life with.' But I think now that that was wrong. MariAngela, you are the one I have been given to live my life with."

She looked delighted. "Thank you! That's exactly right."

The next day at work, I got a call from Diane.

"Hey, Charlie, you'll never guess where I'm calling from."

"You're right. I can't guess."

"Phoenix! I'm in Phoenix!"

"Lucky you. I'll bet you can use a vacation, the way you work."

"Oh, no, no, Charlie. No, no. This is no vacation. I've left him."

"You're kidding, you left Frank? Finally? Why? How?"

"Well, it's probably not exactly what you're expecting. I came to visit an old college friend here in Phoenix in February for vacation, and while I was here, I also talked to a former colleague that works for a big labor law firm here, and bottom line, after I got back to Chicago, he offered me a job!"

"That's wonderful! I just got a new job too, and it's one of Gilbert's competitors, I mean, if he's still in business at all."

"Then you have to come out to Phoenix and we'll celebrate! So anyway, I was so happy, but Frank was furious and refused to consider moving out to Phoenix, which I kind of don't blame him because I sprung it on him, but I only sprung it on him because I guess subconsciously I was thinking of leaving him anyway or else why would I even have considered the job offer, much less take a vacation by myself to Phoenix, right? I mean my friend wasn't even that close. Can I tell you something intimate, Charlie?"

"Of course."

"It makes me a little ashamed, but I'll tell you anyway. My friend is a he, and he is only a friend—I'd never have cheated on Frank the way he did with me and you. But when I got to Phoenix, I don't know, both of us must've had something on our minds, because we ended up getting together, you know? Am I a terrible person?"

"Were you doing this to get back at Frank?"

"I wasn't, honestly! My friend and I just sort of, you know, fell together, though I have to ask myself why it was him that I decided to visit out of the blue. Maybe I was trying to force the issue because I needed out from under Frank. So, this is the weird part, I don't know how to explain it exactly, but the whole week, you know, we were doing it. And for some reason, it was just an inside joke, don't ask me to explain it, but every time we had sex that week, we'd put a little tab of Scotch tape on the inner frame of the door of my hotel room in Phoenix. You know, like we were keeping score."

"Okay, weird, but I sort of get it."

"It ended up being a lot of Scotch tape! So Frank comes the same weekend I was originally scheduled to return, and I'm already doing interviews with the new firm, so I told Frank I'd be delayed in coming back and we're already arguing about whether I should take the job if it's offered to me, so anyway he comes to my hotel where I'm staying to try to force me to come back to Chicago, and the instant, I swear, the *instant* he sees those strips of tape on the hotel door, he says to me, 'That's how many times you've had sex with some guy, isn't it?' I was mortified, but that's the way he is, Charlie, he's amazing. I couldn't say anything, I was just paralyzed, and I knew that even if I didn't get that job offer I'd stay in Phoenix until I got another. He just knew. Like you and that girl."

"MariAngela. Diane, she's asked me to help her die, but I'm not going to do it."

"You're not? Why on earth not?"

"I don't know. I need to think of something else, but I have no idea what it is."

A couple of days after this conversation, I was in a Starbucks after work, on my way to see MariAngela, when I suddenly felt a terrible throbbing in my left temple. It happened very suddenly, as if a switch had been turned on in my brain. I put my cup of coffee down and walked over to the counter to buy a slice of lemon poppy seed cake, thinking that the rushed lunch I'd had at my desk might've brought on the headache. But when I tried to eat the slice of cake, I immediately felt nauseated. And when I looked around the Starbucks for the bathroom in case I became sick, all of the lights bleared in my vision and made me feel disoriented and dizzy.

I called Ludmilla to tell her I wasn't visiting that day, staggered home and went to bed, and didn't get up again until the next afternoon, fortunately a Saturday. I'd been scheduled to go into work anyway—we were that busy—but it wasn't like missing a workday. I'd never had a migraine before, so I didn't quite know how to treat it. By the middle of the afternoon on Saturday, after applying cold packs to the back of my neck and warm washcloths to my eyes and popping six or so Advils, I was feeling a bit better.

It had been MariAngela's migraine.

The next day, I downloaded my own copy of the Roman general's book and read what MariAngela had been reading. There, on my bedside table in the rental house, I'd switched on my iPad, and then it did that thing where the text flipped from horizontal to vertical when I moved it, so I walked around to the other side of the table and read the Roman general's words, and I could read them just as well upside down as I could right side up.

And I found another book too, because I needed an answer to what the Roman general had said about focusing on the waking world, and the book contained these words written by a poet from St. Louis:

And what the dead had no speech for, when living,
They can tell you, being dead: The communication
Of the dead is tongued with fire beyond the language of the living.

On Sunday afternoon, I ventured into the dormer room and discovered that the shutters were gone. The drywall was so crumbly that the little hinges had finally broken away, and the shutters, almost as light as butterfly wings, must have tumbled away in the breeze.

I looked through the now-permanent proscenium in the wall at the little fragment of street that I could glimpse—a bit of concrete stoop, a metal handrail, and a piece of lumpy tree root. It wasn't the same tree root as the one in my dreams, the one from my childhood street that Willa and I had sat on, but there was more that I couldn't see, outside of my peripheral vision. I could sense that all of the trees in the city were connected, underground, by their roots. Not just this tree, but Willa's and mine, and whatever ones had lived beneath the lawn in front of MariAngela's house on the South Side of Chicago.

I lowered myself into the dormer room and gazed for a long time at the fragmentary slice of street below. I watched, wide awake, as MariAngela sat down under the tree in a nurse's uniform, holding a tray of brightly colored test tubes. She looked me in the eyes, searching—for suddenly I was there, under the tree, with her, and her lips moved like Willa's, and before she spoke, I knew what she was going to say. And I agreed with what she said, and I finally had my answer. We looked back up at the house I had been in a moment before, and though it was very small, we could clearly see the opening where the shutters once had been.

And at that moment, she turned into me; I was looking at my own face. And I realized that at that moment, I was her, too.

The next day, I got a call from my mother. She sounded subdued but completely sober.

"Carlos, my dear, I have some news for you."

"Father?"

"Yes, of course. I'm sorry, my dear. This morning."

"I'm sorry too. Are you alright?"

"I'm fine, my dear. It was not expected. I mean to say, no, it was not 'unexpected.' "

"So they killed him?"

"Who is this 'they,' dear?"

"Them. The people he owed money to."

"Oh no. He had a double illness. He had an—I looked up the translations of this word in English, so I will sound it out for you—an 'an-your-ism.' In the abdomen. The doctors say from the drinking of wine."

"Yeah, an abdominal aneurysm. It can happen to alcoholics."

"Carlos, I want you to know that I have completely stopped drinking. And then while he was on the operating table, he had a stroke too, and that was the end of it for him."

"I'm so sorry, Mother. I'll come as soon as I can."

"Three days is the funeral from now. Please be here in three days for me."

The next day, I visited MariAngela for the first time at her Irving Park apartment, where she'd been moved. It was a contemporary three-story brownstone, with a deck in front of each unit. Mari-Angela's deck was hung with potted plants, and they'd flourished unattended all that spring, so that now, at the beginning of summer, the entire deck was screened by green tendrils that grew up and out from under the roof of the deck toward the sun.

She thankfully was still not in one of those complicated high-tech wheelchairs she'd loathed and feared; instead she sat, albeit a bit stiffly and to one side, in a wicker rocking chair, by an open window, near a writing desk she didn't use. The curtains were wide open, and the sunlight was streaming in. Her wrists were strapped to the arms of the rocking chair, and her jaw was distended slightly to one side. But her eyes, and her beautiful espresso-colored eyebrows, remained as always.

Her migraines, blessedly, had faded away. There was an easy chair nearby where Ludmilla sat and knitted. The apartment was warm and comfortable and filled with yet more houseplants that I presumed either Ludmilla or the night nurse watered, and a blue-and-green parakeet they must have fed and talked to that hopped around impatiently in its cage, as if waiting for MariAngela to come and play with it.

MariAngela smiled at me when I came in. She looked happy.

I looked at Ludmilla for permission, and she knew what I was asking and nodded her assent. I unstrapped the Velcro straps from MariAngela's wrists, and then I lifted her up and cradled her in my arms and carried her to the window.

She sighed. "That breeze feels good."

She felt so light that I wanted to carry her back to my house in my arms.

But then I realized that where she was didn't really matter now.

"MariAngela, I understand now what I need to do."

"There's no need to say it, Charlie. I understand it too."

"And it doesn't involve helping you to die."

"No, you're right about that. I have a good year or so left."

"Long enough to see him or her."

"The doctors would never allow it. It's unheard of."

"But you're okay with it anyway?"

"Of course I am, Charlie. And you are too. Because you love me."

"I do love you, MariAngela. I'm so sorry that I'm the first person to say it in your life."

"But now there'll be someone else to say it, won't there, Charlie? Maybe not until I'm gone, but that doesn't matter, does it?"

"You'll just have to hang on long enough."

"I will, Charlie, I promise you that."

"MariAngela, I have to tell you something. My father just died. I have to go back to Buenos Aires for the funeral, and then I'm bringing my mother back here with me. She's stopped drinking —I believe her, I think she really has—and she is going to need something to do with her life. This is going to make her happy, I think, to help us, and it really *will* help us, too."

"I'm sorry about your father, Charlie."

"Well, he was a complicated man."

"You'll be back soon?"

"Of course, in plenty of time. We'll have plenty of time, I promise."

And we did. I came back with my mother as promised, though it took longer than I'd hoped to find an estate agent in order to sell their house. Most of the little profit would go to the men my father owed, but that was fine. My mother was happy to be back in America, and as she had promised, she left the bottles behind. She had another thing to live for now.

And my pretty, parenthetical little MariAngela? She kept her promise too. She got to see the shadow on the sonogram and that kept her going, and of course she got to see what emerged from out of that shadow for several glorious months.

I mentioned before the last time she came into my brain when she was living, but it happened again three more times about fifteen months later, after her death.

In the first dream, she looked exactly as I first remembered seeing her at Berto's, and, as in my early dreams, she did not shift or change into another person or another version of herself. It was her. I was so excited that I wrenched myself awake, and then I cried out in frustration because I realized that she had come to me and I had let her go.

A few days later, I had to go visit a client in Boston, and I was afraid the distance would be too great, but as I dropped off to sleep in the Boston Sheraton, there she was, seated under the tree and waiting for me.

I forced myself to be conscious and yet to remain asleep at the same time. I was terrified that I would lose her again before I asked her the question that was on my mind. And then I remembered, again, to tell myself, "This is a dream. You can do anything you want." And so I reached out and touched her to make sure she was real, but I "missed." I don't know how, exactly, but my hand had failed to touch her. She took pity on me and grabbed my hand and brought it to her cheek, the one I'd stroked while she was still alive, and her skin felt just as warm and real as when she was alive. I asked her, "What is your name?"

And she looked at me for a moment and she said, "It doesn't matter anymore."

But it was her, and only her.

I waited for her to speak. I waited for her to tell me some news from where she was, but she said nothing else.

So I told myself, "This is just a dream. She can speak to you if you wake yourself up."

So in my dream I awakened, and she was still there, sitting under the tree. And this time, before I had a chance to lose her, I kissed her just like I had kissed her the very first time at Berto's. It was a glancing kiss, not a deep one, but it left me with a little tingle on my lip, and I knew that I would not forget it.

Then I asked her, finally, the question that Dr. Nemerov had always wanted me to ask. I said, "What do you want, MariAngela?"

And she replied, "I already have what I want."

There my dream ended.

I'd been to Boston half a dozen times before on business, but as I strolled around Faneuil Hall Marketplace and the Italian neighborhood nearby, the city and its sights trembled with a glorious freshness, as if I were seeing it for the first time, and after a long winter convalescence.

She came to me again last night, and she snuggled in between the roots of the tree next to me, and we held hands like we were children. I wanted her to say something, and while I waited, I noticed that all around me, everything—the elm tree, and the other trees, and the flowers and the shrubs—cast velvety shadows on the sidewalk.

Her lips moved, but I could not hear her speak. Instead, I heard an infinitely distant cry, coming from deep in the basement with all the worms and spades and mangles and harrows, but then, thrillingly, rising in volume as it ascended through the house, through the open shutters and out into the street and into the swaying trees, and then I woke up and remembered that it was the cry of someone real, someone in my mother's arms right next to me as I slept.

Michael Antman is the author of the novel *Cherry Whip* (ENC Press, 2004) and the forthcoming memoir *Searching for the Seagull Motel,* and is a two-time finalist for the National Book Critic Circle's Balakian Award for Excellence in Book Reviewing. He also is the Global Head of Marketing for a Fortune 500 company.

CPSIA information can be obtained
at www.ICGtesting.com
Printed in the USA
LVOW03s1507031217
558470LV00010B/640/P

9 781937 484576